ALTERNATIVE
Holidays

Also from B Cubed Press

Alternative Truths

More Alternative Truths: Tales from the Resistance

After the Orange: Ruin and Recovery

Alternative Theology

Digging Up My Bones,

by Gwyndyn T. Alexander

Firedancer,

by S.A. Bolich

Alternative Apocalypse

Oz is Burning

Stories for the Thoughtful Young

Poems for the Thoughtful Young

Space Force

Alternative War

Alternative Deathiness

Spawn of War and Deathiness

The Protest Diaries

Alternative Holidays

Edited by
Alicia Hilton and Bob Brown

Cover Art
and Design
Francois Vaillancourt

Published by

B Cubed Press
Kiona, WA

Copyright

Table of Contents

Dreidel of Dread: The Very Cthulhu Chanukah

Alex Shvartsman

'Twas the night before Chanukah, and all through the planet, not a creature was stirring except for the Elder God Cthulhu who was waking up from his eons-long slumber. And as the terrible creature awakened in the city of R'lyeh, deep beneath the Pacific Ocean, and wiped drool from his face-tentacles, all the usual signs heralded the upcoming apocalypse in the outside world: mass hysteria, cats and dogs living together, and cable repairmen arriving to their appointments within the designated three-hour window.

"This will not do," said Chanukah Henry. "I will not have the world ending on my watch, not during the Festival of Lights."

"This sounds like a serious problem," said Henry's father the brain surgeon at the dinner table after they lit the menorah. "Maybe let The Guy in the Red Suit handle it?"

'Chanukah' Henry Rabinowitz bristled at the mention of Nick. Henry lived in his parents' basement and put up with the litany of complaints from his mother by day while trying to launch his chosen career of spreading the Chanukah cheer by night. Nick, on the other hand, lived in a mansion and dated supermodels and rode jet skis and everyone inexplicably loved him, despite his propensity for breaking and entering into people's homes via their chimneys.

Henry pushed the matzo ball in his soup around with a spoon. "Absolutely not, Dad. Nick already has the best movies and songs and holiday specials and all the pretty ladies wanting to sit on his lap. All Chanukah has is that terrible Adam Sandler song. We need a great modern Chanukah story, and averting the apocalypse would do nicely."

"I don't know," said his father. "This seems an awful lot like a Christmas yarn to me. "The Very Cthulhu Christmas" even sounds like a better alliteration than "The Very Cthulhu Chanukah."

"I've been reading about this Cthulhu," said Henry's mother. "With his death cultists and his bad temper and his hideous face, he sounds just like Bertha Sheynson from the temple. And what's with the irrelevance of humanity? My husband the brain surgeon is very important. And my son the schlimazel, well he could be important one day, too. Still, going to an underwater city alone at night sounds dangerous."

Henry steeled himself against his mother's usual monologue aimed at making him stay home, but she surprised him.

"You go out there and you make us proud, son. Just don't forget to wear a hat. And some mittens."

Feeling very verklempt, Henry put on his blue-and-white robe and set out for the South Pacific. He rounded up a group of shoggoths and quickly resolved their human resources problem (or rather, their shoggoth resources problem) by putting the red-nosed shoggoth in charge, because nothing works better than elevating the employee nobody likes to mid-level management. The subdued shoggoths pulled his '84 Cadillac and he made it to the green slimy vaults of R'lyeh in no time.

He walked through the chilly cavernous halls of the corpse-city and was very glad to have listened to his mother and brought his hat. Finally, he was face to face with Cthulhu.

"Not cool," he told the Elder God, "initiating an apocalypse on the first night of Chanukah. Between that and H.P. Lovecraft's well-documented views, people might draw certain conclusions."

"What? It's not like that," said Cthulhu. "I'm a progressive and forward-thinking being, and I'm disdainful of all of humanity equally! Besides, I don't even feel like destroying anyone just now. I'd rather go back to sleep, but the neighborhood got so noisy with Godzilla and those Kaiju from the Pacific Rim gallivanting about. And I'm bored. Do you know how hard it is to get ESPN down here?"

"I can keep you entertained," said Chanukah Henry. "We can spin the dreidel." He withdrew the four-sided spinning top from his pocket.

"I don't know," said Cthulhu, examining the dreidel. "Gods" aren't supposed to play dice with the universe."

"Nothing so dramatic," said Henry. "We can play for this Chanukah gelt." He produced a bag of chocolate coins.

It was a Chanukah miracle: the game most people can't tolerate for more than twenty minutes at a time lasted for eight days and eight nights until Cthulhu was bored back into deep sleep.

Chanukah Henry saved everyone and became a celebrity, yet he never let the fame and fortune go to his head. The world was now his oyster, but Henry still kept kosher.

Alternative Holidays

Candy Canes and Brimstone

Alicia Hilton

A murmuration of demons
Flew from the River of Fire
Ninety-eight monsters
Large, small, and microscopic
Shrieking, hissing
Leathery, feathery, and fanged
The most depraved flock of all
Summoned by sleigh bells
And scents of mulled wine
Peppermint and human flesh
Christmas Day in Hades
The most aromatic
And horrific holiday

Fallen Angel Marlene
Swooped and dove
Past stalactites and stalagmites
Leading Lucifer's minions
Through pulsing caverns
The intestines of the great beast
Known as the Underworld
Were coated in luminous slime
Boulders shuddered
Exhaling energizing brimstone
Inhaling demon secretions
A symbiotic relationship
Bound in blood and sin

A giant horned bat
Licked sulfurous powder
From a stalactite
His eyes dilated
Guano shot from his butt
Boils on his back popped
He let go of the rock
Spun like a top
And soared past Marlene
She unlatched the whip
Strapped to her hip
Gave him a lash
Crack!

A zombified raptor hooted,
"Give him another lash!"
Crack! Crack!
A headless witch cackled
At the scarlet stripes
Criss-crossing the bat's back
Demons swooped after Marlene
And the bat
Ten times faster
Than flying reindeer
What a very merry chase
Full of bloodlust
And Christmas cheer

The rowdy murmuration
Landed at the entrance
To Lucifer's confectionary
Hooves stampeded
Through an iron gate
Pushing, shoving
Past evergreens decorated
With severed fingers and toes
Following a cacophony
Of odiferous delicacies
Sweet, savory, and petrified
Luscious meat sacks

Spiced with Christmas fear

Fallen Angel Marlene
Collected fees
At a second gate
Made from hissing snakes
Aisle 1 Sweet—One Incisor
Aisle 2 Super Sweet—One Molar
Aisle 3 Savory—Two Talons
Aisle 4 Special Surprise—Four Talons
Satan's minions tore teeth from gums
Ripped talons from fingers and feet
Microscopic monsters freeloaded
Clung to bloodied demons
As they surged down aisles

Aisle 1 Sweet
Seventy-seven con artists
Were chained together
In a steaming fountain
Filled with mulled wine
The scalded souls shouted
The same lies they'd used
To fleece unfortunate mortals
"You'll double your money!"
"It's a sure thing!"
"You can't lose!"
"Extended warranty!"
"Money back guarantee!"

Aisle 2 Super Sweet
Twelve nursing home orderlies
Packed tighter than sardines
In two stainless steel barrels
Begged for mercy
But Satan never forgave
Cretins who abused old folks
A gong *clanged*
Slots in the ceiling opened
Melted candy canes
Poured into the barrels

7

Drowning the sinners
In boiling peppermint

Aisle 3 Savory
A neon sign advertised
Christmas Sale 50% Off!
Forty-four naked
Serial killers
Hung from meat racks
Hooks speared into their backs
A pack of laughing jackals
And nine demon pterodactyls
Pounced and swooped
Fangs and beaks tore throats
Gored juicy bellies
Coated in caramel

Aisle 4 Special Surprise
Six demons dressed as elves
Led a lassoed Santa
Red-faced, shrieking
The monstrous impostor
With a rented velvet suit
Had invaded two homes
On Christmas Eve
Toting a gun, rope
And cans of gasoline
He trussed and torched
Four adults, five kids
And a kitten

The Dark Lord
Materialized
From a swirling cloud
Of sulfurous smoke
A hammer and nails
Clutched in his fists
Fallen Angel Marlene
Dragged a wood cross
Towards the arsonist
She screamed profanity

As Satan crucified Santa
Demons loathed
Kitten killers

Alternative Holidays

The Santa Trap

Nina Kiriki Hoffman writing as Robin Aurelian

It was Subtraction Eve, and the children went through the house looking at everything they cherished, wondering which things Santa would sneak in and steal that night. Janie's birthday was the week before Subtraction. She hated the fact that her birthday was so close to the holiday. She only got to play with her presents for a week before most of them disappeared forever. Sometimes she thought her parents gave her crummy gifts on purpose—why spend money on something she would lose before she even got a chance to break it? Mike's birthday was in the spring and he always got much neater things.

"This time I'm going to hide the truck behind the toilet," Mike said, cradling his yellow Tonka truck in his arms.

"Don't be stupid. It doesn't matter where you put it. The more you don't want him to find it, the more he can find it. He's got some kind of sniffer to find the stuff you like the best," said Janie.

"He didn't find Monkey Man last year," Mike said.

"You didn't like Monkey Man last year. You didn't like Monkey Man until he was the only toy left." Janie looked at her doll, Brewster. Worn and battered Brewster, with the hair half off his head, his clothes all torn and stained. Janie had her own way of dealing with Brewster and Santa. She had had Brewster for four years now. She roughed him up right before Subtraction, made him ugly and dirty, looked at him and thought bad thoughts. She spent all of Subtraction Eve thinking about anything other than Brewster; if she thought of Brewster, she thought about him as her most hated toy. So far, Brewster had been there each Subtraction morning, and she could get back to taking good care of him.

She wasn't sure her method would work this year. Even though Santa was only supposed to take the good things, the new things and the neat things to give to other kids who didn't have enough money to get their own neat new things, Janie had heard of Santa taking someone's best loved teddy bear even though it was missing both eyes and an ear. She thought Santa took things just for spite sometimes.

She had never heard of a single person who had gotten anything from Santa. She had her suspicions. She thought Santa took everything to the stores so when they opened up the day after Subtraction, the biggest shopping day of the year because people had to go buy replacements for stuff Santa had stolen, the stores would have just what people needed.

She had better put Brewster down. If she carried him much longer maybe Santa would sniff out the stink of her concern on him.

She put him on the mantel, right near the spot where they always left milk and cookies. She tried to make it seem as if she wanted Santa to take Brewster. That was part of her reverse psychology too, but it fueled her worry to leave Brewster there in plain sight.

She had better go play with the toys she liked least.

Mike looked at his Tonka truck and let out a howl. "I'm sick of this!" he yelled. "I don't want Santa taking one more thing from me!"

"Shhh!" said Janie. "He knows if you've been naughty."

"I don't care!" Mike said. "He always takes everything anyway, even when I've been good! I'd like to catch him and take away everything he likes, see how he feels about it!"

"Oh, Mike!" Janie breathed, awed by the idea.

Everyone left their front door unlocked on Subtraction Eve. It was a rule. If Santa tried your front door and found it locked, he reported your family to the IRS. Santa might drive a hyper-toad-drawn sleigh, and steal all your favorite things, but nobody wanted to be reported to the IRS: Unlike Santa, the auditors took away things you couldn't live without.

One year there had been a rash of burglaries on Subtraction Eve. All those unlocked doors! All the burglars had been caught. Janie heard they had been fed to Santa's hyper-toads. This gave her pause.

"We wouldn't be burglars," Mike said. "Catching Santa isn't like stealing from other people. Or maybe it's just stealing from other people after they've been robbed."

"Fed to toads," Janie said meditatively.

"We'll wear masks," Mike said. "He'll never know who did it."

"He knows whose house it is, persimmon-brain."

They looked at each other. Is this worth it? Janie wondered. She stared at the presents on her desk, all the really cool stuff she had gotten for her birthday. A big sketch pad—her mom had told her if she drew on all the pages before Subtraction Eve, she would be able to keep it, and she had doodled on each page with her new markers, the box of thirty-six with colors like aquamarine and celestial blue and crimson and scarlet and chartreuse. She liked the paper and pens so much she was sure she couldn't keep them. Mike had given her a stuffed alligator, and she loved that too, though she had tried not to. She'd named it Wally, even though naming things was a bad idea. Daddy had given her a doll this year, a really neat one she'd seen advertised on TV and had asked for specifically: Talk Back Jack. He came with three outfits: mountain climber, dirt bike rider, and cowboy. If you talked to him, he cussed you. All right, they were wimpy cusses, but still.

Usually she didn't get such neat stuff.

Mike sat on her bed and hugged his Tonka truck.

"Do you think he turns on the lights when he comes in?" Janie said.

They put the trip wire about three feet from the front door so the door wouldn't hit the wire when it opened. Janie held the big pillowcase, and Mike held the electric cord. They sat across from each other, Mike just inside the living room entrance, Janie behind the coat rack in the front hall, and they waited.

Mom and Daddy had gone to bed an hour earlier, after putting Mike and Janie to bed. "Sleep well, sleep deep, sleep late, children," Mom had said as she tucked them in. "Tomorrow afternoon we'll go to a movie, how about that?"

Janie grabbed Mom and gave her a big kiss. Toad food couldn't go to the movies.

Splat-splat-splat-splat, splat-splat. Janie straightened, gripping the pillowcase with both hands. Had to be toads in the driveway.

The front door opened slowly inward. Santa was muttering as he came in. "Blasted bug-grubbing flimflamming distelfinks," he growled, stumbling over the threshold as he grabbed for the front hall light switch and turned on the light. "Yowch!" He tripped quite nicely over the wire. Janie was on him in an instant, pulling the pillowcase down over his head, while Mike wrapped the cord around his wrists, binding his arms behind him. "Burning brands!" cried the muffled Santa. His snatcher-sack had fallen as he fell. "Blistering boards!"

Janie was panting. Fortunately this was a very small, skinny Santa, though all dressed in traditional red.

"Frag mag zigzag," muttered Santa as Janie and Mike rolled him over. "Third time tonight! What do you bleeping want?"

"We want you not to take anything this year, Santa." Janie said.

"Is that all you want?" he said. He had a nice voice, Janie thought, confused.

"I want to see what's in your bag," Mike said. "I want to find something you really like and take it away from you."

"I don't," said Janie.

"There's nothing I like," Santa said.

"That's not fair," said Mike.

"Oh well," said Santa.

"What do we have to do to get you to go away without stealing our stuff this year?" Janie asked.

"There's nothing you can do about it."

"What if we just don't let you go?"

"You're going to let me go, aren't you?"

Well, this plan wasn't working at all, Janie thought. "Are you going to feed us to your toads?"

"No. Of course not."

"You're not going to tell the IRS on us, are you?"

"How much taxes do you pay?"

"None," said Janie.

"There you go."

"What about our parents?"

"Did they help you plan this?"

"No."

"There you go," said Santa, and sighed.

"Untie the cord, Mike," Janie said, pulling the pillow slip off Santa's head. He blinked at her. He was awfully skinny, and had a lot of dark curls, all messy with being tripped and tied up, and he had very dark eyes. His eyes looked nice. How could Santa look nice?

"I will not," said Mike. He grabbed Santa's snatcher-sack and reached into it.

"Don't do that," Santa said. He sounded depressed.

"Ouch!" yelled Mike. He jerked his hand out of the sack.

"There you go," said Santa tonelessly. "Got a future now, young man."

The back of Mike's hand was smoking. Mike began to cry: no sound, but tears rolled down his cheeks.

"What happened?" asked Janie.

"He got the brand. He's going to be a Santa when he grows up. What do you least want me to take this year?" Santa said.

Janie stared at him. Was he going to be nice, just this once, and let her keep what she most loved? After she had tied him up? Not likely. "My new doll," she said, "Talk Back Jack."

Santa sighed. He tensed his muscles. The cord broke and his hands were free. "I hate this job," he said. He stood up, grabbed his snatcher-sack, and headed upstairs.

Janie went into the kitchen and got some ice for Mike's hand. Tears were still welling up from his eyes. On the back of his hand, inflamed and red, was a jagged "S." She gave him ice in a rag to press against it.

She poured milk, put some cookies on a plate, took cup and plate to the mantel.

Santa came back downstairs, his sack bulging. "Sorry about this, kids," he said. He wandered into the living room and drank the milk and ate the cookies. "I hate this job." He looked at Mike.

Mike sniffed. He said, "Do you get to play with the toys before you give them to someone else?"

"I guess you could, if you wanted to," Santa said. He cocked his head, eyed Brewster, glanced at Janie. I hate that doll, she thought as hard as she could.

Santa picked up Brewster.

Hate him, Janie thought.

Santa put Brewster back down and sighed. "You're not going to try this again next year, are you?"

Janie and Mike shook their heads.

"Good," said Santa. He went out the front door. Janie and Mike watched as he climbed into his sleigh. The hyper-toads did a couple of limbering hops and then took off.

Janie watched until Santa was out of sight. Then she went and got Brewster, hugged him tight. She went up to her room. Not a single birthday present left—even the underwear Grandma had sent was gone. There was a note, though, in six different colors, on a page torn out of her sketch pad. "Write me in the pen," it said, and gave the address of the state prison.

Janie sighed and slipped the note into her desk drawer.

Any Sufficiently Advanced Technology

J.C.G. Goelz

The alarm beacon flared on the ceiling of the *Starship Genesis*. The shrill signal drilled into the crew, stirring them like nanobots after a hull breach.

Captain Elo Heem touched the tablet built into the arm of her chair. "Engineer G'brel, what the hell happened? Did the transmat go through?"

G'brel was already in the crawlspace behind the transmat engine, inching forward on his back as he examined the circuitry. He winced as a spark struck his cheek. He touched one of the colored lights on his bracelet. "I'm not sure, ma'am."

"Not sure? That's why we came to this God-forsaken planet." The reciprocal transmat in utero was the only way to spread their ethos without the locals knowing they did it.

"Yes ma'am." He winced again as sparks flared against his chest. He prodded the transmat circuits with his probe. "It has something to do with the anomaly that is holding us in geosynchronous orbit."

"If that wasn't bad enough. We're lit up like a flare. The locals probably think there's another star in the sky."

"Yes ma'am. We probably shouldn't have tried to use the transmat."

Her face tightened into a scowl. "Did it work? Did we trade packages?"

G'brel rubbed where a spark had burned his cheek. "Do you want to hear the good news or the bad news?"

"Give me both."

17

"Our package was sent, but we didn't receive the package from the planet."

"What does that mean, engineer?"

"It means that the Transcendent Being we sent down is sharing existence with the local baby."

"Oh shit, that can't be good. Can it?"

Lucy in the Sky with Helen

Sheri White

Helen gave Lucy her before-bedtime treat. She put the little dish of tuna on the floor and smiled at the cat's obvious enjoyment. Helen talked to her cat as she cleaned up her small kitchen, her hand trembling around the sponge she wiped the counter with.

"You know, Miss Lucy, today I was on a website that listed every holiday celebrated around the world. And not just the regular ones like Christmas or Easter. There are all sorts of strange holidays people like to have fun with."

"There was *Find a Rainbow Day, Tell a Lie Day, National Hairball Awareness Day*—I don't need a holiday for that one, do I? I am very aware of those, especially when I step on one."

"Anyway, Lucy, tomorrow is a holiday called *Answer Your Cat's Questions Day.* Doesn't that sound like fun? You've been with me for almost a year. You must have questions! Oh, I know you can't talk. But how amazing would it be if for just one day we could have a conversation?"

Helen turned off the overhead light and shuffled to her room. "Good night, Lucy."

The black cat ignored Helen's shaky voice, intent on getting every bit of tuna.

#

Helen lay on her side with her back against the couch, watching TV. Lucy was stretched out against her and purred contentedly as Helen stroked her fur.

Come on down! the announcer yelled at someone in the audience.

"I do love *The Price is Right*, but it hasn't been the same since that handsome Bob Barker retired. What do you think, Miss Lucy?"

The cat turned her head and blinked up at Helen.

"Why did you name me Lucy?" she asked.

Helen sat up quickly, and Lucy jumped to the other end of the couch. She tilted her head. "Well?"

"This can't be happening. Cats don't talk. Cats *can't* talk."

"Hey, you were the one who mentioned answer your cat's questions day." The cat walked back over to Helen and sat in her lap.

"Okay. I'll go with it." She took her phone out of the pocket of her fuzzy white robe, which was no longer white because of Lucy's fur. "But I want to put this on the Internet when we're done." She put the phone into a hands-free holder on the coffee table and set it up to record.

"I feel silly doing this." Helen chuckled nervously. "But I named you Lucy because I love The Beatles and one of my favorite songs is *Lucy in the Sky with Diamonds*."

"And why did you adopt me?"

"Oh, you adopted me! I didn't even plan on adopting you or any other cat that day. I had just taken donations to the shelter, and you put your paw out and snagged my sweater. I couldn't leave you there after that. Don't you remember doing that?"

The two of them chatted for quite a while. Helen couldn't remember the last time she had a real conversation with anybody. She would talk for a few minutes here and there with Sandy next door at their mailboxes, but that was pretty much her only human contact.

The house grew dark as the day passed, only the muted TV giving off light.

"Oh, you must be hungry, Lucy!" She took Lucy off her lap and stood up. "Let's go to the kitchen."

"One more question. Why do you live alone?"

Helen's smile faded and her eyes grew sad. "I lost my husband a long time ago. And my children are busy with their own families. I do get email from all of them, though. But I miss them. My grandkids are in elementary school now—I haven't seen them since they were in diapers."

She scratched Lucy under her chin. "But it's okay! I have everything I need, and you bring me so much joy."

Lucy slow-blinked at her, cat language for love and trust. She followed Helen into the kitchen.

#

Sandy knocked on Helen's door a couple weeks later. "Helen? Are you okay? Your mailbox is full, and I haven't seen you check it in a while."

She waited a few minutes, then went home to make a call for a welfare check. When the police arrived, she met the two of them at Helen's front yard.

"I'm Officer Kendall, and this is my partner, Officer James. How can we help you?"

"I'm Sandy. Thank you for coming," she said. "Helen hasn't said anything, but I could see she hasn't been looking well the past couple months. I just want to make sure she's okay."

"You did the right thing, Ma'am," said Officer James. "Stay here while we take a look."

Sandy watched them knock on the door, and call to her just like she had. Officer Kendall was tall enough to stand on tiptoe and look through the front-door windows. He looked at his partner and subtly shook his head. Sandy noticed.

"Officer James? Can you see her?"

"She's laying on her couch. We need to go in and see if she's...asleep or sick."

Sandy chewed on her thumbnail and paced in a circle.

Officer Kendall tried the doorknob, but the door was locked. "Ma'am, we are police officers. We are coming in, so don't be frightened."

The sturdy but builder-quality door was no problem to kick in. Officer James reached Helen first and checked her neck for a pulse. He turned to look at Officer Kendall and saw Sandy standing in the doorway.

"I'm sorry, Ma'am. She looks as though she passed peacefully, though." They began to make calls for arrangements to take Helen away.

Sandy walked over to Helen and perched next to her on the edge of the couch. She noticed Lucy curled up by Helen's feet, awake and watching closely.

"Hi, Lucy," Sandy said softly. She reached over and stroked Lucy's cheek.

Sandy rubbed against her and purred.

The TV was on, so Sandy grabbed the remote and turned it off. She knocked over Helen's phone when she put the remote back. "I should see if there is anyone I should call. Oh, I don't know the password." Then she realized the phone unlocked through face recognition.

"Ugh. I hope this isn't disrespectful." She put the phone in front of Helen's face to unlock it. She quickly changed the password once she got through. She accidentally opened the photo app instead of the contacts app, and a video popped up. Sandy hesitated, then clicked the play arrow.

As Sandy watched, tears rolled down her cheeks at the sight of Helen having a conversation with Lucy, using a different voice to represent the cat's. When Helen talked about her family and how she missed them, Sandy cried for real.

"I'm so sorry, Helen. I didn't realize you were so lonely."

"Ma'am?" Officer James stood in the doorway.

Sandy wiped her eyes. "Yes?"

"The Medical Examiner is on her way. It might be best if you aren't here to watch."

She nodded and stood up. "You're right. Thank you." She put the phone in her pocket to call Helen's children when she got home. She wasn't sure if she would delete the video or not before she turned the phone over to them.

She scooped Lucy into her arms and walked out the door, passing the officers. "Thank you both. You've been very kind."

"You're welcome, Ma'am," responded Officer James. "We're sorry for the loss of your friend."

Sandy snuggled her cheek against Lucy's soft warm fur. "She loved you so much, Lucy. I'm glad she had you. I know you loved her too."

"I did," whispered Lucy, in a voice too soft for a human to hear.

12 Zombie Days of Christmas

Gregg Chamberlain

On the first Christmas zombie day
My partner gave to me
A promise to keep my brain free.

On the second Christmas zombie day
My partner gave to me
Two clips of bullets
And a promise to keep my brain free.

On the third Christmas zombie day
My partner gave to me
Three Molotovs
Two clips of bullets
And a promise to keep my brain free.

On the fourth Christmas zombie day
My partner gave to me
Four good used tires
Three Molotovs
Two clips of bullets
And a promise to keep my brain free.

On the fifth Christmas zombie day
My partner gave to me
Five loaded guns!

Alternative Holidays

Four good used tires
Three Molotovs
Two clips of bullets
And a promise to keep my brain free.

On the sixth Christmas zombie day
My partner gave to me
Six tins of dog food
Five loaded guns!
Four good used tires
Three Molotovs
Two clips of bullets
And a promise to keep my brain free.

On the seventh Christmas zombie day
My partner gave to me
Seven jugs of water
Six tins of dog food
Five loaded guns!
Four good used tires
Three Molotovs
Two clips of bullets
And a promise to keep my brain free.

On the eighth Christmas zombie day
My partner gave to me
Eight shots of morphine
Seven jugs of water
Six tins of dog food
Five loaded guns!
Four good used tires
Three Molotovs
Two clips of bullets
And a promise to keep my brain free.

On the ninth Christmas zombie day
My partner gave to me
Nine packs of batteries

Alternative Holidays

Eight shots of morphine
Seven jugs of water
Six tins of dog food
Five loaded guns!
Four good used tires
Three Molotovs
Two clips of bullets
And a promise to keep my brain free.

On the tenth Christmas zombie day
My partner gave to me
Ten cans of petrol
Nine packs of batteries
Eight shots of morphine
Seven jugs of water
Six tins of dog food
Five loaded guns!
Four good used tires
Three Molotovs
Two clips of bullets
And a promise to keep my brain free.

On the eleventh Christmas zombie day
My partner gave to me
Eleven books of matches
Ten cans of petrol
Nine packs of batteries
Eight shots of morphine
Seven jugs of water
Six tins of dog food
Five loaded guns!
Four good used tires
Three Molotovs
Two clips of bullets
And a promise to keep my brain free.

On the twelfth Christmas zombie day
My partner gave to me

Alternative Holidays

Twelve rolls of T.P.
Eleven books of matches
Ten cans of petrol
Nine packs of batteries
Eight shots of morphine
Seven jugs of water
Six tins of dog food
Five loaded guns!
Four good used tires
Three Molotovs
Two clips of bullets
And a head shot to set my brain free.

Yes, a head shot to set my brain free!

Moderno Inferno

Richard Lau

CANTO I

So, there I was, at the corner of Lower Place and Midlife Road. Approaching me from half a block away was a hulk of a man in a hockey jersey who exuded such an air of hostility that the angry cloud threatened to extinguish the already dim glow of the yellowed streetlamps. From the other direction, a scarecrow figure in dirty rags danced drunkenly towards me, belting out vulgar renditions of Christmas Carols interrupted by shouted obscenities.

Staying at my present location was additionally unadvisable due to a seedy con man vending "high-end" merchandise from the back of his van "at unheard of discount holiday prices." I was certain he was on some sort of naughty list in at least three counties.

Violence, insanity, and fraud all threatened convergence at that one intersection, and the crosswalk lights were red to boot!

I retreated south, against the advice of a blinking DON'T WALK sign, into Dark Woods Plaza.

Alone in the immense parking lot, I quickly became lost, like an abandoned and lonely shopping cart, far off its original and rightful path home to the cart corral.

"Hey there! Can I help you?"

The high-pitched, enthusiastic voice cut through my clouded mind like a laser ray of sunshine. Suddenly appearing before me was a young woman wearing a blue uniform that brought to mind every 60's vision of a stewardess. Her blonde hair was pulled into

27

a ponytail, revealing her fair and freckled face, high cheekbones, and pointed chin. She reminded me of an elf.

"What's your name?" inquired this pixie, as I wondered whether wings could fit under the suit jacket.

"Uh, Dante," I mumbled. "Just call me Danny."

"I'm Virginia," she said. "But you can call me Virg." She continued without pausing to take a breath, "Are you lost? You look lost."

"I guess I am," I admitted. I told her about my failed navigation efforts.

"Oh!" she said brightly, and I got the impression she said everything brightly. "We can take a shortcut through the mall."

She pointed to a huge featureless and windowless building that rose like an intimidating mountain range of tan concrete blocks behind us. In five-foot tall capital letters, a sign on the building said "MALL." There were smaller sized words under the four letters, but I was too far away to read them.

"Uh, I'm not sure I want to risk getting lost in there," I said, suddenly chilled with a touch of Arctic air. Baby, it was cold outside.

"Don't worry," soothed Virg. "I'll be your guide."

I must have still looked reluctant, for she added, "I know my way around in there. I'm a personal shopper!"

A cloudburst of yelling interrupted my thoughts. Coming our way, the beefy giant was beating up the drunken scarecrow for vomiting on him while the van salesman was trying to sell them some expensive cologne to cover up the smell.

"Lead the way, Virg," I said, instantly changing my mind. Maybe I could even get some actual holiday shopping done instead of waiting for the panicked Christmas Eve rush.

Ahead of me, she alighted more than walked. It was as if I was following a fluttering butterfly on a spring day.

As we approached the building's entrance, I looked at the sign again. The middle legs of the "M" had turned sideways, so that the letter now resembled an "H." The inverted "V" of the "A" also rotated 90 degrees, the new letter now appearing to be an "E" in some old English script. They can do some amazing things with digital signs nowadays, though I could swear the sign was made up of neon tubes.

As we passed under the sign, we were now close enough for me to read the smaller words: "Abandon all savings ye who enter here. Cash, checks, and major credit cards accepted."

CANTO II

Once inside, it took a few moments for my eyes to get used to the dim lighting. Lit glass counters and flickering displays left shadowy aisles where darkness lurked and crouched.

I felt duller as the slightly off-key angelic chirpings of a children's choir were piped from tinny speakers, lulling me into a sleepwalker's trance.

I entered a forest of towering tinseled pine trees of all colors, shapes, and plastics. Beneath this artificial canopy, I felt like a shrunken Alice in Christmasland facing an endless stream of vertically bobbing human figures in ugly sweaters. This bobbing flow was only broken up by gift-wrapped boxes the size of small tanks and gigantic boulders resembling ornaments tilted precariously, as if waiting to roll on and crush the unwary and unwanted, Indiana-Jones-style.

I looked to Virg and saw she showed no signs of wonderment. "There be demons here!" I thought, as she led me further inward where horned masses of scarlet creatures pushed randomly about. But as these denizens drew closer, I could see the horns on their heads were merely fake reindeer antlers and their blood-red faces were just flushed, as their wallets and purses had been before they had entered this realm, from never-ending exertion.

When I thought I could stand the compacting crowd no longer, my guide and I arrived at a large lobby, filled with hard and uncomfortable yellow and orange plastic seats occupied mostly by bored-looking men. Each one was buried up to his neck in overfilled plastic bags. Once in a while, a shadowy figure would emerge from the darkness carrying another large bag and drop it by one of the heads and depart again, declaring, "Almost done, dear."

"This is Limbo," Virg explained. "It is for those who have forsaken the joy of shopping and wait endlessly for their loved ones to finish, which, of course, they never do. They are forever condemned to 'watch over purchases' and wait. As we have no Wi-Fi or hotspot signal here, they are additionally tormented by never knowing the score of a current sports game or being able to access their social media."

"That's horrible!" was all I could say, noting that we were being slowly surrounded by more figures carrying more bags. Our empty arms were magnets to these iron shavings of shadowed shoppers.

I sighed with relief as Virg moved us toward what appeared to be the only route of escape, a descending escalator guarded by a pale, thin man.

CANTO III

The escalator steps dropped into a deep, dark pit. The pale man in the security guard uniform moved to block our way as we approached. His badge identified him as "Charon."

"Let us pass, Charlie," ordered Virg. "Mess with me, and you're a dead man."

A groan rumbled and echoed in the ribcage under the guard's tight-fitting shirt, but nevertheless, he stiffly moved aside as if his legs were wooden stilts.

"I'm with Customer Recruitment and Retainment," Virg explained to me. "We trump Security."

I was distracted from her words by the smell of cooked food rising up out of the darkness. I still could not see the end of the moving staircase, but I could feel an updraft of warm air and hear a loud wash of chewing and slurping, punctuated by burping and flatulence.

In the distance, I saw a spot of light growing steadily brighter and larger. As more details came into focus, I could see seated people gathered around a multitude of tables filled with cardboard plates and plastic trays.

"This is the Food Court," announced Virg. "People here eat all they can and then more."

"More?" I repeated, seeing how the consumers closest to us had cheeks that bulged like overinflated beach balls.

"Once they finish a meal, they are tempted to try a different meal or one from a different food stall. You may notice that the food stalls are placed in a never-ending circle."

"What variety!" I commented, taking in all of the proffered cuisine and foreign-sounding eatery names.

"Look closer," Virg suggested, as we passed by a table.

To my surprise, the plates and bowls seemed to be filled with the same thick, gelatinous brown sludge, and so were the cups. As we passed, the diners put their arms protectively around their dishes and growled, as if afraid that we were going to take their food. They didn't need to worry.

"There's just one kitchen for all of them, and it only produces the same slop no matter what the food stalls call it." Virg was stating what I had already figured out.

I felt a little ill. The sight, smell, and sound of all that consumption, concentrated and corpulent, made me nauseated. "Can I visit the restroom before we proceed?" I asked, trying to choke back some bile.

"There are no bathrooms on this level," Virg said, moving toward another descending escalator. "That's part of its charm."

CANTO IV

This escalator wasn't as long as the previous one, and we reached the bottom in no time. A long line of people stood before us, some of them filling out papers in their hands. Pockets had been turned inside out and purses opened to show an emptiness only matched by the eyes of those standing in the line.

The line was orderly and confusing at the same time, as it seemed to wrap all around itself, winding back and forth like a Celtic knot, resulting in people bunched in clusters and facing in all different directions.

"This level is for those applying for store credit cards," Virg announced, pulling some similar forms from her jacket pocket and handing them to me.

I looked over the terms. "Isn't it usury to lend money at unreasonably high interest rates?"

"We call it customer service."

I tried to rip up the application forms, but the paper wouldn't tear. To my horror, I saw that I left a thumbprint in the signature section.

"Thank you!" said Virg, snatching the papers out of my hands. "That's all that's needed. I'm sure you'll be approved."

She moved quickly through the crowd, headed for what I could only assume was the front of the line. "One Mall credit card, coming right up!"

I tried to follow her but quickly lost sight of my guiding pixie. To make matters worse, the people in line were giving me vicious looks. "Hey! No cutting!" "What are you trying to pull?" "We've ALL been waiting for a long time, buster. What makes you so special?" "Back of the line, buddy!"

Yes, but where was the back of the line? Surely, Virg would return to me there. But all I saw was a mass of unhappy people who seemed to be standing more in a huddle than a line.

Suddenly, a blue-jacketed arm snaked out of the forest of bodies and grabbed my hand. "This way!" sang Virg's voice, though I still couldn't see her.

She was beaming as we stopped by yet another escalator. "I was not only able to get to the front of the line, but I'm having them expedite processing your application! A card should be ready for you by the time you leave. The perks of being in..."

"I know, I know," I interrupted grumpily. "Customer Recruitment and Retainment."

"Damned right!" my guide said, waving a triumphant fist in the air.

Shuddering at her use of the word "damned," I moved onto another downward step.

CANTO V

This escalator was well lit and had brightly colored signs hanging over our heads. They were filled with short phrases, like: "Top Quality!", "Limited Time Only!", "Buy One, Get One Free!", "Lifetime Warranty!", "Generous Return Policy!", and "Customer Satisfaction Guaranteed!"

"Wow!" I exclaimed, feeling better than I had for what seemed like hours. "Those sound great! Can all that be true?" I immediately regretted my question.

"True, to a degree." Virg smiled, the way a patient teacher smiles at a child who has been held back a grade two years in a row. She pointed to several of the signs. "See that little star at the end of all of the phrases? The asterisks indicate that there are certain terms and conditions."

"Isn't that a little fraudulent?" I asked.

"Nothing so malicious. Perhaps a little misleading, but that's marketing, right?"

She smiled and waved me on.

CANTO VI

Even before I placed a foot on the descending step of the next escalator, I could hear the thunderous roar of an angry mob. It sounded like a war zone, except the only weapons were whatever parts of the body the combatants were willing to use or sacrifice. Mixed among the shouts of rage and wrath were the wails of people in pain, misery, or loss.

I hesitated, not ashamed at all for being afraid. "Do we have to go down there?"

Even Virg looked a bit concerned and uncomfortable. "We had a candle shop down there. Usually, the scent of pine cones, cinnamon, and ginger spice adds to the festive atmosphere and calms things down."

"What happened to the shop?"

"The mob burned it down," came the answer I had expected but didn't want to hear. "They're so cute when they get so excitable! Just stay close. Try to stay out of their way. And whatever you do, do not, I repeat, do not reach for anything or you'll bring doom down upon us."

With such an ominous warning from my usually chipper guide, I stuck my hands in my pockets and hunkered behind the petite form of Virg, wishing for once that she was the size of a football lineman.

Sure enough, pooled at the base of the escalator was a riotous mob. Arms, legs, entire bodies flailed wildly in some spontaneous dance of violence. Every few minutes, a small appliance or electronic gadget would go flying over their heads with an ocean of arms reaching upwards to bring it down. The boxed item would disappear into the surging mass, and the arms would fall to blows on those unfortunate enough to be in the immediate area.

"This is our big sales level!" Virg shouted into my ear, dragging me off the escalator and over to one side. "People are whipped into a frenzy over slashed prices and huge discounts!"

"Are the prices really that good?" I asked, getting out from in between two women tugging on a wig like it was pull taffy.

"They seem to think so," Virg said, throwing a wicked elbow to the nose of an overweight man with a 24-pack of toilet tissue.

Cartilage crunched. Blood gushed from the poor sap's nose.

Virg continued maneuvering us around the outside of the mob.

We eventually came to a section of wall that contained the sliding metal doors of an elevator. With great relief, we stepped inside.

I noticed there was only one button on the panel, and then I had a revelation. On my entire journey so far, I hadn't seen a single escalator going up.

CANTO VII

It seemed like the elevator dropped forever. And as we fell, the holiday music playing through the hidden speakers grew louder and higher pitched until we were trapped with the continuous drone of Rudolph the Long-Nosed Mosquito.

I grew disoriented and weightless, as if my feet were not touching the elevator floor. I thought I saw Virg floating beside me.

"Oh no!" I muttered. "What fresh Hell is this?"

"There's a patent office on this level of the mall," Virg answered. "A bored clerk is having a thought experiment on his equivalence principle. Don't worry. It'll be over soon."

And it was. Our feet suddenly reconnected with the floor as the elevator stopped moving. Our knees bent with the sudden landing.

"At least Schrödinger's cat wasn't in the elevator this time," Virg said, by way of apology. "I really hate that one. You know how many students think physics class is hell? They have no idea how close they are to the truth!"

The doors slid open, and we exited onto a narrow ledge, high above the floor of a cavernous shaft. The mosquito drone faded as the doors closed, replaced by a repeating series of explosions, as if a cauldron-drum solo was being played by roaring canons. Rum pum pum pum! Rum pum pum pum!

About two hundred yards away, rising up from the shaft's floor was a towering throne of padded purple cushions and gold edging. It stood at least five stories tall. A gigantic red-skinned demon with black hooves and tufts of white fur was seated on the throne. He appeared naked except for a black sash around his waist. Was this the ultimate evil that resided in and ruled this forsaken abyss?

Fearlessly, Virg led us toward a zigzagging series of rocky steps that led to the cavern floor.

Rum pum pum pum!

"Why didn't the elevator go all the way to the bottom?" I asked, shouting into her ear, having had more than my daily allotment of walking.

Rum pum pum pum!

"To build anticipation."

Rum pum pum pum!

Anticipation for what? But that was my guide's only answer. Perhaps she had gotten tired of fitting her words between the relentless drumbeats, like the lyrics of some overly-long song.

As we drew closer, I could see the black hooves were actually shiny leather boots. What I had mistaken for skin was velvet cloth trimmed in white fur. At least I got the fur part correct.

It wasn't a demon or fallen angel, but an overweight bearded man in a chair.

"Santa Claus?" I cried in disbelief.

The giant figure did not seem to hear me. My voice was too tiny or his ears too far away. Probably both.

"Here?" I asked my guide.

"Yes," said Virg. "We trot him out every Christmas. Children want photos with him. Parents are willing to stand in line and pay greatly for the opportunity."

"You mean you take advantage of children by emotionally blackmailing parents into paying for a photo with Santa?"

"Well, we have another term for it," Virg said. "We call it 'Additional revenue stream.' Shouldn't it be Christmas for us as well?"

I stared at the immobile figure, silent and remote in depression or regret. His eyes were open, but he seemed asleep. "Is he always like this?"

"No," Virg replied. "Earlier in the year, the white fur expands and covers him completely. His beard thins to a few thick whiskers, his ears grow ridiculously long, and we trot him out again..."

"As the Easter Bunny!" I finished for her, full of disgust.

I felt like my heart was still in the elevator, still falling.

"I've had enough!" I shouted, so forcefully that it surprised both of us. I didn't want to see any more. The sooner I forgot this, this Hell, the better! "Where's the exit?" I demanded, spinning around but seeing no more doorways or escalators.

Virg pointed upward. "You wish to leave? All you have to do is climb up to his lap and tell him what you wish."

I looked up at the sheer wall of red, black, and white, feeling very much like a tiny child.

Heaven was never so far away.

The Last Reindeer

Katharina Gerlach

Lucy stepped off the ancient motorbike, reached into the sidecar, and gave her brother's head a rub. She tried to ignore the feverish heat. "I'm gonna take a look." She spoke past the pebble in her mouth that helped her cope with the thirst and nodded towards a single long dead tree that rose from the dried ground.

"Okay," Seth sounded tired. Lucy hoped they'd find better shelter tonight than protruding rock. She turned to the tree and climbed.

From her perch on the highest limb capable of supporting her weight, Lucy faced into the wind, glad for her goggles, and stared across the endless plain of dried and broken earth. Shaking the scent of sunburnt dust was as impossible as making out any features of the distorted horizon. The land seemed to be dancing with the sky in the hot air.

"How far do you think it is to the North Pole?" she called down, forcing a note of cheer into her voice.

"Santa Claws manages it overnight, so it can't be all that far," the seven-year-old's voice sounded stronger as he spoke of his beloved Santa Claws. His heart-shaped face lightened briefly into a beacon of hope in the dismal surroundings.

Lucy checked her compass again, but it pointed relentlessly into the wide expanse of cracked soil without even a hint of greenery.

This trip was a horrible mistake. She wanted to be home. It wasn't much with its single room and the sheet iron walls, but it kept out the sand, had a kitchen with running water—a luxury she'd never hoped for—and an outhouse—another luxury.

With a sigh, she tucked the compass away and climbed down. Swinging from the lowest of the dead branches, landing on bent knees.

Seth watched her from the sidecar, his scarf askew and his face lit with hope. How could he be so sure Santa Claws really existed? And that he lived in the north in a snow covered paradise?

It didn't matter. She'd do anything to keep her brother alive, even if just for one more day, even if it meant a trip on their battered bike through the desert. Seth had lain near death when she finally gave in to his pleadings to see Santa Claws. She had expected to bury him in the desert. But for reasons beyond her comprehension, Seth seemed to be improving, despite the toll the trip should be taking on him. His lethargy gave way to the fun-loving child he'd been before taking ill.

She adjusted the scarves on their faces, started the bike, and set out again. The steady putter of the bike and the tires crunching on the cracked soil sent Seth to sleep, but Lucy forced herself to drive. For miles, there was nothing but sand in the air and in her hair, and the taste of heat on her tongue. The horizon scintillated, never drawing nearer.

Seth's dark brown curls fluttered in the wind. With his eyes closed, the dark shadows under his eyes were stronger, his sunken cheeks more pronounced. The traveling doc had said he'd have a month or two at the most, and that they should enjoy the time as best they could.

I just wish he could have asked for something easier to find than snow, Lucy thought and pushed the thought of his imminent death way down.

A dot appeared on the horizon shimmering in and out of existence, finally growing to a blob. She checked her compass, they were still moving north. The closer they got, the better Lucy could identify the blob. It was a small but sturdy building made of wood. A brick-built well stood beside it, complete with a small thatched roof, and a winch. There even was a garden with green plants. Someone lived there, and since they seemed to have water, maybe she could get her bottles refilled. Seth needed more water than they carried.

Lucy stopped the bike at a good distance but left the motor idling. If an owner showed up with a gun, like many did when strangers appeared, they'd be far enough away to evade the bullets and flee. She spit out the sand in her mouth. Sure, it was a waste of fluid, but talking with sand grinding between her teeth was difficult.

"Holla, anybody home?" she called as loud as she could.

The door creaked open, but no one came out, not even when she called twice more. Did that mean no one was home? Something white and flurry wafted out of the hut's darkness, landed on the plants and vanished.

Lucy killed the engine. Maybe that was a stupid idea, but she wanted to know what the white stuff was, and Seth needed more water. She could tell by the sweat on his forehead that he wasn't well. If the building was as empty as it appeared, he could rest inside—out of the sun. And maybe, just maybe, she could convince him to return home.

Bending forward to make herself as small a target as possible, she hurried to the door. The closer she got, the less the heat bothered her. The air smelled fresher and greener nearer the plants. When she looked into the hut, her eyes widened. It was a barn as empty as the desert surrounding it. It looked bigger on the inside than on the outside, but what was most surprising was the distinct drop in temperature. As fast as she could, Lucy returned to the bike, picked up her brother and carried him inside. She lowered him onto the straw covering most of the ground so carefully that he didn't wake.

It was the perfect place to spend the night. The cool temperature would ease Seth's pain, and they'd both feel less thirsty. With luck, the well would provide them with water, too.

Behind her, a gentle voice said, "You know he'll die soon, don't you?"

She shot around, switchblade in hand.

The weirdest antelope she'd ever seen stood in front of her. It was quite big with wide shoulders and split hooves. Its head was lowered as if too heavy to lift, the thick fur seemed to be made for much colder weather, and the horns split like the branches of a tree. The pointy ends looked vicious, so she lifted her knife a little higher.

"Attacking me won't help," the animal said, and for a moment Lucy's knees trembled. Who'd ever heard of a talking antelope? But she had to be strong for Seth.

"He's got cancer." She was surprised how defiant her voice sounded. "And I'll make his final wish come true or die trying."

"Santa Claus hasn't granted wishes in..." The antelope shrugged. Its fur shook with the gesture. "I don't know ... in several centuries?"

Lucy frowned. "How do you know we're after Santa Claws?"

"It's Claus, not Claws." The animal cocked its head, staring at her and her knife with deep, brown eyes. "Why don't you put that away, so we can talk?"

Hesitantly, Lucy obeyed, but kept her hand curled around the switchblade's heft in her pocket, just in case.

"Very good." The animal stepped past her and nuzzled the sleeping boy. Lucy nearly pulled her knife out again, but Seth just smiled as if he had a pleasant dream. The animal looked up at her. "No one comes here unless they've got a request for Santa. What's yours? Saving his life?"

"He could do that?" Lucy's eyes opened wide. "But the doctor said there's no cure."

"Not in this world, no." The animal settled down beside her brother. "So why did you come, then?"

"He wants to see snow. Just once." Lucy blushed. "He thinks there's snow at the North Pole where Santa Claw—Claus is living. I'd hoped we'd get there if we traveled north long enough."

"He won't make it that far. One way or the other, you'll return home alone." The animal's words were a blow. Tears painted tracks in the dust on her cheeks. "You love him much, don't you?"

Lost for words, Lucy unsuccessfully tried to stop crying. She nodded. For a moment they both looked at Seth in silence.

"I'll make you a deal," the animal said suddenly and stood up again. "You will not like it, but it's all I can do."

Lucy looked at it wordlessly.

"I can take your brother to Santa Claus. He might or might not cure him from his disease, but at least your brother will see snow. That much I can promise." It shook its head. "However, it will mean farewell here and now for you."

"Why would you help?" The words wobbled past the lump in Lucy's throat.

"Life has been...", its great head lifted and held still as if seeking an answer from beyond, "...boring ever since Santa gave up on the children." The animal sighed. "Your love for your brother might shake him into action again. I can make no promises."

Something icy landed on Lucy's hand. As she looked at the tiny star, it melted. She'd never seen anything so delicate, so beautiful, and so fleeting. Was that snow? Her heart pounded and the lump in her throat grew. Blinking away the tears, she turned to wake her brother.

It took her two weeks to return home, much longer than the trip out. The sun was near setting when the last sputter of the fuel told the bike would go no further. Lacking the strength to push it, she set out on foot. Home was less than an hour away.

The head of the day cooled rapidly as she put one foot ahead of the next. The heat had not only eased up, but she felt a damp chill in the air that reminded her of the barn where she left her brother. Eventually she found herself walking down the slope toward the small settlement with her home, a smile spread over her face and even though it was tinged with sadness, it contained hope. The village and surrounding lands were powdered with a thin layer of white.

Alternative Holidays

Santa's Dog

Kevin McCarty

'Twas the day after Christmas
And all were asleep,
Full bellies, quite warm,
Nary even a peep.

But for one little dog,
Floppy ears, brown-red,
His muzzle was white
And low hung his head.

His paws were so sore
From thistles and rocks.
His nose was near frozen,
Traveling the blocks.

They once called him, Rusty
He longed for that sound.
Many had loved him,
But not one was around

Had he been abandoned,
Forgotten, replaced,
Too old to be useful,
A memory erased?

Well, no matter the cause,
He breathed a great sigh

And closed his sad eyes,
Then lay down to die

But then in the distance
Arose such a sound,
Poomp, poomp, it was rubber,
Blue-ish and quite round.

Russ lumbered in pursuit
To capture that ball.
But where to return it?
He knew not at all.

He looked left, he looked right,
That ball in his mouth
And spied an old elf
A bit to the south.

He was dressed all in green,
A little red cap,
And a broad, beaming smile,
A right friendly chap.

At his feet the ball dropped.
Rusty wagged and barked.
His eyes tried to say
Please play as they sparked.

"Good fellow," the elf said
"Why you have a knack."
He threw it again,
Russ brought it right back.

"You shouldn't be alone,"
Nick said as he frowned
"So tired and hungry."
He looked all around.

"No master, no family
I'll not let this be.
It's no longer Christmas
But this gift I give thee."

He picked up that old hound
Looked at him up close
The dog wagged his tail
Then he licked Santa's nose.

"My fine little dachshund
Alone for no longer.
You're coming with me,
And you'll grow even stronger."

"Chasing balls every day
And night if you choose.
I must ask the missus,
But I doubt she'll refuse."

With a wink and a grin
A flash through the fog
The two headed northward
Saint Nick, with his dog.

Alternative Holidays

Christmas Fare

Kelly Piner

Chaz braked at the stoplight and squinted at the boarded-up front window of Delaney's, the once elegant 1950s bistro. Sacks of trash were stacked at the gate that had led to the lavish patio. "We're bound to find another restaurant around here."

Olive groaned. "I hope it's soon. My blood sugar's dropping."

"You and your blood sugar." He pulled a miniature Hershey bar from his pocket and passed it to her. They rode in silence as Chaz drove down one cobblestone street after another in the old section of town, slowing at each intersection to glance at storefronts.

Their Christmas tradition had always been to dine out at a posh uptown restaurant, followed by a visit to Saylor's tree farm, where she and Chaz would stroll hand-in-hand past rows and rows of pine trees, careful to select just the right one. Afterwards, they'd warm themselves by the old granite fireplace at Lily's Café, where they'd enjoy a piping hot pot of ginger tea and crumpets. Given Chaz's busy schedule as an airline pilot and hers as a hospital administrator, it was one of the few days they had all to themselves.

She slipped on her black leather gloves with the faux fur trim, determined to salvage the lunch. "Don't stop at just any restaurant." She spoke loudly, so as to be heard over the rumble of the brick pavement. "This is our Christmas luncheon. We've been coming to Delaney's forever. How could it close after 70 years?"

"Probably the recession. I'm not finding anything down here. Maybe we should just head back and eat at Ralph's Tavern?"

"Ralph's Tavern! You've got to be kidding. That's not special. We go there every Friday night for fish and chips."

"Do you have a better idea?"

She gently backhanded him. "Don't you have any imagination?" Then, with no forewarning, she shouted, "Look!" Olive pointed at a quaint brick cottage decorated in white shimmering lights, sitting on the corner of Plymouth Street. It seemed to have come out of nowhere. A massive spruce adorned the large picture window, wrapped in strands of blue and green lights and covered in icicles, reminding her of the large Christmas trees at her grandmother's clapboard farmhouse, so many years ago. From a Mercedes up ahead, a handsomely dressed couple emerged. The valet handed the man a ticket and sped away in the car.

"*London's Eatery*. How come we've never seen this before?"

"Beats me. Maybe it just opened." Chaz cruised up to the valet parking, and a young man opened Olive's door.

"Welcome to London's, ma'am." He spoke with a perfect British accent.

Olive slid from the SUV and hooked arms with Chaz. She took cautious steps in her new black suede pumps through the freshly fallen snow on the slick sidewalk. A doorman in a pressed black and white uniform opened the heavy oak door, complimented by a stained-glass window. From inside the foyer, the dining room looked festive, cozy and comfortably arranged, and in the corner, a roaring stone fireplace warmed the room. Wreaths made of pinecones and red ribbons adorned the old brick walls.

They approached a young hostess dressed in a red velvet dress and Santa hat. Her shoulder length blonde hair and sparking hazel eyes reminded Olive of their own daughter, Morgan. "Lunch for two?" The hostess had the same warm, inviting British accent as the valet.

Chaz nodded and squeezed Olive's arm. "Is this special enough for you?"

Olive smiled. "Thank God I found it."

Chaz rolled his eyes. "What would I do without you?"

"Follow me." The hostess lifted two leather-bound menus and led them to a roomy burgundy booth by the picture window, near the fireplace. "Your server will be right with you."

Olive slipped off her coat and slid into the booth. She adjusted one of her pearl earrings. "I've never seen such a beautiful restaurant. The building looks exactly as it must have looked in the 1890s."

Chaz peeked over the top of his glasses. "Yeah. It still has the original tin ceiling."

"I don't ever want to leave."

"That could get expensive."

Olive laughed and delved into the menu. "Oh my. A traditional English meal. They even have pureed parsnips and Yorkshire Pudding."

A tall, lanky waiter approached their table, his full lips and piercing steel blue eyes reminiscent of a young Paul Newman. "I'm Jacob. I'll be taking care of you today. May I start you with a cocktail?"

Chaz turned to Olive, who nodded, and then said, "We'll have a bottle of Veuve Champagne."

"Good choice, sir." The waiter retreated.

Olive inched closer to Chaz and grasped his hand. "What a perfect day. An enchanting restaurant. Champagne."

"Let's make London's our new Christmas tradition."

"You don't have to twist my arm."

Jacob reappeared seconds later and popped the champagne cork. He filled two sparkling crystal flutes, and carefully placed the remainder in a chilled bucket nearby. "Enjoy."

They clinked their glasses together. "To London's." Chaz said.

"And to a lifetime of Christmas luncheons," Olive added. She was taking her first sip of champagne when she went still.

"What's wrong?"

"Our waiter, Jacob."

"What about him?"

"He was young, early twenties. But look at him now. He's at least forty and has a paunch. His pants won't even fit over his stomach."

Chaz turned. "It's just the muted lighting. It's hard to tell from this angle."

Olive forced a smile. "I guess you're right." But she had her doubts. Chaz's methodical, practical mind refused to believe anything but the obvious.

"Of course I'm right. Now, let's order." He signaled to the waiter.

When Jacob approached their booth, Olive's jaw went slack.

His blonde tousled hair was a dingy gray, and dark circles rimmed his eyes.

She glanced at Chaz who stared down at the menu. She cleared her throat. "Are you Jacob, our waiter from before?"

"Yes, ma'am. Is there a problem?" His voice had turned gravelly.

There was something about his eyes, a vacantness. Olive shook her head. "No, you just look different, somehow."

"Probably a little frazzled, the lunch rush and all."

After they had ordered two turkey entrees with all the trimmings, Olive leaned over and whispered. "You're going to tell me that this is the same young man who greeted us?" She glared at Chaz, daring him to disagree.

Chaz cleaned his glasses with the white cloth napkin. "I admit this guy looked quite a bit older. Maybe there's two Jacob's who work here?"

"Please."

"Don't worry about it. Let's just enjoy our fabulous lunch." Chaz took a big gulp of champagne.

For a few minutes, they admired the décor. Then Olive poked Chaz's arm. "Look." She motioned toward the couple in the corner booth.

"What now?"

"It's the couple who came in ahead of us; the ones driving the Mercedes."

"What about them?"

"Don't tell me you don't see it." Her voice held a hint of disbelief.

Chaz glanced. "I don't see anything but two old people drinking wine."

"Exactly! They weren't old when they came inside. Can't you see it?"

"Maybe you've had too much champagne."

"Two glasses? I've had two glasses. You always blame everything on me having too much champagne. They're not even the same people who came inside. Chaz, they resemble...your parents."

Chaz barely stifled a laugh. "Now I know it's the champagne. Come on, Olive."

Chaz's parents had been killed in an auto accident five years earlier, and Chaz rarely spoke of it. His mom, also a Brit, had prepared many an English meal for them.

With shaky hands, Olive poured herself another drink and lifted it to her lips. The earlier festive bustling had morphed into film clips of grainy black and white, vibrant shades of red and green now muted shades of gray, and heaviness clung to the air. Overhead speakers piped in Bach's Toccata and Fugue in D minor, but The Hallelujah Symphony had played softly in the background only a few minutes earlier, she was certain of it. Dread marred waiters' faces as they moved in and out of the dining room, as if in slow motion, through the swinging door that connected to the kitchen.

A waiter old enough to be Jacob's dad emerged from the back, clutching two plates, which he placed in front of them. "Will this be all?" He looked off into the distance, as if he had somewhere else to go.

"This'll be just fine," Chaz said, without looking up.

When Jacob had retreated from ear shot, Olive pressed her hand to the small of her throat. "I won't even say it."

Chaz placed a napkin in his lap. "Good. Let's eat."

Olive looked down at her meal and froze. Small bits of spoiled meat filled one side of the plate. The putrid stench made her gag. In disbelief, she set her fork aside. Decomposed parsnips had turned to slime, and a greenish film covered the sourdough rolls. She pressed her hand to her mouth. "Chaz!"

"Now what? Can't you let me eat in peace?" Seemingly unaware, he lifted a forkful of decaying turkey to his mouth and then another.

"How can you eat it? It's rotten."

He threw down his napkin and slid out of the booth. "When I return, I don't want to hear another word. This isn't like you. It's just not like you." He marched off in the direction of the men's room.

The room spun slightly. Olive leaned her head back against the high back booth.

Had she drunk too much champagne? But this place wasn't right; first, their aging waiter, and then the couple in the corner. And now, the spoiled food. And Chaz hadn't even noticed? And when she next looked, the young hostess had transformed into an elderly woman, hobbling along on a walker as she ushered a family to a table. Was she hallucinating?

Olive flinched when the waiter interrupted her thoughts.

"Yorkshire pudding, ma'am." An aged Jacob wore a patch over his right eye. A trickle of blood ran underneath it, smearing his cheek. "Enjoy." Small black insects crawled along his apron and his youthful hands were now bony with loose, crinkled skin.

Olive trembled. She wanted to speak, but no words would come. And what was taking Chaz so long? She turned to the pudding and gaped. Hundreds of tiny spider eggs sat in the middle of it, encased in a spun silk blanket. The egg sac quivered slightly, as if the babies were eager to burst into life.

Out of nowhere, a dead rodent dropped from the ceiling and landed on a nearby table.

Olive pushed the dish away and dashed toward the men's room, whimpering. She could kick herself for leaving her phone in the glovebox. When she found Chaz, she'd drag him out of the hellish eatery and into the street if she had to. If only she'd agreed to lunch at Ralph's Tavern. But, no. She always had to have it her way, no matter the price.

A sign that read *Gents* hung over an old wooden door. She banged loudly. After a good fifteen seconds, she banged harder. An elderly man with a full beard emerged, dressed in tattered clothes.

"Sir, is my husband in there? I have to find him."

The old man shook his head. "No one in there but me."

Olive cracked open the restroom door. "Chaz! Chaz!" When he didn't respond, she peeked into the kitchen through the swinging door. Her eyes opened wide.

A legion of black mice raced across an old stone floor, darting over staff's feet who seemed not to notice.

Tall Mason jars filled with a blackish fluid lined a wooden shelf. Inside the jars, something resembling intestines floated.

Blood rushed from her head.

In the distance, what looked like discarded limbs, arms and legs, were piled high near a large boiling caldron.

Filled with dread, she squinted and leaned in for a closer look.

"May I help you?"

Olive screeched.

Jacob stood behind her, looking older than ever. His blood-tinged eye patch stared back at her. He swiped his hands against his white apron, leaving a large red stain.

"I can't find my husband. I must find him."

"Have you checked your booth?"

"Of course I checked the booth," she said, becoming hysterical. "He left for the restroom, but never returned."

Jacob emitted the most unholy odor, recognizable to Olive from the days when she'd worked in the hospital morgue.

She backed away. "You're right," she said, her voice quivering. "I'll go back and check our booth." She waited until Jacob disappeared, and crept back and peered into the kitchen. She had to find Chaz.

In the distance, Jacob tossed limbs into the boiling caldron and used a log to press the arms and legs down into the water. He stirred them around with a large black spoon.

Olive opened her mouth to scream for help, but no words would come, as if a dark force had engulfed her and rendered her speechless.

She charged for the front door. She'd get the car and call Chaz from the road.

At the oak entryway, the muscular doorman stepped forward, blocking her way. "Sorry, ma'am, but no one's allowed outside." He held his hands behind his back and rocked back and forth on his heels.

"But I have to find my husband," she faintly said.

"You'll not find him out there." He motioned with his head toward the street. "Kindly return to your booth, ma'am."

Despite her determination to flee past the doorman, her legs suddenly felt as if thrust into quicksand, heavy, and unable to carry her. Had a spell been cast that left her immobilized? She frantically scanned the restaurant from one side to the other, searching for some clue, until the elderly hostess approached. "Follow me."

"May I use your phone? I left mine in the car."

"Sorry, but ours has been out of service for weeks."

With nowhere to run, Olive limped on wobbly legs behind the old woman who only an hour earlier could have been a sorority girl, in her prime. The hostess gestured with her blue-veined hand when they reached the burgundy booth.

Olive shook her head. "This isn't right. I was sharing a booth with my husband, but he's gone."

"This most certainly is your booth, number 31."

But the elderly man from the bathroom sat at the booth, eating lunch. Rotten vegetables clung to his beard. "I don't know this man," Olive told the hostess.

The man looked up and spoke with his mouth full. "Don't be an idiot. What are you waiting for? Sit down."

Olive glanced around for help.

No one met her gaze.

She perched on the edge of the seat, careful to keep her distance from the stranger. "I don't understand. Who are you?"

"Olive, it's me. Chaz."

"Chaz! You're not Chaz. You're old enough to be his father. Why are you doing this to me?"

"Look closely, dear." He leaned over and stared at her.

Olive pressed her hand to her mouth. There was something familiar about him, his eyes. "Please tell me what's going on. My husband's disappeared."

"He hasn't disappeared. I'm right here. You said that you never wanted to leave London's." He jabbed his index finger at her. "Those were your exact words. You never wanted to leave. A lot of years have passed, Olive."

The room spun as she looked around, praying that she was being secretly filmed for some TV reality show, but the bleakness of the situation told her otherwise. Tears collected in her eyes. "But we just got here, an hour ago."

"No, Olive. We've been here a lifetime. London's is so special, no one ever wants to leave. People age and die here. Their bodies have to be processed."

"Good Lord!" Olive wept into her hands. "What do we do now? Can't we just drive away?"

The old man shook his head. "Too late. If only you'd agreed to lunch at Ralph's Tavern, but you wanted something more special. I died years ago. I'm just waiting to have my body processed. It's not yet your time." He motioned to an elderly man who limped to their table. "Jacob, bring us a bottle of your best champagne."

"Right away, sir. The occasion?"

"I'm being processed tonight. My time has finally come."

"Very good, sir. Very good indeed. I'll bring two bottles. Drink them quickly, and you won't feel a thing."

Olive watched in horrified silence as staff rolled Chaz into the back room where his limbs were chopped off one by one and tossed into the caldron.

As the room grew dark around her, Olive caught the first glimpse of herself in a silver teapot.

Alternative Holidays

Paradise Misplaced

Samuel Marzioli

Forrester and I took our positions on the ramp just beyond the ship's main hatch, our weapons glistening in the light of towering infernos. A swarm of Hell prisoners clashed and floundered as they raced in our direction, their screams manic, deranged. It didn't take a genius to realize they wanted out and we were the only ride.

"Ready Ryan?" said Forrester, priming his energy dispersing gun.

"If not, I guess I'll see you in Heaven," I said, priming mine.

A man-spirit scrambled up the ramp. Gelatinous ooze matted his hair against his forehead. When he snarled, the square mustache perched upon his upper lip pressed into his nostrils. He looked haggard, scalded to a merlot-red, ravaged by scars befitting an afterlife of torture. Nevertheless, I knew exactly who he was.

"Give my regards to Goebbels, *Herr Fuehrer*!" I said, and fired.

A beam of light ripped into his chest.

He dropped to his side, floundering like a fish out of water.

I fired again.

He rolled and struck the ground with the silence one would expect from the barely tangible.

"You do realize that was Charlie Chaplin, right?" asked Forrester.

I shrugged. "That's not the story my future kids will hear someday."

From then on, we focused only on the "plang" of our guns and the careful aim we threw at the advancing horde.

With every passing second, they shaved the gap between us, drawing closer to their escape—and our capture. Not for the last time, I remembered it was Father's Day. If only my dad could see me now. I kept an eye out for him, just in case.

#

Earlier that day, my boss Mr. Fudder called me in to work at his bookstore down on Main, aptly—if unimaginatively—called Mr. Fudder's Books. Being fatherless on Father's Day, I had nothing planned. Besides, what better way to distract oneself than with friendly blather and mindless repetition?

Six hours of mundanity ensued. I trust I don't need to mention the questions I answered, the directions I gave, the books I bagged, or the spicy burrito I ate at lunchtime—which greeted me like an old friend when I unwrapped it, but then shamed me with an early, angry exit—to make my point?

Once my shift ended, I nodded at Mr. Fudder, who waved and smiled, and wished my father "health and happiness."

"If I ever see him again, I'll be sure to let him know," I said, and made a beeline for the door.

No sooner did I take a step, than my cellphone rang. Without bothering to check the screen, I took a calming breath and answered.

"Hey Mom," I said.

"Hi sweetie. How are you doing?" she said, her voice dripping thick and sweet as molasses.

"Fine."

"Are you sure? It's Father's Day you know."

Briefly, I turned to scan the sales floor. Small cardboard placards had been taped to every shelf, and a ten-foot banner stretched across the ceiling, their messages proclaiming: "Looking for that special gift for Dad? We got it!" Just in case I didn't get the hint, a father standing in the center aisle embraced his son, a scene so heartwarming it might have been the subject of a Rockwell painting.

"Is it? I hardly noticed," I said.

"Well if you need to talk, you know I'm here for you."

"Thanks. I just clocked out. I still have a few errands to run, but then I'm coming home."

"That's fine. Take all the time you need."

After we said our goodbyes, I cut the line and stowed the phone back in my pocket.

My mother meant well, but even after all these years, she didn't understand: the last thing I needed was a torrent of reminders of what I'd never had.

"I love you, Dad," the son down the center aisle said.

His father ruffled his hair, and a too-pleased grin spread across his face. "I love you too, Son."

"Oh for Christ's sake," I muttered, and headed outside.

#

Out front, the street had been cordoned off from Dwight Way all the way to Channing. Onlookers, newsmen, and an army of cops gathered around, forming a semi-circle in front of a new building erected in a once-empty lot. For years, a steel edifice forty feet high had hidden it from plain view, but now it had been removed, and its insides revealed.

It appeared to be a restaurant shaped like a flying saucer, like Planet Hollywood with a sci-fi twist. While I'd never been a fan of kitsch, I was famished, so I pushed my way through the crowd and trudged up the restaurant's entrance ramp. The cramped interior had no tables, only three rows of black leather chairs bolted to the floor. All of them faced a man seated in a cockpit with an impressive display of toggle switches and blinking buttons. He punched a few, flipped others, and a pervasive thrum sounded from beneath the flooring.

"Engines primed," the man announced.

Only then did I realize my mistake; this was no restaurant. I tried to apologize and leave, but a couple of flight attendants ushered me into an empty seat, and once they started passing out complimentary drinks and hors d'oeuvres, I didn't have the heart to protest. There were five passengers in all, including me, but a man in an orange jumpsuit sealed the hatch before anyone had a chance to get acquainted.

He turned to us, swept his arms out with a theatrical flair, and said, "Welcome to Heaven Cruise! I'm Doctor Forrester and our ship is the *Spirit of Adventure*, a luxury craft designed to make your trans-dimensional journey as safe as an average car commute. Is everybody ready?"

The others nodded; I offered up a why-the-hell-not shrug.

"Hold on, Doctor," said a man seated in front of me, wearing a black suit so shiny I could almost see my reflection. "You made a lot of impossible claims about what this ship could do. Before I go anywhere, I want proof that it's safe and functional. Theory, schematics, anything!"

"Nicholas Trent, is it?" said Forrester.

"Yes."

"That information's classified. But if that's unsatisfactory, you can always take the portal." He pointed to a transparent, cylindrical booth set into the back wall, no bigger than a coffin. "It's voice activated. Just say 'I lack the spirit of adventure' and you'll be transported back from whence you came, no questions asked."

Nicholas crossed his arms, his glare fierce, a look like he was trying to bend spoons with his mind.

"No? Well then, moving right along," said Forrester.

#

I watched our ascension through the windows surrounding the cabin's spherical interior. At first, the city lay sprawled around us, a tribute to human ingenuity, but then it shrank into a splotch of gray as if a reminder of man's true cosmological significance. Before I had a chance to truly wax philosophical, Forrester said, "Anyone up for a game of *Go Fish*?" and the ideas were swallowed. Because, dang it, I was up!

Forrester, Debra—a prim African-American woman in a flannel skirt—and I played ten frustrating hands where no one confessed to having fours or tens. I quit once the stakes raised from fun to a thousand dollars a round. Cardinal Strang—an older gentleman wearing a red cassock—took my place.

In the meantime, Nicholas and his shiny suit traipsed around the cabin. He loomed over the control panel in the cockpit until the pilot said, "No loitering, chief," and later settled by a window.

"This is unbelievable," he said.

"I know what you mean," I said, after sidling up beside him. "I can't believe I'm actually in space!"

"No, I mean this whole excursion. My father coerced me into this. He called it reconnaissance for when he passed away. But I have better things to do than waste my time on this superstitious nonsense."

An awkward silence followed. I'd never been good with those, so I blurted out the first thing that came to mind. "I didn't know my father. He abandoned my mom and me shortly after I was born."

Nicholas's face shifted to a grimace, equal parts dismissive and displeased. "Who are you supposed to be, anyway? I recognize everyone here but you."

My heart thumped like a hammer on a gavel. While the legal consequences of my uninvited presence weren't clear, I could almost hear the voice of my future cellmate crooning "Hey pretty boy" into my ear. Thankfully, the pilot interrupted before I had a chance to answer.

"We're shifting into altered space. Everybody buckle up."

Nicholas shook his head. "You can count me out!" He made for the portal, pried the sliding door apart, and stepped inside. "I sure as hell lack the spirit of adventure," he said.

And he was gone.

#

Once we entered altered space, the ship was caught in turbulent vibrations. It reminded me of that time my buddies dragged me to a back-alley massage parlor, and the violent unease the masseuse caused molding my buttocks into some misshapen form. The fact it came free this time did nothing to relieve the tension.

With fingers clenched around the armrests, I darted anxious glances from window to window.

The others handled it better than me. Forrester attempted to catch everyone's attention, grinning like a boy who'd just flipped through his first nudie magazine. Debra rested her hands over her lap with the same composure as the Queen at teatime. Dawson—about as young as me, but with a pinched, bulldog face–tapped his toe, and Cardinal Strang whispered a prayer in Latin.

"Leaving altered space," the pilot said.

When the ship eased into smoother sailing, everyone strained for the closest view.

Instead of the roiling, black void of altered space, the scene was drenched in perfect white, details etched by the barest hint of fine, gray lines.

"So this is Heaven. No busty, bikini clad angels? How disappointing," said Dawson.

"No, it's Purgatory, our first stop," said Forrester. "I figured it would be easier to enjoy the best when you can compare it with something less."

"Like sipping Ovaltine before having a proper glass of chocolate milk," I offered.

"Exactly."

We gathered around the exit. When the ramp lowered, Cardinal Strang rushed out first. He reached the ground and fell to his knees, lifting his hands like a wide receiver who'd just scored the winning touchdown. "It's beautiful. A lifetime of faith justified," he said, voice wracked with emotion.

We stepped around him. Once he finished with his impromptu celebration, he caught up to us in a hobbled run.

The farther we walked, the more details emerged: streets of alabaster lined by chalky sidewalks, and beyond them rows of single-story ivory buildings of the exact same proportions. Only, it was muted, phantasmal, a mere suggestion of something real. The moment I turned away, whatever I had seen faded from my mind like the content of a dream.

"Jeez, the window view kind of summed it up," said Dawson.

"Agreed. It's not much to look at," said Debra.

Forrester shrugged. "It's as it should be. Purgatory was never meant to be grand. It's a place—"

"Of quiet contemplation," finished a man who, like everything else, appeared only when approached within a certain distance.

The man had a blank expression, neither calm nor alarmed by our presence. The same couldn't be said for us.

Debra gasped, Dawson chuckled, and I took a profound new interest in the pristine skies above us. Because the man was naked. With each step, his limp penis swung like a dog's happy tail. Once he paused, he rested his hands on his hips and allowed his manhood to dangle with the confidence of porn stars.

"Doctor Forrester? Your servant, sir," he said, his bow the only modest thing about him.

"Likewise, Reginald. As you can see, I've brought the first group."

Reginald studied us closely. "I cannot say I miss clothing much. Here, we exist only as God intended." He waved a hand in front of his crotch, and winked at Debra.

Debra took a step back.

"Keep it classy, Reggie," said Forrester. "It's time for the tourist bit now. Exactly how long have you been here?"

"From 1860 until now. Maybe two hundred years?"

"A nice place, decent neighbors?"

"Not bad, but then again not all good either." He smiled, this time winking at me.

I took a step back too.

"So what's Purgatory all about?" said Dawson.

"A fair question," said Reginald. "Some have described it as a simple place of holding, others as a realm of meager tortures. In reality, it is somewhere in between. Here we are forced to confront the greatest disturbances of our mortal lives, to settle once and for all the things that made us unready for union with the Maker."

"And what does that entail?" said Debra, placing a timid hand against her cheek.

"Why not find out for yourself? Close your eyes. Do not think. Let Purgatory lead you."

We all did as directed. In the quiet of my mind, I found only those questions about the afterlife that have plagued humanity for generations. Did they eat? Did they laugh, and play, or love? And the big one: was sex allowed?

The more I let go, the more my mind fixed upon a single scene. I saw myself as a baby, swaddled in a blanket, cradled in my mother's arms. A man leaned over her hospital bed, his gaze like pride, like rapture. His hair was black, and his skin and eyes were brown, Spanish at a stretch, but most likely of Filipino descent. While I didn't recognize him, I knew he had to be my father.

Did that mean his absence was my so-called mortal struggle? I couldn't believe it. I'd had a decent life, with a caring mother who'd provided all the comfort and emotional stability I could have asked for. I didn't miss my father because I never knew him, and yet—

Debra screamed. My eyes snapped open. I found her on her hands and knees, face planted to the street, with Forrester crouched beside her.

"Get me out of here!" she shrieked.

"Yes," said Forrester. "I suppose we've stayed long enough. Thanks, Reggie," he called over his shoulder as he ambled back the way we came.

"At your service," Reginald said, waving goodbye. As if to emphasize the point, his penis waved as well.

#

"Are you sure you won't stay, Debra? It only gets better from here on in," said Forrester.

"Yes, I'm sure. I have a lot to think about and I doubt even Heaven will change that. Goodbye." She stumbled to the portal.

Her hands trembled as she slid the door open. Once inside, she said, "I lack the spirit of adventure," and disappeared.

Forrester chuckled.

"What's so funny?" said Cardinal Strang.

"There's no verbal command. The portal triggers upon entry, with a slight delay. I only said that before because Nicholas was a ninny."

"Real cute, Doc," said Dawson.

"I thought so."

"Debra may have the right idea. I think maybe I should join her," said Cardinal Strang. "When His Holiness assigned me to investigate Mr. Forrester's claims, I never dreamed it would be like this."

"Better make your decision quickly. We need to press on," said Forrester.

We all strapped in again, even Cardinal Strang. Once we took off, he seemed nervous, shivering in his seat, muttering what seemed to be, "*Dominus Meus, Deus Meus*" over and over.

"Take us out," said Forrester, and the pilot responded with a two-finger salute.

Soon, the white of Purgatory faded to black, and the uncomfortable vibrations returned.

"No, I've changed my mind," said Cardinal Strang, fumbling with his seat belt. "I can't face the Maker yet. I'm not ready."

"Easy, Your Eminence. It's not safe to move around," said Forrester.

"I can't stay," he said, rounding the chairs to the rear wall.

"It's too dangerous to use the portal while in altered space," said Forrester. "Your body could break apart and be lost in oblivion."

Cardinal Strang lumbered toward the pilot.

"Get back in your seat, Your Eminence," said Forrester.

"You heard the man. Sit down!" yelled the pilot.

Cardinal Strang tried wrestling the controls away from the pilot, and failing that he yanked the control stick hard.

The cabin's vibrations grew until every object became a ragged blur of motion. The engines hummed, the sound low at first, but as seconds piled on it rose into a high-pitched bleat.

Details appeared outside the window: lakes of fire, black terrain spanning from horizon to horizon, a series of metal walls that separated the land into a patchwork quilt of grays and blacks.

And all of it swelling, a barrier of earth and stone rising up to greet us.

"Here it comes!" yelled the pilot.

I shut my eyes. My heartbeat thumped in my head like a steady slap against my ears.

The ship lurched and collided with the ground once... twice... three times. The hull skidded, a sound like nails on a chalkboard boosted to infinity. One more feeble crash and the ship slid into a rest.

Forrester tore his seat belt off. "Is everyone okay?"

Though dazed, I nodded.

"Once I find my severed head, I'll let you know for sure," said Dawson, massaging his temples with both hands.

The flight attendants gave him thumbs up, and the pilot made his way to the hatch, muttering, "Better see where we landed."

"No, don't!" shouted Cardinal Strang. He stumbled after him. "I'm not ready to see the blessed lands yet!"

The pilot tossed him a withering stare. "Brother, you got your wish." He pressed the hatch release. "Welcome to Damnation," he said and headed outside.

The smell of smoke and sulfur poured into the cabin, along with a wave of broiling heat. The ground was endless, a flat and desiccated expanse punctuated by skyscrapers that appeared to have been carved from the very stone they sat upon. And now that we were at ground level, the flames of the lakes of fire towered over us, as stark and daunting as any mushroom cloud.

"No busty, scantily clad demon babes? I'm disappointed," said Dawson.

"On Earth, you squeeze boobs. In Hell, boobs squeeze you," said Forrester.

"Terrifying. And yet I'm intrigued. Is that true?"

"I don't know. But I certainly have no intention of finding out. Hey, pilot, what's the damage?"

"Surprisingly minimal," he called out. "A thruster's been torn loose. I'll need to weld it back in place. Someone give me a hand?"

"I'll go," I said. Since technically I didn't belong, it was the least I could do.

"Wait," said Forrester. He approached a wall panel, which snapped open with a hiss, exposing a column of gadgets all pressed into individual nooks. "This is for him," he said, holding out a welder. "And this is for you."

He handed me a gun. Though it was leg-length, with a barrel the circumference of a dinner plate, it felt light as Styrofoam.

"What is it?" I said, rubbing my hand over its slick, cool surface.

"Energy dispersing gun."

"What am I supposed to do with it?"

"Cock the forend, wait until you see the reds of their eyes, and blast those so-and-sos into spirit bits."

"Got it."

Once outside, I handed the welding torch to the pilot. He slipped on a helmet, gloves, and padding, and got to work on the repairs.

I stood guard on the ramp, making sidelong glances at the empty buildings only a few miles away. Hell's heat was suffocating, ripping so much sweat from my pores I shined with the luster of a honey-glazed ham.

Soon, I spotted a native. A man—or at least the spirit of a man, as he was slightly transparent–poked his head out from a window. Others did the same, and dozens more exited through doors, a stream of curious gawkers. I waved. It seemed like the proper thing to do. After all, if someone had crashed a car into my yard, an apologetic wave was the least I would expect. On hindsight, not my brightest moment.

Their gazes locked on me. Worse still, as they began a frantic race in our direction, their body language didn't convey an ounce of reciprocal politeness. They were like dogs chasing the only cat, cannibals tearing after the lone anthropologist, or Brits scrambling for the last cup of tea.

"Pilot," I said.

"Yes."

"Is this as bad as it looks?"

He turned. "Worse! Doctor Forrester?"

"I see it. I'll be right out," yelled Forrester, grabbing a gun.

"I think I left my stove on," said Dawson, stepping into the portal. "I lack the—" he started, but slapped his forehead and grinned, disappearing before the laughter could roll out from his throat.

"Your Eminence?" said Forester, motioning to the last gun still resting in its nook. The old man shook his head, huddling between the flight attendants behind the backmost row of chairs.

Forrester hustled out to join me, and said, "Looks like it's up to us, kid. I didn't catch your name."

"Ryan," I said.

#

"For the love of God, Ryan, get your head back in the game!" said Forrester, blasting a red-scaled demon off the back of a spirit that bore a striking resemblance to Vlad Tepes.

"Sorry. I was just remembering how this mess began."

"You have an impeccable sense of timing. And just so there's no confusion, that was sarcasm."

"Noted."

I continued firing, a caricature of tough-guys that would've made Schwarzenegger in his prime jealous. Or at least that's how I imagined it—I'm open to the possibility I looked more like Gandhi in a slap fight.

"What happens if they get into the ship?" I said.

"They might escape Hell," said Forrester.

"What happens if they capture us?"

"Torture. Death. Who knows? They left that part out of my Bible, smart guy."

A girl clambered up the ramp on hands and knees. When she lifted her head, a bestial growl escaped her throat and I jolted. Not because her flayed and barbecued body reminded me of the floating chunks left in a kitchen fryer, but because I recognized her.

"Amber Ferranger!"

She was my first love. We went out from junior high to my sophomore year in high school, and broke up when I caught her making out with Tom Drake in the back row of our local theater. I'll admit, once I knocked her back with an energy beam, I felt a warm glow of satisfaction. After her, I didn't recognize anyone else, so I started giving the spirits false identities to take the edge off.

That neighbor who played his drums until four in the morning. *Plang*!

Whoever scratched "Cool Beans" into the hood of my mother's car last week. *Plang*!

My father, who missed every important moment of my life, without a single phone call or letter of explanation... I tried to pull the trigger on that one, but something held me back. So, instead—

My English teacher, who gave me a "C" on my mid-term project last semester. *Plang*!

I heard Forrester call out, "At your leisure, pilot!"

"Almost there," said the pilot.

For every spirit we picked off, another dozen took their place. The Hell prisoners drew within a stone's throw.

I gulped and braced myself for the worst when dispersal beams erupted from between Forrester and me in rapid succession. They had the accuracy of a master marksman— headshots, every one.

Briefly, I turned to glimpse our new ally.

"Cardinal Strang?" I said. Because, let's face it, I had my money on a flight attendant.

"This is my fault. I can't let you do it alone," he said.

"But how are you so good?"

"Faith can be offensive no matter how well intended. Therefore, they train us in more than just theology these days."

As unlikely as it seemed, we managed to hold the Hell prisoners back, covering the wastelands with a carpet of their destabilized bodies.

My gun went empty first. For good measure, I hurled it at the closest attacker.

He caught it and fell back, tripping up the mob behind him.

I thanked my obsession with old actions flicks for that one.

"Almost out," said Forrester.

"Me too," said Cardinal Strang.

The pilot announced, "I'm finished. Let's get the *Hell* out of here!"

I chuckled, despite myself.

We retreated into the cabin. Forrester and Cardinal Strang laid down suppressing fire with the last of their "ammo." Once we made it inside, Forrester mashed the hatch button while the rest of us strapped in.

The pilot initiated the take-off sequence and we blasted away, leaving Hell behind.

#

When we reentered the space above Earth, Cardinal Strang said his farewells, along with a heap of apologies for the trouble he'd caused.

"Think nothing of it, Your Eminence," said Forrester. "We'll bill you for the damages."

After the portal whisked him away, I was the only passenger remaining.

"Where to now, boss?" the pilot said, drumming his fingers on his armrest.

Forrester turned to me. "Well Ryan? Still up for Paradise?"

I gave him a meek smile and shook my head. "Look, Forrester, I have a confession to make. I never paid for this cruise. I didn't even know this was a cruise before we took off. It's all been a misunderstanding."

He smiled. "You didn't think it was strange that security didn't hold you back when you tried to board?"

"I didn't notice any sec—"

"Or that with an expensive venture of this sort, I wouldn't know every passenger backward and forward? You were meant to come."

"How do you mean?"

"Your father. He arranged for everything."

"I don't understand."

"Somehow, he learned about this trip back when I was still smoothing out a contract with the Maker. Your dad said he wanted to meet you, begged me to let you come. We worked out the details and, with no objections from God, we all agreed that *if* happenstance or fate led you to my ship, no one would stand in your way. I didn't believe it would happen, but lo and behold, there you were right on our maiden voyage."

"So my father is dead?"

"Dead as a doornail, as they say."

"And he never abandoned my mom and me?"

"That's a story better left for him to tell."

"Well then, what are we waiting for? Let's go!" I said, strapping in again.

"You heard the man, pilot. Engage!"

The pilot gave a two-finger salute. The ship sped up. The sun, stars and planets shifted back into a black velvet curtain.

We entered altered space, in all its butt-abusing glory.

I hardly noticed. Again, I realized today was Father's Day, and for the first time in all my years, I didn't mind one bit.

Alternative Holidays

A Visit at Saint Nick's

Gregg Chamberlain

"Is that so?" Santa Claus asked.

The little girl nodded. "Uh, huh."

"A time traveler!" Santa exclaimed. "That's what you're going to be when you grow up?"

Another nod.

Santa chuckled. "Well, isn't that wonderful? Smile now."

He gestured, and together they turned to face the camera. There was a flash. The little girl's eyes blinked with the after-glare.

"Maybe we'll cross paths again during one of your trips," Santa said, still chuckling. "Time to go now."

He helped the little girl slide off his lap and into the waiting arms of a pretty, tall, young elf standing beside Santa's throne. She led the little girl by the hand over to where a harried-looking woman waited at the exit from Santa's Christmas Workshop in the crowded mall.

"Ready to go, Lizzy?" the woman said. Already she was looking around the huge mall foyer, searching for her next destination and also the one after that.

The little girl nodded and took her mother's hand. The smiling elf held out a clipboard and a pen.

"Just mark whether you'd like prints or digitals," she said. "Also fill in either the email or the postal address line."

She watched as the woman's face scrunched up in thought, forehead wrinkling with stress lines. A single strand of silver hair showed among the brown. Still smiling, the elf reached out, placed a hand on the woman's shoulder, and gently squeezed.

"Hey," she said, as the woman looked up. "It's okay. You're doing fine." Her smile broadened. "You're a very good mother."

The woman blinked in confusion. Then smiled slowly in return. "Thanks," she said, and finished filling out the form.

After getting back her clipboard along with the advance payment from a debit card swipe, the elf watched the mother and daughter quickly vanish into the mall crowd. She returned to Santa's Christmas Workshop, taking up a position beside another girl dressed as an elf. A third helper elf manned the camera while a fourth was stationed beside the throne waiting to escort yet another child away after his visit with Santa.

"How you doing Kara?" she asked.

Her fellow elf groaned. "My feet hurt. My legs hurt. My back hurts. I think even my smile hurts. So looking forward to break time. Don't you just hate this Christmas Eve shift, Liz? It's like a freaking madhouse."

"Always is when everyone's in a rush to get things done," Elizabeth said. "All those last-minute items we all have to check off our lists."

She looked back at the crowd, just in time to see little Lizzy's mother give her daughter a surprise hug. Elizabeth the Elf felt a warm, new memory slip suddenly into place. A sad smile appeared on her face.

"Especially if there's something important you need to do."

Invitation

Jenniffer Wardell

Santa's workshop had a dick drawn on it.

Matt snorted at the graffiti, poorly hidden by a cardboard Christmas tree. Next to him, Abbie immediately looked up in interest. "What's so funny?"

He looked down at his little sister, instantly sure he would rather stand on a lunch table naked than admit what he'd actually been laughing at. "The elves' shoes are stupid," he muttered finally, caught without a better answer.

She curled her hand through his, careful not to pull on his aching shoulder. "It's the bells. Boys don't like cute shoes."

Well, now he felt guilty. "Sorry." He squeezed her hand, resolving to try harder to fake this whole Christmas spirit thing. Maybe he could steal her some lights or something. "I know how much this means to you."

Abbie beamed up at him. "Which is why you brought me." She moved closer against his side, making sure not to lean. "Even though you didn't have to. I could have missed it one more year."

Despite the bruises, Matt pulled her closer. "You know you can always ask me to do stuff like this, right? No matter what."

She shot him the most loving "you're an idiot" look he had ever received. "I know who takes care of me."

He cleared his throat, trying to pretend it didn't have a lump in it. "Tell me more about the elephant book you've been reading."

Eventually, they were close enough to get a good look at Santa. Abbie leaned forward, eyes wide with awe, but Matt was sure he'd seen better. The beard made him look more like an old wizard guy than Santa, and he wasn't nearly fat enough. Still, the padding mall Santas had to wear probably stunk. He couldn't blame the guy for going without.

There might be other things to blame the guy for, though. The boy sitting on Santa's lap right now was one of those kids who said "why?" every other word, and the answers the guy came up with were strange. When the kid asked if he really ate all the cookies kids left out for him, Santa went into a whole routine about the spirit of Christmas.

"The cookies and milk children leave out for me always radiate so much love and excitement," he told the kid, using that weirdly calming voice of his. "There's so much happiness in the air during the holidays, and the nicer emotions are sweeter and more delicious than any Christmas treat. I drink it right up." He smiled. "It keeps me alive."

This time, Matt managed to keep his snort just inside his head. The guy would probably have a blast talking to his English teacher about chakras and healing crystals.

Finally, it was Abbie's turn. She ran up to stand just in front of Santa, waiting until he held out his arms before crawling into his lap. "Did you know that elephants are smarter than any animal except for big monkeys?" She leaned closer, her voice dropping to a whisper. "We also count as big monkeys."

He laughed. "I had not known that." He smiled down at Abbie. "Now, little one, what would you like for Christmas?"

Abbie's shoulders fell, her voice turning wistful in the way that always broke Matt's heart. "You can't bring me anything. Dad told me that the reason we don't get Christmas presents is because he'd shoot you if he ever saw you anywhere near his property. I don't want you to get hurt."

Santa went still, the same way adults always did when they were thinking a lot more than they were saying. "That wouldn't stop me, child. Bullets can't hurt Santa Claus."

"We probably shouldn't risk it." Abbie leaned forward, wrapping her arms around him. "I just wanted to give you a hug and make sure you were okay."

Santa hugged her back tightly, meeting Matt's eyes over the top of her head. Matt braced himself for questions he didn't want to answer, but in the end it didn't matter. Family Services was worse than useless, and even if the guy tried to call he didn't have either of their names.

When Abbie pulled away, Santa smiled down at her. "How would you like to be an honorary elf? My friend over there needs help handing out candy canes, and I think you're just the person to do it."

Abbie happily agreed—big surprise there—and ran off to help give candy to strangers. Once she was out of earshot, the guy put up a "Santa on break" sign before turning his attention to Matt. "And what do you want for Christmas, young man?"

Matt tore his gaze away from his sister's beaming expression, focusing on the old man. "Unless you're down for murdering my dad, I don't think there's anything you can get me."

Rather than look offended, or even horrified, the guy only looked more kind. "It must be dire circumstances indeed, for a son to want his father dead."

Matt's throat tightened at the sheer compassion in the man's voice. Knowing he was being stupid but not able to stop himself, he yanked down his collar to show the ugly purple bruise spread across his shoulder. He'd gotten good at popping it back in the socket, all on his own.

The man looked more solemn now. "I see," he said quietly. "And your mother?"

"Last time she tried to leave, Dad beat her so black and blue she couldn't go to work for a week." He swallowed. "She could probably get out if it was just her. But she won't go without us, and one of Dad's old Army buddies is a lawyer."

"I see." There was no judgment in the words, and he stayed silent long enough to let Matt's heart settle a little. Then he took a deep breath. "You know, your sister didn't make a request of me."

Matt blinked, thrown by the sudden change of topic. Maybe the guy was just desperate to stop an uncomfortable conversation. "I know. It was nice of you to let her help with the candy canes, though."

His expression softened. "Your sister is a delight, but that isn't what I meant." He leaned towards Matt, intent. "Requests for gifts are invitations welcoming me into the homes of children I visit. I have no invitation into your home."

Matt held his breath, feeling like all his hair was standing on end. It would be easy to do what he was asking—a few simple words, said in his most sarcastic tone—but he couldn't look away from the guy's eyes. They were too old for his face, which was saying something with a guy this old. They'd seen things.

Centuries of things, even.

He shook away the thought, but he couldn't shake away the strange feeling that accompanied it. "I, uh..." He swallowed. "I should go."

He hurried toward his little sister, trying to pretend he couldn't feel Santa's eyes following him.

#

The guy was a wackjob.

That was what Matt told himself, over and over again, in the days following their visit to Santa. He was just some New Age-type who took out his frustration at the hordes of ankle-biters by saying weird crap to them. Hell, there were worse hobbies out there.

There were some things, though, he'd long ago stopped trying to convince himself about.

That night, the sound of something crashing in the living room jolted him awake. His heart pounded like a jackhammer as he listened to his father scream at his mother, his body torn between the urge to race in there and hide under the bed. A heavy thud had Abbie scrambling out of her bed and into his, burrowing her face against his chest to hide her tears. He squeezed his eyes shut and wrapped his arms around her as tight as they would go, the sound of his mother's pleas like glass in his throat.

Finally, it had been quiet for long enough that Abbie's breath had slowed into sleep. He eased back, careful not to wake her as he slipped out of bed. With practiced, silent feet, he made his way into the kitchen.

His mother was sitting on the floor, a ratty bathrobe around her shoulders and a worn pack of frozen peas pressed to her eye. He'd seen that package a lot, over the years, even though he didn't think they'd ever actually eaten peas.

When she saw him, she smiled. It looked as tired as she did. "Hey, kiddo."

Matt sat down beside her. That way, if his hands clenched, she wouldn't see it. "What was it this time?"

She sighed, the smile disappearing off her face. "It doesn't matter."

His fingers curled, mirroring the tight ball of rage in his chest. "He shouldn't do it at all."

She looked solemn. "No, he shouldn't." Moving the bag, she leaned over carefully and pressed a kiss against his cheek.

His eyes burned with all the tears he'd never let himself cry. "There has to be something I can do."

His mom looked like she was about to cry herself. "Just keep protecting your sister. Please."

Over the next few days, Matt thought long and hard about a lot of things he'd told himself not to think about. He stole a soda and a mini pack of sandwich cookies from the convenience store on the corner, hiding it in his secret stash spot. They never had a Christmas tree, but he cleared off space on top of the cardboard box next to his bed.

On Christmas Eve, after his dad had safely passed out, Matt got one of his mom's coffee mugs from the kitchen. He carefully filled it with half the soda, setting it next to the unopened package of cookies. Then he sat back on his heels, looking at his meager offerings.

It was stupid. He was stupid.

Still, Matt closed his eyes. "Dear Santa," he whispered into the darkness, "please make sure he can't hurt us anymore."

He made himself go to bed after that, staring at the ceiling and trying hard not to think about anything at all. He had no idea when he went to sleep.

#

He woke up to Abbie shaking him. "Matt," she whispered furiously, half trying to drag him out of bed. "There are people in the house. They look like police."

Matt was out of bed in an instant. Motioning for her to be silent, he snuck over and pressed his ear against the crack of the door.

"... probably died in his sleep, ma'am," a stranger's voice said. "We won't know details unless you want an autopsy, but we didn't see the usual signs of a heart attack. It was more like he just ran out of energy."

Matt's own heart stopped.

Abbie crowded in around his legs. "What is it? What's happening?"

He closed his eyes, dizzy with emotion. "Dad's dead," he managed.

She gasped, flinging her arms around his middle. "Promise?"

They waited, breathless, while they took the body out of the house and drove away. When it was quiet, Mom finally opened the door. She still looked utterly overwhelmed, but he could also see the first sparks of hope in her eyes. "Kids, I need to show you something."

They followed her into the living room. There, right next to the TV, was a brightly lit Christmas tree about as tall as Abbie. Underneath it was a small collection of unwrapped gifts.

Abbie shrieked and ran forward to throw her arms around a huge stuffed elephant. Slowly, Matt went over and picked up the silver-embossed card sitting on top of a pair of new tennis shoes.

"Thank you for welcoming me into your home" was written across the front. Inside was a spidery, surprisingly refined scrawl. *Consider this a thank you for the holiday meal. I tend toward sweeter nourishment these days, but there's no harm in indulging older cravings when occasion calls for it.*

He looked up to see his mom staring at him. "Who did this?" she whispered.

Matt looked back down at the card, desperately trying to come up with an answer that didn't sound insane. Abbie, arms still around her elephant, answered for him.

"It was Santa Claus, Mom." She beamed at them both. "It turns out we just had to invite him in."

The Effect of Place on Love and Death

Gerri Leen

All you know is the slide of flesh over sheets and the joining of bodies as your lover murmurs his feelings to you. You came to Mexico to be together; it might as well be Cleveland. You wonder if you'll ever leave the hotel room.

It's your first time vacationing together. He's wooed you, and you've been caught. He has the money to fly you down for a weekend in Paradise, to this hotel that lies on the plaza, that has views of the hills surrounding the town. His favorite place, he told you as you boarded the plane. Does he expect it to be yours, too?

The smell of the flowers in the plaza drift up into your room; your lover has left the window open, and it captures the scent of marigolds, of dripping wax candles, of sweets and breads being baked and sold. These scents mix with the smell of damp hair, of his cologne and your perfume, of sex and heat and touching. You finally fall away from each other, chests heaving, sweat glistening, and in the plaza below, a hubbub of voices rises to your room. It's the Day of the Dead. One of them, anyway. You're still not sure which day is for what, or why they don't call it the Days of the Dead or the Time of the Dead.

"One day is for the young. One day for the adults. All death is specific," your lover told you on the plane when you asked. As if that explained anything.

"Is love specific?" you wanted to know, but he didn't answer, and by his look, you understood he didn't see any reason for you to have asked.

You try not to think about how general you might be to him now that you're not trapped under him, not lying with your legs wrapped around him, giving him a pleasure specific to this room. The ceiling fan blows a cool breeze to sweat-streaked skin, and you know the words he would use to assuage your doubts: I love you; I adore you; I want you.

But for how long?

If love is specific, then your love will belong to skeletons and altars and portraits of the dead. If love is specific, then your love belongs to this place and it will be a lesser thing when you leave it.

"What are you thinking about?" His voice is throaty, raw.

"You," you say. "I'm thinking about you."

He appears to like that. Ego, it seems, does not need time or place: it just is. It endures. As long as you worship him, will he love you? Will he at least need you?

The smell of marigolds fills the room, pungent spice being dispersed by the gentle circles of the ceiling fan. You're not sure you'll ever get the smell out of your head.

#

You've roused, showered, dried your hair and perfumed your body. You've made up your face. You look beautiful both because he told you so and because you can see it in the faces of the men you pass. You thought you saw it in the mirror as you finished getting ready, but your own judgment is usually suspect.

Beauty is relative. Who will you be compared with? What lens will your lover wear as you walk? The gentle filter of love that makes all you do and say seem witty and enchanting? Or the more harsh reality that says you're not so clever, not so pretty. That you're not what he wants.

You live in fear that he'll realize you're not what he wants. You'll run before he can realize it: it's your way. You fear being left more than watching love die before it's ready.

"The altars are gorgeous," he says.

All you can see is the gaudiness of the things. Remembrance should be somber, should be respectful. A woman pours out two glasses of tequila; a man sets a brightly painted guitar on the altar. In your lexicon, the only bright thing death brings should be flowers—and not the raucous gold and orange of the marigolds. They should be white flowers. Lilies and roses and other things that glow at night, not in the day. That fill your head with their sweetness—a sweetness that does nothing to ease pain.

"This would be a good tradition to take with us," your lover murmurs, and it should fill your heart that there's an us and a future to fill with things like this incomprehensible festival. But you hear his words and filter them into, "When we end, we should build an altar to our love."

"Which is your favorite?" he asks, and you point to one at random. It's bright and covered with things from the sea.

"Mine's that one," he says, and leads you to an altar that has a family of dolls on it, surrounded by the remnants of a full life—toys and clothes and books. An old man keeps watch over it all.

You feel a pang. You've told your lover you don't want children. And here's the evidence he wasn't listening.

"It's like my family. See. Two adults. Three boys. Just like Jim and Roger and I."

You swallow the panic and pain that wells up in you. It's all right. It's only his family. His family, not your family—a family you've said you don't want.

"What's wrong with you?" You imagine his tone is less forgiving.

Because this is what happens. You're good at luring; you're not so good at keeping. Interacting with intent is easy, but just being with someone—just enjoying the moment—eludes you.

"There's so much to see. Just so overwhelming." It's almost the right thing to say, so you continue. "I love it."

His beautiful, luminous smile breaks through, and he pulls you closer.

There. You've appeased him. For now.

#

"Fortune?" a woman asks. "Pay me what it's worth when it's over."

Your lover has gone to fetch drinks. This woman holds out her hand, and you place your palm in it. The fortunetellers are all the same—none of them see deeply enough inside you to get it right.

"You lost everyone you cared about when you were young." This is correct. One car trip that you were too young to go on. "But you've never lost a lover."

You laugh. You've lost every one of them and will lose this latest, too. You try to pull your hand away; the woman holds on tightly.

"You chase them away before you can lose them."

You stop pulling. This is truth on all fronts. Can this woman be for real? "Is that bad?"

"Don't you know the answer to that?" The woman gestures toward the altars. "Yours would be empty. Colorless and sad."

"It's not sad to have never lost a lover." This is the mantra of your life; it must not fall in the face of this woman's attack.

"It's sad to have never loved anyone enough to feel their loss."

"I love. I do love." But you know the woman is right. Even your current lover, now that he's caught, is bumping up against the spikes and razors that surround your heart. He'll flee eventually. Glad to escape. And your altar will stay empty. You try again to yank your hand away. "I won't build an altar. I won't gather flowers. I have no one to honor, not anymore."

They all piled into the car and left you. They laughed and waved, and you were stuck with your sitter. They never came back. Their altar would be crushed metal and gravel.

"The Dia de los Muertos is as much for us as for those who have passed over." The woman drops your hand. "If we make our peace with them, we give ourselves permission to go on."

"I go on." That's the one part you have no trouble doing. Going on is freedom. No one can catch you.

No one can hurt you.

"Perhaps you should tarry a while with your dead, your forgotten, your lost. It might make your sojourn with the living easier."

"And then again..." You fish out coins, have no idea if you're being generous or stingy, and the woman's expression as you drop them into her hand tells you nothing. "Thank you."

The woman moves on, and your lover appears. "Who was that?"

He perks up when you tell him; you didn't know he was interested in such things. "Is she any good?"

You take the soda from him and drink heartily. "No. She isn't."

"Too bad." His look is wistful. "I'd like to know our future."

You could tell him all about that, but you won't.

#

Shadows fall across the floor. From below, the sound of singing, humming, and low talking fills your room.

"This is the night for children," your lover says as he stares out the window.

"I don't want any," you say, blurting out what has already been stated.

82

"I know. God, I know." He turns to look at you. "I wasn't criticizing. I was just saying that tonight is reserved for them."

"I'm sorry. I thought—"

"Why did you come here with me? Do you even love me?"

This is how it starts. They question your love. Then they question your worth. Then they leave because you've already left them. No man can be trusted with your heart. And you trust no man with your heart. They are, of course, slightly different things, but being aware of the difference is not the same thing as being willing to bridge the distance.

"Do you love me?" He moves closer and tries to pull you into his arms, but you resist. "Is there someone else?"

This question has been asked before. It always breaks your heart. For you are—if nothing else—faithful. You find it hard enough to love one person, much less two. "There isn't anyone else."

You change into your nightgown, crawl into bed, and turn off the light on your side of the room. When you made love, there was no space between you; now there will be a demarcation, the beginning of the schism.

"I'm going out for a bit." He grabs his jacket and hurries to the door.

You take a deep breath, then beat the thick down pillows into submission before closing your eyes and drifting off.

#

The fortuneteller sits in the plaza when you wander out, unable to stay asleep. Your lover hasn't come back.

The woman rises, takes your arm as if you are old friends, and says, "Walk with me."

You resist. This woman is a stranger.

"Honey, please?"

The voice. The lilt of the word. For a moment, you're back in the past, on a porch, waving goodbye to a father and sisters and a mother who would never come back.

Over the years, it's been your mother you missed most, your mother you've had the most trouble pushing down into the murkiness of memory, rather than living in some higher level of pain.

You're afraid to look at the fortuneteller. Afraid to see, in this land of mystery, on this night that belongs to dead children, what might be standing next to you.

Or maybe you're just afraid of what might not be standing there. You want her to be your mother. Want magic to exist and love to transcend boundaries—you want her to be able to push past the walls between life and death and come back to the little girl she abandoned.

Abandoned. Your breath catches at the thought. Your mother died, sitting on the passenger side, the one the other car plowed into. She wasn't driving; she had no choice. There was no abandonment.

But your heart says differently, and you feel the fortuneteller squeeze your arm.

"You're not ready," she says, and she kisses you on the forehead. "Go back to sleep."

You wake in your bed. It's morning and your lover is next to you. His hand is on your arm, lying gently, and you feel a pang deep inside. It's almost painful to feel this safe, even for a moment.

"Good morning," he says. "You were dreaming." His eyes are wary, his smile not a full one.

You slide over, into his arms, hugging him close, and hear him breathe out. In relief? Is he off balance now? Does he wonder why he brought you here?

"I dreamt of my mother." It's not precisely true, but he knows enough of you to understand.

And then you start to cry. You don't want to and you try to stop, but the tears come as if you've never cried in your life. You think he'll pull away in the face of this bizarre storm of emotion. You think he should pull away.

He only holds on tighter. When you stop crying, he makes love to you, his eyes never leaving yours, stroking your hair, kissing softly and sweetly, and you cry again because it feels good, and because you wish you were worthy of his tenderness.

You'll hurt him. It's what you do. One night and one morning won't change that.

#

He takes you away, rents a car and drives into the hills until you reach a new town, but you can't escape the dead. Altars fill the plaza; the cemetery is busy with women cleaning the graves.

He drives farther, his speed increasing, and you finally put your hand on his arm and say, "It's okay."

He sighs, a sound of defeat. He would have spared you this, you know that.

"Take us back to town. There was a restaurant on the way, in that last village we passed. Let's eat there."

You eat outside, and the proprietor is gregarious, his two children peek out as if they've never seen gringos. A small dog plays on the edge of the terrace. The food is hot and spicy, and the beer is cold, and you smile at the children as they laugh and duck for cover.

You see your lover staring at you. "What? I do like them."

"Then why don't you want them?"

"It's not fair to them. Life is uncertain."

"It is. But not all families die."

There it is. The bald-faced truth. Not all families die.

"Mine do." That's the other side of this harsh truth. Or at least your article of faith. If you have a family, it will be taken from you. Because it happened before.

He looks down. There's no argument to change your mind, and he's smart enough to realize this. "I love you," he says, as if it's a challenge to the gods.

"I know."

You can see by his expression that this is a shabby response, but it's the best you can do.

#

It's you who stands at the curtains now. He sits in bed, reading.

"I'm going out," you say, and he looks at you but doesn't move to get up.

You wonder if he knows this is the end. This is the last moment between you where things might be saved. He's getting too far in, too fast, and to protect yourself, you'll strike first.

He'll be glad to say goodbye at the airport. He won't want to share a cab the way you did on the way in.

You practically flee the room. Against your will, you cry, and brush tears away as other tourists crowd the elevator. As the next bunch pushes in, you begin to feel claustrophobic and have to concentrate on your breathing to keep from screaming and pushing and kicking.

On the day after your family died, your sitter's mother turned you over to child protective services. The elevator ride up to their offices was long, and the woman let go of your hand as more people pushed onto the car. You remember the panic, the loneliness, the anger—how could they do this to you? How could they leave you?

The woman didn't take your hand again. "You'll have to be a big girl from now on," she said on the walk down the gray and yellow hall to the window where an unfriendly man sat reading.

You feel the need to scream now, for yourself, for that child who did what she was told. Who grew up far too fast.

"It's time now," a familiar voice says as you nearly run off the elevator and through the lobby.

The voice is in your head, and then it's at your side. The fortuneteller takes your hand and holds it tightly. "Come on."

You don't want to go, but you're caught up in the crowd. You're heading for the cemetery and you pull back: you never visit your own family, why visit anyone else's? But the fortuneteller's grip is like iron.

Then she squeezes your hand. "I'll tell you a story. Once upon a time, there was a little girl with blonde curls. She laughed and smiled, and she was the pet of her family. They doted on her, her father who would come home and scoop her up, and her two older sisters who liked to dress her and arrange her hair as if she was their doll. And especially her mother. Her mother loved her so much."

"I don't want to hear this story."

"Well, this story wants to be heard." Her grip intensifies, and you're pulled into the cemetery, past the candles that light every nook and cranny. The graves are decorated, the white stone gleaming, the marigolds filling the air, and a new flower, a white one, adds its own particular scent.

You register that this is beautiful, perhaps the most beautiful thing you've ever seen. But there's too much panic and fear and age-old pain rushing up for you to enjoy the spectacle.

You're drawn into a dark corner of the cemetery, where no graves lie, only grass and trees. Then you see a lone candle burning, held up by a pile of rocks.

"This is for the forgotten ones," the fortuneteller says. "This is for those who have no grave to polish, no flowers to set out, no food to offer."

You sink to the ground, and in front of you the candle gives way to the porch light. You're sitting on the kitchen floor, staring out the screen door at the carport. Your family should be home by now. Where are they?

Your sitter is cranky with you. She's not the girl your parents usually use. She's older and meaner, and you hope your parents never call her again to come watch you.

The phone rings, and the sitter goes quiet as she listens to whoever has called, and then she hangs up and calls someone else, and there are words that hang heavy and dark. "Accident. Everyone. Dead."

You get up and walk to the door, trying to unlock it, to run out to the carport and wait there. But your sitter grabs you and closes the door and puts you to bed with threats of bad reports to your parents if you're not good.

That's the cruelest thing of all. That she would invoke your parents when she knew they were dead. You've never forgiven that girl, would spit on her now if she were here.

Only, it's probably not her fault. She was just babysitting, just a kid herself. The deal was that the parents would come home and she'd be released. Not get stuck with the kid. Not have to take her home to her mom the next day so she could walk her down to the government offices.

"We never meant to leave," the fortuneteller says, and you're afraid to look at her.

"*They*. They never meant to leave." They because they is far away, and we is close; we is a choice, we is your family, and family go away.

"*We*." Her voice is firm and loving and full of sorrow.

You turn and look up at the woman standing next to you. As you grew older, your mother's image faded from your memory, so you kept photos of her close so you'd never forget.

But you did forget. For the fortuneteller's face hasn't changed: you just couldn't see it for what it was.

"In this place, at this time, the dead walk when the living call." Your mother's smile is luminous.

"I didn't call." But you did. You've been screaming for her in your heart since that night.

"I heard you. We all did. We've just never been in a position to come back." She crouches and pulls you into a hug, her arms strong and firm. She's dead; she's alive. She's not gone.

She will be gone, though. This is temporary.

You tear yourself away from her embrace. "You left me!" The words come out in a cry that resembles the howl of a jungle cat.

You scramble away, scuttling along the ground as if there's escape on this night that you understand now is for the adult dead.

"Yes, I left you. I'm sorry for that."

"I had to go on without you." Without anyone. Still, now: alone. Alone with this specter who can walk among the living.

"He saw me. Your young man." Your mother smiles. "He's a good one. You should hold on to him." She kneels next to you and takes your hand. "I see a long, happy life. If you just let him in." She kisses you, her lips soft and filling you with warmth. Her hands trail along your face, as if memorizing it by touch.

And then she's gone, her body giving way to smoke that drifts across the space like the black mist from a fireworks display. Your lover steps through the smoke, his eyes meet yours as he takes in the candle, and you, sprawled across the grass, eyes starting to fill.

"Everyone I love leaves me," you say, and it's the deepest truth you own.

He sits beside you and doesn't try to tell you that you're wrong. His arms are strong, his breath warm and comforting, and he holds you and whispers things that have nothing to do with the past. The future, he sees a future for you.

"You don't want me. I'll run. It's what I do."

He opens his arms, letting you go. His eyes never leave yours as he says, "Run, then."

Part of you wants to. Your heart's beating fast and you can feel the call of freedom—of protection. Who will defend you now, if you love him? Who will keep you from losing him?

"Please don't run," he whispers. His voice cracks, and his eyes are moist, and you're lost. You clutch him and hold him, and fear that if he doesn't run now, you'll never let him go.

But he's stronger than you are, and he drags you to your feet and says, "Let's look at the altars."

You walk together because there's no other way to walk, not with him holding you so tightly or you hanging onto him as if he's the bridge that will see you through life.

As you pass altars, as you nod to families celebrating their dead, you gradually loosen your grip on him, and he lets go of you.

Finally you're holding lightly, hands clasped, and every so often he pulls you in so your shoulders bump up against each other. Your panic fades, and it's replaced by something you're not sure how to identify.

You finally decide it might be peace.

"I lied." You smile up at him, a strange expression for the declaration you've just made.

"You did?" He doesn't seem worried, either at the dichotomy or the fact you lied. "What about?"

"That fortuneteller? She was very good."

You walk on, the scent of marigolds burning itself into your brain. You hope you'll never lose it.

Alternative Holidays

The Stockings of Santa River

Daniel Ausema

We still put out stockings, Kate and I, just like the old days. Huge stockings. They used to be commercial laundry bags or something. We don't hang them by a fireplace of course—we don't have a fireplace—but in the river as nets.

I keep saying I'll catch a salmon someday. Kate rolls her eyes at me whenever I say it, which is probably every day, I suppose. Sisters, right? They never let you imagine something impossible. I wouldn't kill the salmon. I'd probably tell it the story of what happened to its ancestral rivers, the ones that dried up in the heat, the ones drained to quench the thirst of the soldiers, the ones that filled with fallout dust, choked with debris. We'd cry together for a while, and then I'd set it free.

But I don't think there are salmon left alive anywhere. Certainly none that visit our river.

Kate caught a corpse one year. Its boots were still good, good enough that I still wear them.

We call the river "Santa River." That wasn't its old name. I don't remember what it used to be called.

Kate reaches the stockings first. "Hurry," she calls as she hauls hers to the riverbank. Water seeps through the tears in the cloth, pouring down the bank in rivulets of tiny erosion. We don't check what's inside before we exchange them. That would ruin the ritual.

We drag them to our shelter. It's made of sun-bleached logs and scraps of tarps. Whatever we can find to give us some shelter. For a little while, part of the roof was the corpse's tattered shirt, spread open and lashed to other flotsam. It didn't last very long.

Once there, Kate pulls to a stop. She holds her stocking behind her back, posing. I face her. Our parents had us do something like this. We can't remember it much, but we try to do it anyway.

Pulling my stocking around in front of me, I cry, "Merry!" and hand it to her.

She pulls out a turtle shell. For a moment I dream of meat. Can we make turtle soup? I don't even know what that is, but it seems like something I've heard of. But I already know that the shell is long empty. Its husk is light in her hands. "You're so thoughtful," she says. "I'll clean it and make a serving dish. It will look beautiful. Now, your turn!"

She hands me her stocking. It smells... metallic.

I open it slowly, dreaming of holiday presents of old. Bikes and toys and shiny things still in their packages. Gifts that don't come tarnished by river mud and fallout soot. I'd celebrated toys like that before we'd started running, before... everything. Maybe it will be a tool that can help make life here easier. I'm old enough that I should want that instead of toys. Maybe it will be a magic wand to make it all change back or change to something better, something new. Each is as likely as the other, and as likely as the fabled salmon of my imaginings.

I pull out something wrapped in riverweeds and fishing line and quickly brush the mess away.

It's a grenade. We stare. I swallow at the terrible thing, at the memories that come and go as fast as the ripples on the river. For a moment I'm my own age, and I remember the darkened skies, the fear, the flight to this place where we two, ragged siblings finally stopped. There's nothing else to say, as if the whole sad history of the last decade is told in that mud-smeared weapon. Is it only ten years? Time has lost its grip on my thoughts. I place it gingerly under a needle-less tree and manage a quiet, "Thanks."

The ritual releases the memories from my thoughts, though it takes an effort to push them entirely away, to reclaim the daily sense of our life here. I pick up my empty stocking. "Come on. Tomorrow's Christmas again. Let's set the stockings now!"

We race, and I reach the Santa River first. Next year—tomorrow—I bet I'll catch a salmon.

Nessel

Jeremy Mallory

Ceremonial Magicians are PITAs. I would say they are the bane of my existence, but let's face it—I'm not one of the angels they call up very often. Poor Zadkiel.

I dawdled on a lawn across the street from the house of one Frater Solidus Nemquo. The sky was the pale grey that precedes snow, and the air had a thin bite to it, like a hungry child. A light breeze caressing the back of my neck set me on edge.

As if on cue, the first small, hard flakes began to fall. The silence that fell with it was not the enveloping quiet one feels on a hot summer evening, but a small, peaceful, insistent quiet that begs for silence rather than forcing it.

The place did not draw me. The magician's mumbled and incanted words of summoning did not draw me. No command bade me go there. All I knew is that this would be a crossroads of time, a key moment, a *kairos*—and I had to be present.

Nemquo, usually called Harvey Pemberton of Waukegan, Illinois, was no different from other Ceremonialists: demanding but ultimately pitifully unaware of what he wanted (or whom he was actually summoning). Were he a lady, he would be of an age where one does not inquire; being anything but, he was a fifty-two-year-old schlemiel who divorced his previous wife after eight months of trial (for her)/marriage (for him) and went to seminary, convinced that he had "a calling." The calling, apparently, was to waste taxpayer money aping bigger minds than his own. Now he had student loans, a passable income as a legal assistant, and a secret life in his basement, where he was presently trying to summon a demon—or at least, something more powerful than himself to bring him riches.

Some rebellious part of me wanted to leave him alone, to sidestep this crossroads, to let this cup pass. But the *kairos* led me inside, feet pulled first slowly then in strides. I could not be bothered to sigh, so I drifted up to the door and knocked hard.

Harvey stopped in the middle of his peroration.

I sensed him blinking at the "coincidence."

He cleared his throat and started again: "*O ye who are yclept Niklas, I do sumone ye avaunt!*" His voice was thin, barely audible against the wind outside. I rolled my eyes and knocked again.

He restarted the sequence. "*Lo, threes I do sumone ye who are—*"

"Oh, for fuck's sake, Harvey," I bellowed, utterly losing my temper. "Open the door!"

Splat. In my mind's eye he sprawled on mottled beige linoleum.

The door flew open.

He struggled to stand, using the doorknob for support. The look on his face was priceless and unique, like a melting pug.

He wore a crimson ceremonial robe that hadn't been washed nearly enough, and a headdress that looked like a child's Pharaoh costume.

The house smelled of cabbage and sausage, likely last night's dinner, and the unmistakable mustiness of books everywhere. Books piled on the floor against each wall, even up the stairs, and collected in corners like snowdrifts.

Harvey had seen better days, and his pursuit of power and glory had led him into a place in his life where he no longer had the resources to pull himself out, a Narrow Place of his own making. I did not need to know the details, but I knew it was time.

"It's impolite to look so disappointed when a guest arrives," I commented.

He shook his head. I've only seen one person sadder, and he had to be marked so the nations would not slay him on sight.

I raised my eyebrows.

With a start, Harvey remembered the customary politeness. "Please come in."

"Thank you." I stepped over the threshold. "I smell honey," I said curiously, and started down the stairs to the basement.

"Did... I do something wrong?" Harvey said with a worried tone in his voice.

"Less than you think. My Name isn't Niklas, or Nicholas, and I know I'm not who you expected to show up." I stepped into the candlelit basement and walked around his Circle. He had kicked over one of his candles in his haste to get upstairs.

I walked right through his Summoning Triangle, which should hold fast any demon. What a Nimrod. "But other than that, you did fine." I pushed at the greenery around his chalked Circle with my steel-toed boot. "The holly is mine, ever-green yet red as blood against the white of snow. The ivy is as well, crowning saints and sinners alike and twining around the oldest buildings like a scholar in love. And this..." I picked up a shallow dish of honey from a small side table. "This is indeed my favorite." I dipped a fingertip in and sucked on it, looking squarely at Harvey.

He stared at my leather jacket, and widened his eyes when he took in the torn jeans and motorcycle chaps. "But you don't look like—"

My barking laugh embarrassed him too much to finish his sentence. I stood up, shook out a cigarette, and placed it in my mouth. "Of course I don't. If you think an angel is going to look like what you expect it to look like, you're as stupid as the people of Sodom." Smoke spiraled up from the cigarette.

His eyes widened. He realized that I had never pulled out a lighter.

"They didn't figure it out until too late. Let your hospitality not be as deficient as theirs."

The loosely gaping mouth was a sign that he might be starting to get it.

"But I... I wanted—" Harvey stuttered to a stop.

The rebellious part of me had not stopped resisting. I wanted to finish the honey first. I wanted to embarrass Harvey more. I even wanted to just turn and walk out, to fly away. But the moment urged, and would not be countermanded.

"Fine." I put down the honey and drew myself up to my full height—always five inches taller than the other person. "Harvey, there is an angel for every time. You know that, Frater Solidus Nemquo. Ecclesiastes." I waved my hand and the lit cigarette vanished, the smoke turning fragrant—frankincense and pine. "This time is known for one thing: it is a time like no other." I slipped out of my jacket and dropped it; it turned into rolling, boiling mist as it hit the floor.

"Whatever is expected—" the rest of my clothing melted away and I stood before him, naked but not in the least bit vulnerable "—is transcended."

He blinked. Twice.

Good.

I'm no Zadkiel, but my countenance is striking in its own way.

My voice had changed by now, hollowing out and becoming quieter, more peaceful. And the wings had appeared. "Is this more what you expected?" I asked, but honestly didn't care what the answer was. I felt pity toward him, soft and cold like snow.

I sighed, and a cold breeze blew through the room, a midwinter frost indoors. The rebellious part of me could not resist educating. "All right. The Name. I'm not Chaucerian. Olde Englysshe is beautiful, but not liturgical. You know the right languages to use—use them. I am not 'yclept Niklas'—I will show you the Name you may call me by."

With four paces I walked toward Harvey and stood next to him, each step leaving a letter in its wake.

He shrank as I placed my hand on his back and gestured toward the letters of frost on the floor. "Focus ...." He hadn't done well in Hebrew, but he could manage this. "Sound it out."

"N... ss... ehl." He blinked and nodded once. "Nessel?"

"Yes. Miracle of the One," I said, stepping behind him. Once more, Harvey seemed disappointed.

"B-but—"

His voice cut off when I put my hands on his shoulders. Time to finish this. The *kairos* subdued my quarrelsome corner and forced my hand.

Ordinarily, having a tall, strong, naked person behind oneself might feel intimate, whether or not it is welcome. But *intimate* and *angel* are not concepts that coexist well, not even for that hound-dog Zadkiel. The utter inhumanity of my touch set every single reptilian nerve in Harvey's hindbrain shrilling with fear. But at the same time, angels still bear the Glory, which roots humans to the ground and compels their attention.

I whispered gently in Harvey's ear. In profile, his face was stricken, eyes bulging and mouth helplessly wide open.

"I Name you true: Harvey Louis Dunkirk Matthews Pemberton, known as Frater Solidus Nemquo, and also known by the Divine alone as Eosphoros. You have called me up and asked for my Gift, offering a gift in return. This I accept. You shall see the Gifts of my time as they are, and realize they are *for you.* Charity will bring you to your knees in awe. Warmth and kindness will move you to tears of wonder. For every person you know as small, bitter, angry, demanding, fretful, worrisome, querulous, or miserly, you will see a spirit in them that will slice open your soul and release those same bindings in yourself, leading it from this Narrow Place. Your spirit will burn with the same light of the reborn Sun in the midst of darkness. This is the Gift of my time. And you will receive it completely."

I released my hands from his shoulders and took one pace back. He did not move. His jaw hung open and his eyes did not even twitch, as if he were completely paralyzed.

I circled around once, relighting the candles that had fallen, then moved up the stairs.

By the time the fire had started in his basement, I was half a block away, my boots leaving prints in the snow behind me. Old books, alas, burn brightly and quickly.

Harvey, miraculously uninjured, would indeed find more charity than he ever imagined in his life, more goodness and wonderful kindness in response to his grave loss and the destruction of everything he owned.

Were Zadkiel's appointments like this? How could he keep it up?

I did not want this crossroads. This end was not of my making—angels are not authors, merely plot devices. The making is between the human and the Other. This was my job because this is my time, my *kairos*, and this time is like no other: whatever is expected shall be transcended.

And I am not the one who chooses how.

Alternative Holidays

He's Coming

Louis Evans

He's coming to judge both the young and the old.
He's coming as day after day it grows cold.
His coming is certain and foretold with dread.
He's coming. His banner is winter stained red.
He's coming, unheeding the plea of the tyke.
He's coming regardless, so cry if you'd like.
He's coming: our fortresses mean less than sticks.
He's coming, unhindered by vault, cave, or bricks.
He's coming. His mounts gallop through time and space.
He's coming and soon he will be in this place.
He's coming and none may his judgment defy.
He's coming and grim is the gleam in his eye.
He's coming—and whether you wail, gnash, or frown—
It just doesn't matter. He's coming to town.
O, Santa Claus is coming... to town.

Alternative Holidays

Lancelot Wednesday

Judy Lunsford

For over 100 years, on the first day of May, all of the parents in the village dressed their daughters as boys so that the fairies wouldn't take them away.

But in a household of a poor family, Millie, who was oldest of the girls, ran out of clothes to hide her gender. Being the oldest, Millie gave her May Day clothes to one of her younger sisters and hoped that she was too old for the fairies to take away.

For the whole of the day, Millie and her sisters stayed huddled in the house and sighed with relief as the golden sun dropped below the mountains in the distance.

As darkness fell over the village like a curtain, Millie's mother deemed it safe to send Millie to the well for water.

When she got there, a little man was sitting on the rocks beside the well. He couldn't have been over two feet tall, and he was wearing a pointy brown hat and his purple shoes had bells on their toes. His brown leather jacket covered him all the way down to his red and orange striped socks.

He smiled at her with crooked teeth and pink cheeks. He smoked a small pipe and blew smoke rings towards her as she approached.

Millie knew immediately that he must be some kind of fairy, but beneath the fear that she felt rising in her chest, she was curious. No one in the village had ever actually seen a fairy up close before.

"Hello," the little man said.

"Hello," Millie said. "Who are you?"

"You can call me Lancelot Wednesday," he said. "What's your name?"

Millie knew that it was dangerous to give her name to a fairy creature, so she decided to use another name. But she panicked and the only name she could think of was one of her younger sisters.

"My name is Rose," she said.

"Ah." The little man nodded. "Does your kind make a habit of lying?"

"What?" Millie was stunned that he knew she was lying.

"I happen to know that your name is Millie, and that Rose is one of your younger sisters." He eyed her in the light of the silver moon that made the little man's dark eyes sparkle with an eerie twinkle of starlight.

"How do you know that?" Millie asked.

"I listen," he said. "I have heard your mother and your father call each of you by name."

"Then why did you ask?" Millie said.

"I wanted to know which sister would be surrendered to me," he said.

"No one is being surrendered to you," Millie said. "You have no power over me or my sisters."

"On the contrary," he said. "This is my well, and those who drink from it have always been under my power."

"This is our well," Millie said. "We've been drinking from it for years. I've never seen you before."

"That's because I *hide*," Lancelot Wednesday said. "I watch. I have been waiting."

"You can't have my sister," Millie said. "Take me instead."

"No." Lancelot shook his head. "You have already given me Rose. She will come with me at the stroke of midnight."

"No," Millie said. "You can't have her. You will take me instead."

Lancelot Wednesday shook his head. "I don't take liars."

"Is your name really Lancelot Wednesday?" Millie asked.

Lancelot smiled. "I merely said that you could call me Lancelot Wednesday," he said. "That is not a lie. But you said that your name was Rose. That is a lie."

"You tricked me," Millie said.

She could feel the tears and panic rising. She couldn't believe that she had been so gullible as to fall for a fairy's trickery. Her mother had taught her better than that.

"That's what fairies do," he said. "Weren't you taught to ignore fairies? Your mother advised you to ignore us if you ever saw a fairy. Not to engage. You should have listened to your mother."

"You will not take my sister." Millie swung the wooden bucket that was in her hand with all her might at the fairy's head.

He raised his arms to block the blow, but he was too late, and the bucket smashed him in the side of the head, knocking him backwards, and he and the bucket fell down the well.

Millie gasped at the sight of the little man falling backwards. The last thing she saw were his little purple shoes as he toppled down the dark hole. She could hear the distant jingling of the little bells that dangled from his toes.

She rushed to the edge of the well and looked down.

The moonlight shone down the well just enough so that Millie could see the silhouette of Lancelot clinging to the side of the well.

"Help me up," he pleaded.

"Only if you release Rose from her bond ," Millie said.

Lancelot grumbled, "Are you still willing to take her place?"

"Yes," Millie said. "I am willing."

"Then help me out," Lancelot said.

Millie got the rope that she used to tie to the bucket and lowered it down to the little man. He grabbed the rope and she grunted and groaned as she pulled him back to the surface.

He climbed out of the well and shook the moisture from his clothes like a dog and glared at her.

"You will come with me," he said.

"You will leave Rose alone," Millie said. "And the rest of the girls of the house as well."

"Agreed," Lancelot said.

"Then be on your way," Millie said.

"You are coming with me," Lancelot said.

"No," Millie smiled at the fairy. "That was not part of the agreement."

"You agreed to come with me," Lancelot said.

"No, I didn't," Millie smiled in the moonlight. "I said I was willing to take Rose's place, but you agreed to leave Rose and the rest of the girls of the house alone. I am one of the girls of the house."

Lancelot Wednesday's face filled with rage.

"You double crosser," he yelled.

"No." She shook her head. "I tricked you, just as you did to me. And you fell for it."

"That's not fair." Lancelot stomped his foot and glared at Millie.

"Be off," Millie said. "You are no longer welcome here."

"I will be back," Lancelot said. "I will figure out a way to take you or one of your sisters."

"No, you won't," Millie said. "You agreed to leave all of the girls of the house alone."

"Then you all should plan on living there forever, because at some point, you will each marry and leave your father's house," Lancelot said. "And for your granddaughters, I will be waiting."

Millie grinned and turned back towards the house.

"Don't walk away from me," he bellowed.

"Our granddaughters will be ready when you come for them," Millie said. "And you will come away as empty handed as you did tonight."

Lancelot stuck his tongue out at her and disappeared into the darkness.

Rose was waiting inside the doorway for Millie.

"Did you really outsmart a fairy?" Rose asked.

"Yes," Millie nodded. "And we must always be prepared, because I have a feeling that we haven't seen the last of Lancelot Wednesday."

MOJO DAY

Marie Noorani

In the summer of 2000, just before boarding a plane with my children for a 10-day trip to grandma's house, I asked two simple, but specific, favors of my husband: "Yusuf, while we're away, try to remember to water the flowers, and please, please don't buy a car." I was concerned because my hanging petunia planters lacked automatic driplines to keep them from drying out in the desert sun, and my husband had a vexing penchant for haggling with used car salesmen.

Upon our return, we met Yusuf at baggage claim.

"How are my flowers holding up?" I asked.

"They're all dead," he confessed, then shrugged, a little chagrined, "Sorry."

In familiar resignation, I sighed, predicting what was coming next. With no trace of joy, I said, "What color is the new car?"

A few minutes later, we were loading our suitcases into a late model, gray-blue Jeep.

On the way home, Yusuf and I discussed—yet again—what I felt was the unreasonable refresh rate of the cars in our garage. I tried to make my point by explaining how frequently I found myself wandering grocery store parking lots, unable to remember the make or color of the car I owned. I shared my frustration at having to constantly memorize new license plates.

None of this impressed him; he was unremorseful, even hurt that I was trying to squelch his "hobby."

With impotent intensity, I gritted my teeth and warned, "Okay, then, Mister. I'm takin' this car, and you aren't gonna trade it away anytime soon!" My words were unknowingly prophetic, since he would never again replace a car of mine.

When we got home from the airport, although I was still annoyed about the Jeep, I noticed a morsel of compensation: the license plate. As a latte addict and early American history buff, I was able to memorize it instantly. Obviously, mojo (MJO) was slang for coffee, and July 23rd (723) was the day British General William Howe began his campaign to invade Philadelphia.

Knowing my strategy for memorizing the plate, my kids took notice a couple of weeks later when the license numbers matched the actual date: "Oh, look, Mommy! It's Mojo Day!"

Since it was a gorgeous summer afternoon, and my irritation over the Jeep had subsided by then (I must acknowledge that I actually enjoyed driving it), I declared an instant holiday: "Kids, go grab the neighbors, and let's celebrate Mojo Day!"

In our backyard, slurping mango smoothies, playing lawn games, and dancing to Muddy Waters singing "Got My Mojo Working," we created the sort of spontaneous celebration that the best childhood memories are made of.

The next July 23rd, I was still miraculously in possession of the Jeep, so we celebrated Mojo Day again. And, for two more anniversaries after that, we continued to happily recognize the benevolence of the mercurial stable master who had not yet traded away my ride. The fourth year, however, although I was still driving the Jeep, we celebrated for a different reason: Mojo Day was the welcome antipode of Christmas.

When my children were young, our family's Christmas celebration was the singular, incontrovertible possession of my husband. The fact he was Muslim had absolutely no bearing on his devotion to the day; Yusuf loved celebrating Christmas. He precisely engineered the placement of each electric windowsill candle and the hanging of each glass ornament; he curated a constantly playing, ever growing collection of dreadful Christmas CDs; and he grew giddy at the prospect of freely purchasing extravagant gifts for his family.

For Yusuf, Christmas morning was the pinnacle of orchestrated delight.

While other children, in other households, were deep into a frenzied "greedfest" of torn wrapping paper, ripped open boxes, and squeals of delight, Yusuf held our two children hostage for hours in the glow of the Christmas tree. With disco "We Three

Kings" playing in the background, he forced them to suffer through an excruciatingly slow-paced, one-at-a-time, gift opening ordeal that he videotaped for posterity: "Okay, Sofia, it's your turn to choose a present to open," "Now, look at the camera and tell Grandma how much you like the pretty bracelets," "No, Adam, put that back, it's not time for you to open anything."

They endured this, as I had endured the parade of new cars, because Yusuf was at heart, a wonderful man and we loved him. But, our love did not keep us from brazenly and unapologetically referring to him as "The Christmas Nazi."

On more than one Christmas morning, my children and I threatened to engrave that epithet on his headstone. (We didn't.)

Yusuf died suddenly of a heart attack one Sunday morning while the kids and I were at church, and our hearts shattered.

As much as we always purported to hate the way Yusuf commandeered Christmas, staging the holiday without him was tedious and hollow.

On our first Christmas morning as a family of three, I hoped that my children might discover a bit of freedom in not having to accommodate "The Christmas Nazi's" rigid, gift-opening protocols.

Instead, I was anguished to find them intentionally listening to a danceable version of "Silent Night" and solemnly directing each other in their own one-at-a-time unwrapping ritual. There was no denying what happened to Christmas after Yusuf died. It became unbearably sad.

As we entered July after that first awful Christmas without my husband, I was surprised by how much the kids and I were anticipating Mojo Day. Our annual commemoration of a random summer day based on a license plate certainly seemed silly on the surface, but it offered us a familiar, emotionally unencumbered, and much needed reason to make merry.

In contrast to the Pit of Despair in December, our special day on the opposite side of the year rested lightly on our hearts and demanded very little from us. Celebrating Mojo Day was our brave refusal to surrender to grief.

Thus, year after year, decade after decade, we have continued to mark the day.

As my children have grown up, cultivated busy lives, gone to college, acquired jobs, and eventually married and moved away, we have never missed a Mojo Day. Admittedly, sometimes we celebrated it a day or two late (it doesn't matter), and often circumstances kept it pretty low key. Occasionally, we hosted guests to an extravagant brunch, and every now and then we "went old school" with mango smoothies and Muddy Waters in the backyard. Recently, my grandson joined the first ever "Zoom edition" of Mojo Day.

As my family has remained ardent Mojo Day revelers through the years, "sects" of fellow devotees (including the neighbors who attended the inaugural festivities) have sprung up in various locations to help us celebrate.

Today, when I walk through the upstairs hallway of my empty house, I see mounted above the door of my son's old bedroom the original 723-MJO license plate—merely a dusty keepsake of the gray-blue Jeep and the man who brought it home. But the holiday inspired by that license plate lives on.

Mojo Day occupies a permanent place on our calendar alongside birthdays, Mother's Day, daylight savings, federal holidays, the first day of Spring... and, of course, Christmas— which we are learning to enjoy again in our own ways.

Mojo Day taught us that the value of holidays is not what they celebrate or how they are celebrated, but simply that there is celebration—something most of us could desperately use more of in our lives. Happy Mojo Day!

Quicksilver's Last Job

Simon Kewin

Quicksilver the thief clung to the shadows of the towering pines. Ahead, across a short stretch of open snow, his prize awaited. The greatest of prizes. It really existed. He had doubted his sanity more than once on the long trudge north. But there it was, sitting in the open. People said he could steal *anything*. If he completed this job, he might believe it himself.

He watched and waited, studying the tableau before him, picking out potential dangers. The likely locations of traps, the hiding-places of guards. Great braziers dotting the snowy landscape filled the scene with shifting shadows. He was used to scaling the walls of imperial fortresses, but here there was only a series of low, log cabins. Still, there would be eyes watching from within those brightly lit windows. He could *feel* them.

He couldn't make out any obstacles between him and his prize, but open ground was never good for a thief. He thought about charging in, relying on simple surprise.

He could ghost across, position himself so one of the braziers hid him from the cabins.

No. Too dangerous, too exposed.

Cause a diversion, start a fire? That only alerted people, put them on edge.

A disguise? No one up here to disguise himself *as*.

Being a thief often meant doing the opposite of what people thought you'd do. People saw what they expected to see. His name was a part of that: a deception, like so much else. He *could* move quickly if he had to—he had outrun enough arrow-traps over the years—but the solution here was to do the opposite. Fortunately, he had prepared: practised this very thing for two long months in his mountain hideaway.

He pulled the hood of his specially prepared white suit over his head. The material had been very carefully chosen: just the right reflectivity, just the right sparkle. A circle of white gauze fitted over his face so he could still see, but the light couldn't reflect off his eyes. He was completely covered.

He lay down in the snow and began to crawl out of the shadows towards the treasure, hauling himself over the ground.

He moved a hand with infinite slowness, placing it a little way in front of him. Then one of his feet. Inch by painful inch he crept forwards.

Anyone looking would see no movement. They would see the stretch of whiteness and then, the next time they looked, the same stretch of whiteness. They wouldn't notice the small drift of snow that had shifted its location. He hoped.

It took him two hours to complete the crossing. His legs and arms and back burned with the effort.

The line of beasts tethered to the sleigh began to paw the ground as he approached. They could smell him even if the snail's pace of his movements hadn't alarmed them.

Quicksilver stood slowly, keeping the sleigh between him and the cabins.

Steam rose from the beasts as they stamped or whinnied. A motley collection: a great black bear, antlered caribou, a mountain lion of enormous size, shaggy forest ponies, wild boar, and timber wolves. They watched him with yellow eyes.

Quicksilver reached into his pocket and began to hand out the treats he had brought with him: sweet berries, dead mice, truffles, depending on the species.

He moved down the line, making gentle, reassuring noises, patting flanks. Finally, he was there. He grasped the wooden rail of the sleigh and sprang up into the driver's seat. Behind him, loaded and ready, countless riches of every description. It would be his crowning achievement. What songs would be sung about him now?

In truth, he felt a little disappointed. It was almost too easy. And—a worse thought—what could he possibly do next to top this?

He picked up the reins and called softly to the beasts.

They didn't move.

He flicked the reins across their backs and called again, a little louder.

Still they didn't move. One of the caribou looked back with a mournful stare.

"Oh, you can't make them move just like that. You need the right outfit, for one thing. The hat." A deep voice from the shadows, bear-like in its growl. Amusement in it too, though, like this was all some fine joke. It could only be one person.

Quicksilver's hand moved to his favourite dagger. As if that would help him. He weighed up options. Fight, flight, talk his way out of it. He didn't like any of them. The thing about meeting your victims was not to do so in the first place.

"I don't think any clothes of yours will fit me, old man."

The figure laughed. "Oh, they fit whoever wears them. And you'll need them if you're to take over from me. It can get cold up here." The man stepped in front of one of the smoking braziers.

There was something of the forest beast about his form, too. A deep, looming power. Quicksilver half expected to see antlers on his head. But, as he ambled forwards, he became just an old man, his beard white. Strong once, maybe, but now with his muscle turned to fat.

"What do you mean, *take over from you*?"

"That's why you're here," said the old man, delight in his voice.

"I'm here to take your sleigh and so steal from every single person in the entire world at the same time," said Quicksilver.

The old man laughed, walked along his line of beasts to scratch behind ears. "Ah, so you're a thief? I was a killer. A hired sword. Damn good one, too. I slew hundreds and none ever drew blood from me. Not one of them."

"What are you talking about? You're the Yule Father. The Spirit of Winter. The Gift Giver. Father Frost."

The old man waved a dismissive hand. "Oh, the role is eternal. But we actors come and go. Everyone gets what they want, you see. What they need. Not necessarily what they ask for. That's how it works. I came here fifteen years ago, sword in hand, to make a dark name for myself. So I thought. But what I really sought was rescue. And that's what I was given."

What was this? Some sort of trick? Quicksilver needed to escape. If he could just goad the creatures into flight he could be away. Go *anywhere*. The cut of a knife on one of those flanks might do it.

He readied his blade while keeping the old man talking. "So, can I go or do you intend to set the elves on me?"

The man walked right up to look into Quicksilver's eyes. "I can see the weight of guilt that bows you down. Have you carried it long?"

"You can't see guilt, old man."

"Oh, I can. What is it, all the people you've impoverished, made homeless, starved to death? Do you see them at night, when you sleep?"

"I sleep very well."

"Ah. I used to wake up reliving every limb and head I'd hacked from someone's body. So let me see how it is with you. You set yourself these impossible tasks, breath-taking acts of thievery, each more daring than the last. And you're good, aren't you? Damn good. No one catches you. No one keeps you out. But there's your problem. You're trapped. All you live for is the next job. You have wealth uncounted you will never spend. And where will it end? In your death. You take on the impossible knowing you'll eventually meet your match and get yourself killed."

"I steal because I can. Because I like it."

"I'm sure you did once. But now you can't stop. If each job isn't more outrageous than the last it bores you." The old man sounded genuinely sad as he spoke.

"No," said Quicksilver.

"Fortunately, I have another way out." The old man pulled off his fur hat and handed it to Quicksilver. "Here. It's yours."

"You're giving me it?"

"That *is* what I do. Take the coat too. I won't need it now. It isn't what you asked for, but it is what you want."

Quicksilver studied him, expecting some trick. The old man held out the furs and waited. The caribou with the baleful eye waited, too.

"It's midwinter," said the old man softly. "The turning point. The death of the old and the birth of the new. *That's* what I'm giving you." He leaned closer, whispered conspiratorially as if he didn't want the beasts to hear, "and, just between you and me, the flying is a lot of fun."

Quicksilver looked at the animals tethered to the miraculous sleigh. They would only move for the Yule Father. The *real* Yule

Father. He saw now. He slipped his blade away. He could probably make a dash for the safety of the forests. But then it would just be the long trudge home. Finally beaten.

"I don't know what to do," he said.

"Oh, it's easy," said the old man, laughing. "Truth is you don't really do anything. You're a totem. A figurehead. The beasts know the roads to take and the elves make everything. You sit there and look the part. An occasional laugh is good."

"A laugh?"

"A laugh."

He'd forgotten how to laugh. When did he last laugh?

"How long would I have to do this?"

The old man shrugged. "Until you've balanced everything up. Each gift given will lessen the weight on your shoulders. One day—five, ten, twenty years from now—someone will come to replace you. Sneaking through the woods, not even knowing why."

Quicksilver hesitated. *The turning point.* He'd been a thief for a long time. And he had been the greatest, hadn't he?

He reached out and took the hat from the old man. It felt comfortable as he pulled it onto his head. He stood and worked his way into the fur coat, too. It fitted well. Strangely, he felt lighter with it on. The beasts become more restless, ready for flight, bucking their heads in anticipation.

The old man nodded his head, his beard wagging. "It suits you."

"What happens to you?" asked Quicksilver.

"I've lived a lonely life. It's time I found a woman. Time I had children of my own. I'm not *that* old." He chuckled at his own words.

"Will I see you again?"

"Of course. Every year. But I won't see you. Now off you go. You've a long way to travel, my friend."

Quicksilver picked up the reins once more.

The beasts lurched forwards, scrabbling over the snow, throwing him back into the seat.

They began to pick up speed. The cold air rushed into his face.

A dizzying lurch, and they left the ground, hurtling into the cold northern sky.

Quicksilver's stomach thrilled with the exhilaration of it. And, as they climbed, he found himself roaring into the darkness with unexpected laughter.

Alternative Holidays

@Elijah5782

Lawrence Miller

"What the fuck is a *Mukbang*?" booms the Metatron as I take a seat in the guest chair facing Their hand-carved mahogany desk.

The Metatron takes the form of an amorphous blob, hovering over the leather executive chair tucked behind the desk, Their internal glow casting a faint green light over the desk occasionally highlighted by tiny spark-like flashes of intense blue light. Some say the Metatron used to be a human (like me) named Enoch. Some say They are an Angel, perhaps even a Malach. Some say there's no "the," that it's just "Metatron," like "Facebook." All I know for certain is that They speak with the Voice of Adonai. And that I'm here because we missed a Messianic Window. Again. The last time we had a Messianic Window was like 40 years ago (I know, ironic). Jewish tradition dictates that I, Elijah the Prophet, will herald the arrival of the Messiah on Passover by visiting every Seder dinner, drinking a glass of wine at each one, checking the IDs of all the men present (if you know what I mean), and visiting the local synagogue and blowing the shofar. This was a much better idea before the concept of a Global Diaspora.

On the last Messianic Window, I made it to 7 or 8 houses on Long Island before I was pulled over and blew a 0.12 on the breathalyzer. I was hauled off to jail with a DUI and that was the end of that.

The third house I visited pressed charges against me for breaking and entering; I'm like, you literally opened the door for me, how is that 'breaking' anything? But certainly it was proof that given the modern Jewish diaspora, even allowing for time zones, there was simply no way I could visit every seder in the world, and, crucially, *drink a glass of wine at each one*, in one night. I'm not fucking Santa Claus.

Technically, we had a Messianic Window last year and the year before also, but with a global pandemic in full-swing, it seemed ill-advised to go door-to-door. Besides, "huddling in your home to avoid a plague" was a little too on-the-nose. But I digress.

"A Mukbang is like a *kaffeeklatsch*, only digital, and has real food rather than just coffee and cake. The biggest ones attract millions of viewers! It seemed like a good fit."

"I see," the Metatron intones, which is technically true. They see everything. A video begins to play on the monitor that materializes on Their desk and also had always been there.

Hi everyone, welcome back to my channel! My name is Deb, and today we have a very special guest. Before we bring them in, I want to tell you about this magnificent dish we have in front of us. My fiancé texted me a few weeks ago OMG have you seen this brisket that's all over TikTok? I watched and it looked AMAZING. So today, just in time for Passover, we're eating this amazing Jewish Brisket. But I want to tell you a short little story before about how FreshCrate came to the rescue.

"You can skip forward about 3 minutes." I say, "she's telling a story about how her fiancé's mother got a flat tire on her way home and she was planning a dinner party that night, but luckily she had a specific meal-kit service and dinner came together super-fast and we thank them very much for sponsoring this episode."

The Metatron doesn't have eyes per se, but I swear They roll them anyway. They skip forward 3 minutes.

On screen, Deb, her fiancé, and I chat and drink wine and eat brisket for the next 47 minutes. The camera is stationary. The brisket remains in the foreground the entire time, growing steadily smaller as we consume slab after slab. We mostly chat about whatever Deb wants to talk about. Finally, in the closing moments, Deb asks me where her subscribers can find me.

Hey, thanks Deb, I've had so much fun! You can find me @Elijah5782 on all the regular platforms, and I'm really excited to announce our latest project, a Messianic Age, is Nigh! Find my link in the description!

"We actually got a lot of clicks," I say, "but the feedback was mostly that our listicle '11 Signs the Messiah Is Coming (#7 Will

Shock You!)' was a bit dated. People dismissed it as clickbait and bounced without reading."

The Metatron gives no indication that They heard me. "That one was on YouTube," intones the Metatron, "and this next one was on Twitch, but the videos premiered at the same moment. How is that possible?" They are referring to the 9-hour livestream I did with a Twitch chef/gamer on Pesach.

"The *Mukbang* with Deb was pre-recorded and edited, but the livestream was, well, live. I cooked a brisket from start to finish. While it was braising, we played Fortnite for 8 hours. I'm not very good, but that's not strictly necessary on most of these sorts of channels."

On the screen, the streamer watches me unwrap a beautiful 16 pound full brisket from butcher paper.

I season it thoroughly with salt, pepper, and garlic powder, then sear it top and bottom on a cast-iron griddle. I upend a bottle of generic "Tangy French-Style" salad dressing and a bottle of generic chili sauce into a mixing bowl, then refill each bottle almost to the top with boxed red wine, shake them, empty them into the mixing bowl, and stir to combine. I've already lined the bowl of a large slow-cooker with sliced onions, baby carrots, and like 40 whole cloves of garlic, and I lay the brisket on top, fat side up of course, then coat the meat with the dressing/chili sauce/wine mixture. I set the slow cooker for 8 hours on LOW.

On the stream I say, "This is my favorite way to prepare a brisket; it's easy, it comes together super-quickly so most of the cooking time is totally hands-off, and not only do you flavor your brisket with the onion and garlic, but *you flavor your onion and garlic with brisket.* Shmear a clove of that braised garlic on some matzo with a tiny bit of horseradish and [chef's kiss]."

The Metatron allows that my brisket recipe at least is pretty good.

"This TikTok says you have a 'Signature Cocktail'. Please prepare it for Me." The Metatron turns Their gaze upon the fully-stocked bar that materializes next to me but also has always been there.

I grab a glass shaker and drop in a few celery leaves and a small chunk of horseradish. The muddler is exactly 1.0 cubit in length, honestly a little too long, made from wood of the same acacia tree as the original Tabernacle.

With three quick twists, the leaves are wilted and fragrant and the horseradish has released its essence into the glass. I add a generous pour of Manischewitz Blackberry wine and a few ice cubes, then cover and shake. I pour the cocktail into a red wine glass and add a celery stick.

"This looks like the worst [They don't call it a "Bloody Mary," because we don't celebrate people who kill other people in the name of Adonai but They mean "Bloody Mary"] I've ever seen. And I quite literally have seen them all." I hand Them the glass, which levitates in a green mist.

They take a sip, I think. "This is awful." They take another sip. I think.

"Right? Weird foods can generate a lot of Engagement! We got mad FYP on that." And no, I'm not at all certain that I used that term correctly, but the Metatron didn't know that. I figured it was as good a time as any to drop the hammer. "All told, we got 21.3 million views on Pesach across all platforms, which significantly exceeds the number of actual Jews currently alive!"

"That is quite impressive," allowed the Metatron, "but as you did NOT manage to usher in a Messianic Age, I cannot help but think something was lacking in the execution. Perhaps," added the Metatron extremely sarcastically, "your brisket was under-seasoned?"

"I think it has to do with our business intelligence," I replied. "Next year with improved analytics—"

"You are Present at every *Brit Milah* in the world, and have been for thousands of years. You maintain the list of all males who have remembered the Covenant. What earthly 'analytics' can compare with that? How can so-called Channel Analytics enable you to testify that those participating in the Paschal Meal are on that list, if you are not present at the meal itself?"

It's important to note that I have NEVER inspected the genitals of attendees of any seder to see if they are circumcised. I am Spiritually Present at every bris (long story) so I simply *remember*, like oh, hey yeah I was at your bris and your bris, but this person I've not met before. It's not always this simple though.

"I've been meaning to talk with You about that whole Covenant Verification thing," I began. "There are plenty of men who never had a foreskin, and plenty of women who did and are circumcised. I think it's time we update that requirem—"

"This experiment was noble in purpose. I commend you for your ingenuity." The Metatron looked up from Their cocktail, I think, and I got a sinking feeling in the pit of my stomach. "It was, however, a failure. Next year you shall return to the traditional methods of visiting each seder in person, verifying that each male present is part of the Covenant, announcing the Messianic Age, and consuming the glass of wine provided for you. You are excused."

I rose, pinching the bridge of my nose in a futile attempt to hide my disappointment as I turned to leave.

Next year in Jerusalem.

Alternative Holidays

Chrysalis

Richard Thomas

John Redman stood in his living room, the soft glow of the embers in the fireplace casting his shadow against the wall. He wondered how much money he could get if he returned all of the gifts that were under the Christmas tree—everything—including what was in the stockings.

The wind picked up outside the old farmhouse, rattling a loose piece of wood trim, the windows shaking—a cool drift of air settling on his skin.

Couple hundred bucks maybe—four hundred tops. But it might be enough. That paired with their savings, everything that his wife, Laura, and he had in the bank—the paltry sum of maybe six hundred dollars. It had to be done. Every ache in his bones, every day that passed—a little more panic settled down onto his shoulders, the weight soon becoming unbearable.

Upstairs the kids were asleep, Jed and Missy quiet in their beds, home from school for their winter break, filling up the house with their warm laughter and echoing footsteps.

The long drive to the city, miles and miles of desolate farmland his only escort, it pained him to consider it at all. Video games and dolls, new jeans and sweaters, and a singular diamond on a locket hung from a long strand of silver. All of it was going back.

It had started a couple weeks ago with, of all things, a large orange and black wooly bear caterpillar. He stood on the back porch sneaking a cigarette, his wife and kids in town, grocery shopping and running errands all day. The fuzzy beast crawled across the porch rail and stopped right next to John—making sure it was seen.

John looked at the caterpillar and noticed that it was almost completely black, with just a tiny band of orange. Something in that information rang a bell, shot up a red flag in the back of his crowded mind. He usually didn't pay attention to these kinds of things—give them any weight. Sure, he picked up *The Old Farmer's Almanac* every year, partly out of habit, and partly because it made him laugh.

Owning the farm as they did now, seven years or so, taking over for his mother when she passed away, the children still infants, unable to complain, John had gotten a lot of advice. Every time he stepped into Clancy's Dry Goods in town, picking up his contraband cigarettes, or a six-pack of Snickers bars that he hid in the glove box of his faded red pickup truck, the advice spilled out of his neighbor's mouths like the dribble that used to run down his children's chins. Clancy himself told John to make sure he picked up the almanac, to get his woodpile in order, to put up plastic over the windows, in preparation for winter. For some reason, John listened to the barrel-chested man, his moustache and goatee giving him an air of sophistication that was offset by Clancy's fondness for flannel. John nodded his head when the Caterpillar and John Deere hats jawed on and on by the coffeepot, stomping their boots to shake off the cold, rubbing their hands over three-day old stubble. John nodded his head and went out the door, usually mumbling to himself.

Christmas was coming and the three-bedroom farmhouse was filled with the smell of oranges and cloves, hot apple cider, and a large brick fireplace that was constantly burning, night and day.

Laura taught English at the high school, and she was off work as well. Most of the month of December and a little bit of the new year would unfurl to fill their home with crayons, fresh baked bread, and Matchbox cars laid out in rows and sorted by color.

John was an accountant, a CPA. He'd taken over his father's business, Comprehensive Accounting, a few years before they'd finally made the move to the farm. The client list was set, most every small business in the area, and a few of the bigger ones as well. They trusted John with their business, the only history that mattered to them were the new ones he created with their books. Every year he balanced the accounts, hiding numbers over here, padding expenses over there, working his magic, his illusion. But

122

Laura knew John better, back before the children were born, back when their evenings were filled with broken glasses and lipstick stains and money gambled away on lies and risky ventures. Things were good now—John was on a short leash, nowhere to go, miles from everyone—trouble pushed away and sent on down the road.

John made a mental note of the caterpillar, to look it up later in the almanac. Right now he had wood to chop, stocking up for the oncoming season. He tugged on his soft, leather gloves, stained with sap and soil, faded and fraying at the edges.

Surrounding the farmhouse was a ring of trees, oak and maple and evergreen pine. For miles in every direction there were fields of amber, corn on one side—soybeans on the other.

John picked up the axe that leaned against the back porch with his left hand, and then grabbed the chainsaw with his right—eyeballing the caterpillar, which hadn't moved an inch, as he walked forward exhaling white puffs of air. One day the fields were a comfort, the fact that they leased them out to local farmers, no longer actual farmers themselves, a box checked in the appropriate column, incoming funds—an asset. The next day they closed in on him, their watchful stare a constant presence, a reminder of something he was not—reliable.

John set the axe and chainsaw next to a massive oak and looked around the ring of trees. There were small branches scattered under the trees—he picked these up in armloads and took them back to the house, filling a large box with the bits of wood. This would be the kindling. Then he went back to look for downed trees—smaller ones mostly, their roots unable to stand up to the winds that whipped across the open plains and bent the larger trees back and forth.

A fog pushed in across the open land, thick and heavy, blanketing the ring of trees, filling in all the gaps. The ground was covered in acorns, a blanket of caps and nuts, nowhere to step that didn't end in pops and cracks, his boot rolling across the tiny orbs.

"Damn. When did these all fall down, overnight?"

John stared up into the branches of the oak trees, spider webs spanning their open arms, stretching across the gaps, thick and white—floating in the breeze. He looked to the other trees and saw acorns scattered beneath them all, and more spider webs high up into the foliage. Spying a downed tree, he left the axe alone for now and picked up the chainsaw, tugging on the string, the bark and buzz filling the yard with angry noise.

Several hours later, the cord of wood was stacked against the side of the house, the tree sectioned down into manageable logs, which were then split in half, and then halved again. It was a solid yield, probably enough to get them through the winter—the box of kindling overflowing with twigs and branches that had been broken over his knee. They would keep an eye on the backyard, and over the course of the winter, they would refill the box with the fallen branches and twigs.

The winds picked up again as John took a breath, a sheen of sweat on the back of his neck, night settling in around the farm.

#

When he finally went inside, the wife and kids home from their errands, the house smelled of freshly baked cookies, chocolate chip, if John knew his wife. The kids were up on barstools around the butcher block island, hands covered in flour, their faces dotted with white, his wife at the kitchen sink washing dishes. In the corner of the window was a singular ladybug, red and dotted with black.

"Daddy," Missy yelled, hopping down off her stool. She ran over to him, painting his jeans with tiny, white handprints.

"Hey, pumpkin," John said. "Cookies?"

"Chocolate chip," she beamed.

"Jed, could you get me a glass of water?" John asked. His son didn't answer, concentrating on the cookie dough. "Jed. Water?" His son didn't answer.

"I'll get it, Daddy," Missy said.

"No, honey, I want Jed to get it. I know he can hear me."

John lowered his voice to a whisper, his eyes on Jed the whole time. "I'm going to count to three," John hissed, his daughter's eyes squinting, her head lowering as she crept out of the way. "Get me that water, boy, or you'll be picking out a switch."

Jed didn't move, a smile starting to turn up his mouth, the cookie dough still in his hands.

"Daddy?" Missy said, her face scrunching up. "He doesn't hear you, don't..."

"Honey, go," John continued. "One," John peeled off his gloves and dropped them by the back door. "Two," he whispered, unbuttoning his coat, pulling his hat off and dropping it on the floor. He inhaled for three, a thin needle pushing through his heart, this constant battle that he had with his son, the grade school maturation placing in front of John a new hurdle every day.

The boy got off the stool, leaving behind the cookies, and tugged on the back of his mother's apron strings.

"Mom, may I have a glass of water for Dad, please?"

Laura stopped doing the dishes, her long brown ponytail swishing to one side as she turned to look at the boy. She handed him a tall glass and pointed him to the refrigerator.

Off he went to get the water and ice, pushing the glass against the built-in dispenser, a modern-day convenience that they all enjoyed. Jed walked over to his dad and held the glass out to him, eyes glued to his father's belt buckle.

"Jed?"

"Yes, Dad?" he said, looking up, brown eyes pooled and distant.

"Thank you," John said, leaning over, hugging the boy.

The little man leaned into his father.

"Thanks for the water," John said, kissing the boy on the cheek. It just took a little more work, that's all.

Later that night, John sat in his study, while Laura put the kids to bed. He thumbed through the almanac, looking at the index, studying the upcoming months, the forecast for the Midwestern winter.

There were several things that got his attention. When the forecast was for a particularly bad winter, harsh conditions to come, there were signs and warnings everywhere. For example, if a wooly bear caterpillar is mostly orange, then the winter coming up will be mild. His caterpillar had almost no orange at all.

He kept looking for other signs. If there is an inordinate amount of fog, if there are clouds of spider webs, especially high up in the corners of houses, barns or trees—the bigger the webs, the worse the winter. If pine trees are extra bushy; if there are halos around the sun or the moon; if there is a blanket of acorns on the ground—these are the signs of a rough winter to come—rumors, and legends, and lore.

John closed the book and set it down, a chill settling in across his spine. A draft had slipped through the study window, the plastic sheets he'd meant to put up, forgotten. It was nothing. The stupid almanac was a bunch of crap, he thought. He stood up and went down to the basement anyway.

Along one wall were several wooden shelves—he'd built them himself when they moved in. There were jars of preserves and jam, jellies and fruit, all along the top shelf. Farther down, on the second shelf were soups and vegetables and other canned goods. It was almost empty, maybe a dozen cans of diced tomatoes and chicken noodle soup. On the third shelf were boxed goods, everything from pasta to scalloped potatoes to rice. It was fairly packed, so he moved on to the second set of shelves. It was filled with family-sized packages of toilet paper and paper towels, napkins and cleaning supplies. Then, he turned to the ancient furnace and stared.

Settled into the center of the room was the original furnace that came with the house. Built in the late 1800s, the farmhouse came equipped with a coal chute that opened up on the back of the house. Concrete poured into the ground on an angle, stopped at thick, metal doors—which if pulled open revealed the long abandoned chute that ran down to the basement floor. It was a novelty, really—historic and breathtaking to look at, but nothing more than a pile of greasy metal. The massive, black ironworks dwarfed the modern water heater and furnace, doors slotted like a set of enormous teeth, squatting in the middle of the room. Maybe he'd talk to Clancy.

#

It was fifteen miles to the nearest big city and the national chain grocery stores. John simply drove in to town. Clancy was about the same price, a couple cents higher here and there. But he felt better putting his money in the hands of a friend then a faceless corporation.

He felt stupid pushing the miniature grocery cart around the store. A flush of red ran up his neck as he bought every can of soup that Clancy had.

"Jesus, man," Clancy said, as John brought the cart up to the counter. "You done bought up all my soup."

"Order more," John said.

"I guess so," Clancy said, ringing him up.

"Can I ask you something?" John said.

"Shoot, brother. What's on your mind?"

"That furnace we have out at the farm, the old one? Does it work?"

"Well, let me think. It's still hooked up to the vents as far as I know. The little valves are closed off, is all—easy to flip them open. Helped your dad out with the ductwork a long time ago, he showed me how it all went together. But, you'd have to have a shitload of coal. And I have no idea of where you'd get that, these days. Does anyone still burn it?"

John nodded his head. He knew where he could get some coal. But it wasn't cheap, that's for sure.

"Just curious," John said. "How much are those gallons of water, by the way?" John asked, pointing at a dusty display at the front of the store. There were maybe two-dozen gallons of water.

"Those are .89 cents a gallon, can't seem to move them."

"I'll take them," John said.

"How many?" Clancy asked.

"All of them."

#

John was supposed to be down at his office. Instead, the back of his pickup truck was loaded up with soup and water, and he was headed down to the river. About two miles east, a small branch of the Mississippi wormed its way out into the land. A buddy of his from high school had a loading dock out there. Sometimes it was just people hopping on there in canoes, or boats, paddling down to the main branch of the river, or just buzzing up and down the water. Other times it was barges, loaded up with corn or soybeans—and sometimes coal from down south. There was a power plant upstate from where they lived, and it burned off a great deal of coal. Sometimes it was a train that passed by the plant, offloading great cars of the black mineral. And sometimes there were barges, drifting up the water, shimmering in the moonlight.

John pulled up to the trailer and hopped out. It was getting colder. He looked up at the cloudy sky, a soft halo wrapping around the sun, hiding behind the clouds. All around the tiny trailer were evergreen trees, fat and bushy, creeping in close to the metal structure, huddled up for warmth.

John knocked on the trailer door.

"Come in," a voice bellowed.

John stepped into the trailer, which was filled with smoke.

"Damn, Jamie, do you ever stop smoking? Open a window, why don't you."

"Well, hello to you too, John. Welcome to my humble abode. What brings you out here?"

John sat down and stared at his old buddy. Jamie was never going anywhere. Born and raised here in the northern part of the heartland, this was it for him. And it seemed to suit him just fine.

No college, no aspirations, no dreams of the big city—happy to live and die where he was born.

"Coal," John said. "I'm just wondering. You sell it to people?"

"Not usually. Got a few guys with old pot belly stoves off in the woods. They buy a sack off of me, now and then. You know, I just kind of skim it off the top, the electric company none the wiser."

"How much does it cost?"

"Depends. One guy I charge $20 cause he's broke and has a hot sister. Other guy is a jerk, and his sister's a hag. I charge him $50. I could cut you a deal though, John. Happy to help out an old friend."

"What about a larger quantity"

"How much we talking about, John?"

"Like, filling up my pickup truck?" John said.

Jamie whistled and tapped his fingertips on his mouth. "That's trouble. Can't skim that. Have to pay full price, actually talk to the barge man. Unload it. Not even sure when the next shipment will be rolling through. Getting cold."

John shivered. "If you had to guess though, any idea?"

Jamie took a breath. "Maybe a grand?"

#

John drove home, almost dark now, his house still miles away. When he pulled up the driveway, the tires rolling over more acorns, the house was dark. Where the hell were they? He pulled up to the back of the house, and hurried to unload the truck.

Into the kitchen he went, armloads of soup cans, hurrying to get them downstairs. Why was he sweating so much, why did this feel like a secret? He dropped a can of tomato soup but kept on going. He loaded the soups on the second shelf and went back for more. Two trips, three trips, and the dozens of cans of soup filled up the shelf with a weight that calmed him down.

Back upstairs, he picked up the can he dropped and looked out the window to see if they were home yet. A handful of ladybugs were scattered across the glass, and he scrunched up his nose at their presence.

Back to the truck, a gallon of water in each hand, this was going to take a little while. The soup he could explain—an impulse buy, Clancy running some kind of stupid sale: buy a can of soup get a stick of homemade jerky for free. But the two-dozen gallons of water looked like panic. He didn't want them to worry, even as he contemplated the coal, the thing he may have to do in secret, the risk he'd have to take.

Up and down the steps he went, pushing the water to the back of the basement, covering it up with a stained and flecked drop cloth. He stared at the canned goods, the water, and the coal powered furnace. A door slammed upstairs, and his head turned.

The kids were yelling for him, so he pulled the string that clicked off the light, and back upstairs he went.

"Hey, honey," he said. "What's up, guys?"

The kids gave him a quick hug and then ran on to their rooms. Laura leaned into him, looking tired, and gave him a kiss on the lips.

"You smell like smoke," she said. "You smoking again?" she asked.

"Nah. Saw an old friend. Jamie, you remember him? Chain smokes like a fiend."

Laura eyeballed John.

"Why are you all sweaty?"

"Just putting some stuff away, couple trips up and down the stairs, no big deal."

Laura puckered her lips, swallowed and moved to the sink. She turned on the water and washed off her hands.

"Why don't you go take a shower and get cleaned up? You stink. Dinner will be ready soon."

Later that night John watched the news, Laura in the kitchen doing the dishes.

The weatherman laid out the forecast all the way up to Christmas and beyond. Cold. It was dipping down, probably into the teens. Snow. A few inches here and there, but nothing to cause any alarm.

He switched over to another station, the same thing. He tried the Weather Channel, watching the whole country, the Midwest especially, storm fronts rolling down from Canada, but nothing to worry about.

"How much weather do you need, hon?" Laura said, sticking her head in from the kitchen. "You've been watching that for like an hour."

"Oh," he said. "I was just spacing out, wasn't really paying attention. You wanna sit down and watch something with me?"

"Sure. Want some tea?"

John got up and walked into the kitchen, Laura's back still to him, and wrapped his arms around her waist. She relaxed into his arms, and leaned back. He kissed her on the neck, holding her tight, his mouth moving up to her earlobe, where he licked and nibbled at her gently.

"Or, we could just go up to bed early." She smiled.

"We could do that," he said.

Behind her on the window there were several dozen ladybugs now, bunched up in the corner, a tiny, vibrating hive—and beyond that a slowly expanding moon with a ghost of a halo running around it.

#

The next day they woke up to snow, three inches on the ground, heavy flakes falling like a sheet, white for as far as he could see. The kids were screaming, laughing, excited to get out into it, his wife calming them down with requests to eat, to sit still, to wait. For John the snowfall made his stomach clench, the way the tiny icicles hung from the gutters, the pile of dead ladybugs covering the windowsill, the sense that he had blown it, missed his opportunity—the claustrophobia closing in.

All day John walked around with his temples throbbing, his trembling gut in turmoil—his mouth dry and filled with cotton.

To keep his hands busy, he pulled a roll of plastic out of the garage, and sealed up every window in the house. When the sun came out and melted everything away, the children were disappointed.

John was not.

When Laura fell asleep on the couch, the kids watching cartoons, John made a call to Jamie. Three days for the coal, the day before Christmas, still a thousand dollars for the weight. If the weather held, it gave him time. He told Jamie to make it happen. He'd have it for him in cash.

The afternoon couldn't pass fast enough, Laura constantly staring at him from across the room.

He cleaned up the dead ladybugs, then went downstairs and placed a cardboard box on the tarp that covered up the gallons of water, trying to hide his anxiety with a plastic smile.

The middle of the night was his only chance, so he crept downstairs with his pocketknife in his robe pocket, and slit open the presents one by one. He peeled back the tape gently, no tearing allowed, and emptied the presents from their wrappings. Where he could, he left the cardboard boxes empty for now and prayed that nobody shook the presents. For others, he wrapped up new shapes, empty boxes he found stacked down in the basement.

Grabbing a large black trash bag from under the sink, he filled it up with clothing and gifts, the tiny jewelry box going into his pocket. When he was done, he opened the cookie jar, the green grouch that sat up high on one of the shelves. He pulled out the receipts and stuffed them in his pocket, and slunk out to the truck to hide the loot.

When he stepped back into the kitchen, Laura was standing there, arms crossed, watching him.

"Dammit, Laura, you scared me."

"What the hell are you doing, John?"

"Taking out the trash."

"At three in the morning?" she asked. She walked over and sniffed him.

"You know," he said, smiling. "Christmas is only a couple days away. Maybe you don't want to look so close at what I'm doing. Maybe there are surprises for wives that don't snoop too hard," John said.

Laura grinned and held out her hand.

"Come to bed," she said.

Out the window the full moon carried a ring that shone across the night.

\#

John got up early and left a note. It was the best way to get out of the house without any questions. He left his wife and kids sleeping, and snuck out the back door, the wind whipping his jacket open, mussing his hair—bending the trees back and forth.

All day he drove, one place to the next, his stories changing, his stories remaining the same. Too large, too small; changed my mind, she already has one; got the wrong brand, my kids are so damn picky. The wad of bills in his pocket got thicker. The pain behind his eyes spread across his skull.

What was he doing?

He stopped by the bank, the day before Christmas now, and cleared out their checking and savings, leaving only enough to keep the accounts open. He took his thousand dollars and drove out to the trailer, Jamie sitting there as if he hadn't moved.

"All there?" Jamie asked, leaning back in his chair.

"To the nickel."

"Tomorrow night then," Jamie said. "Christmas Eve."

"Yep."

"What the hell are you doing, John?" Jamie asked.

"The only thing I can."

When John got home, Laura rushed out to the car.

"The fireplace," she said, "It's caved in."

John looked up to the tall brickwork that was now leaning to one side, the winds whipping up a tornado of snow around him. A few broken bricks lay on the ground, a trickle of smoke leaking out of the chimney.

"Everyone okay?" he asked.

"Yeah, some smoke and ashes, I swept it up and the fire was out at the time. But no fire for Christmas now, the kids will be disappointed."

"It'll be okay," John said. "We'll survive."

\#

It was a Christmas tradition that John and Laura would stay up late, drinking wine and talking, giving thanks for the year behind them. Laura would glance at the presents and John would wince. Every time she left the room, he poured his wine into hers, preparing for the night ahead.

At one o'clock, he tucked her into bed and went out to the truck. It was cold outside, getting colder, the layers he wore giving him little protection. There was a slow snowfall dusting the crops, his headlights pushing out into the night.

John was numb. Where was the storm, the epic snowfall, the crushing ice storm—the arctic temperature littering the countryside with the dead?

He pulled up to the trailer and Jamie stepped outside. On the river was a single barge filled with coal. A crane was extended out over it, teeth gleaming in the moonlight.

"Ready?" Jamie asked.

"Yeah."

Jamie manned the crane, back and forth, filling it up with coal and turning it to the side, a shower of black falling on the truck bed, the darkness filling with the impact of the coal.

Over and over again, Jamie filled the crane with coal and turned it to the truck bed, and released it. In no time the bed was overflowing.

"That's all she'll hold, John," Jamie said.

"Thanks, Jamie. You might want to take some home yourself."

"Why?"

"Storm coming."

#

At the house, he backed the truck up to the chute, glancing up at the sky, clear and dark, with stars dotting the canvas.

He opened the heavy metal doors that led into the basement and started shoveling the coal down into the chute where it slid down and spread across the floor.

Fat snowflakes started to fall, a spit of drizzle that quickly turned to ice, slicing at his face. He kept shoveling. The bed of the truck was an eternity stretching into the night—one slick blackness pushing out into another. He kept on.

The snow fell harder, John struggling to see much of anything, guessing where the mouth of the chute was, flinging the coal into the gaping hole, feeding the hungry beast.

When he was done, he didn't move the truck. He could hardly lift his arms. And his secret wouldn't last much longer, anyway.

In the kitchen, he sat under the glow of the dim bulb that was over the sink, sipping at a pint of bourbon that he had pulled out of the glove box, numb and yet sweating, nauseous and yet calm. It was done. Whatever would come, it was done.

He fell into a fitful slumber, his wife asleep beside him, the silence of the building snowfall, deafening.

#

The morning brought screams of joy, and soon after that, screams of panic and fear.

The children climbed in bed, excited to open their presents, bouncing on the heavy comforter as Laura beamed at the children. John sat up, dark circles and puffy flesh under his red, squinting eyes.

"John, you look terrible, are you okay?"

"We'll see," he said. He leaned over and kissed her. "Just know that I love you," he said.

Laura turned to the kids. "Should we go downstairs?"

"Mommy, look at all the snow. Everything is white," Missy said.

Laura got up and walked to the window.

"My God. John, come here."

John stood up and walked over to the window, the yard filled with snow, a good four feet up the trunk of an old oak tree. The snow showed no sign of stopping. The limbs were covered in ice, hanging low.

John walked to the other window that faced into the back yard, and saw that only the cab of his truck was visible above the snow.

The kids turned and ran down the stairs. Laura turned to John and opened her mouth, and then closed it.

When they got to the bottom of the stairs, the kids were already at the presents, starting to rip them open.

Coal dust and fingerprints were on the stockings, a small bulge at the bottom of each.

They stopped at the bottom of the steps and watched the kids as their smiles turned to looks of dismay.

"John, what's going on?" Laura asked.

The kids looked up, the boxes empty. Missy went to her stocking and dumped the lump of coal into her hand.

John didn't remember putting those lumps of coal in the stockings. Some of last night was a blur.

Outside the wind picked up. The loose bricks shifted in the fireplace, a dull thud scattering across the roof, and a blur of red fell past the window.

Missy began to cry.

"John, what did you do?" Laura's face was flush, and she walked to Missy, pulling the girl to her side.

Jed kept ripping open boxes, his face filling with rage—any box, big or small—his name, Missy's name, he kept ripping them open.

Empty, all of them.

John sat on the couch and clicked on the television set, all of their voices filling the room, the paper tearing, Missy crying, Laura saying his name over and over again.

"...for the tri-county area. Temperatures are plummeting down into the negatives, currently at minus 20 and falling, wind chill of thirty below zero. We are expecting anywhere from six to ten feet of snow. That's right, I said ten feet."

"Shut up!" John yelled, turning to them, tears in his eyes. He turned back to the television set.

"Winds upward of fifty miles an hour. We have power outages across the state. So far over fifty thousand residents are without electricity. ConEd trucks are crippled as the snow is falling faster than the plows can clear them. Already we have reports of municipal vehicles skidding off the icy roads."

John looked up into the corner of the room where a large spider web was spreading. A ladybug was caught in the strands, no longer moving.

The weatherman kept talking, but John could no longer hear him. The map, the charts, the arrows and numbers spread across the television screen, warnings and talk of death on the roads.

"...could be anywhere from six to ten days before..."

Outside there is a cracking sound, a heavy, deep ripping and the kids ran to the window and looked out. Icicles and branches fell to the ground, shattering like glass, half of the tree tearing off, one mighty branch falling to the ground, shaking the foundation, sending snow flying up into the air.

"John?" Laura said.

"...do not go outside for anything..."

"John?"

"...blankets, huddle together..."

Somewhere down the road, a transformer blew sending sparks into the sky, the bang startling the kids who started to cry, burrowing deeper into Laura's side.

"...police and a state of emergency..."

The television set went black and the Christmas tree lights winked off.

Wind beat against the side of the house as a shadow passed over the windows. Outside the snow fell in an impermeable blanket, the roads and trees no longer visible.

The room was suddenly cold.

John got up and walked to the kitchen, taking a glass out from the cabinet, turning on the water. There was a dull screeching sound, as the whole house shook, nothing coming out of the tap.

"Pipes are frozen," John said to himself.

On the windowsill was a line of candles, and three flashlights sitting in a row.

He grabbed one of the flashlights and opened the basement door, staring down into the darkness.

John walked down the stairs to where the coal spilled across the concrete, grabbing a shovel that he had leaned against the wall. He pulled open one furnace door, then the other, and setting the flashlight on the ground so that it shot up at the ceiling, he shoveled in the coal.

In no time, the furnace was full.

He walked around the basement, the band of light reflecting off the ductwork, turning screws and opening vents.

Behind him on the stairs Laura stood with the children in front of her, each of them holding a lit candle, a dull yellow illuminating their emotionless faces.

John lit a match and tossed it into the furnace, a dull whoomp filling up the room.

Turning back to his family at the top of the steps, John smiled, and wiped the grime off of his face.

Merry Chrithmuth

Kevin McCarty

Tilda the Tooth Fairy moped, watching yet another Santa Claus movie on the telly. It was a typical star-studded, Oscar-worthy affair with a typical A-lister and his excellent teeth playing the Big Guy. With all her fairy might, Tilda heaved a half-eaten pot pie in the screen's direction, only to watch it dash onto the floor, along with her dreams.

Fred Astaire played Santa, Tom Hanks played Santa, hell, even Kurt Russell played Santa! Nobody would ever make a movie about a Tooth Fairy.

She needed a gig like Santa had.

An idea came to her. She grabbed a pen and quickly scribbled a letter. In a toothy flash, she was at the old man's palatial mansion in the North Pole, pushing the letter through the gilded mail slot, listening as he opened the letter and read it aloud.

Dear Santa,

You have tested positive for Covid-19. In light of your many preexisting conditions, we estimate your chances of survival to be roughly zero. Current CDC regulations require you to quarantine until you test negative. Considering your situation, we suggest you get your affairs in order, but please don't forget our new beakers. Long stems. We've been very good this year.

Your friends at the Centers for Disease Control and Prevention

She heard weeping and wailing and dashed off to his workshop. All the elves were there. Tilda pulled out a large bucket of superglue, liberally applying it to the locks. It didn't take long before there was more weeping, more wailing. She could hear them drawing straws to see who would have to get eaten first.

Elves.

Off to the sleigh. She was all set until Rudolf turned his head. "Where's Santa?"

"On vacation. He asked me to fill in for a bit."

"Uh, OK."

Reindeer.

On to the first house. Toys? Ah crap! Tilda was sure the toys were still in the workshop behind layers of superglue and desperate, hungry elves. What's a tooth fairy to do? Tilda thought long and hard, digging through her fairy pockets for an idea. She pulled out a tooth. Sally's little molar, the third one this month. That's it! People were always giving her teeth. Why not give some back? Brilliant!

Unfortunately, she barely had enough for the first house. She needed more teeth. But where to get them?

Rudolf turned to look back at her. "So where ya' wanna go next?"

An idea struck. A desperate, wonderful idea.

"Take me to the nearest hockey game, pronto!"

In barely an eyeblink, she was fluttering next to a goalie. He was a giant of a man, smelly, spitting, swearing and surly as a cat in a hot tub. In other words, he was perfect.

She whispered in his ear, "The other team says you listen to Taylor Swift music—and *like* it."

"Whaaaa!" he roared, throwing off his mask and swinging his stick at the nearest opponent. Within moments, both teams jumped in and teeth dropped like hail stones onto the ice.

Hockey players.

Tilda fluttered over to a fan behind the now empty team bench. Pointing to another fan wearing the other team's jersey she said, "Hey, I'm just a fairy so what do I know, but that guy over there says you look like somebody who eats hummus."

In moments he was on his feet, pushing her aside and tearing at his jersey. Invoking the wrath of his god. He leaped across the bleachers, hands searching for the other fan's throat.

Fights broke out everywhere. By the time police restored some semblance of order, Tilda was long gone with armfuls of molars, incisors and canines.

Fans.

But it wasn't enough. There were only so many hockey games, so Tilda visited bars, nightclubs, TV sets of Real Housewives and Mike Tyson's house.

It still wasn't enough. She visited old folks' homes for dentures and implants, orphanages for baby teeth. Pretty soon she was swiping everything she could, from bridges to extractions to root canals. Once that was all gone, she pilfered healthy teeth, teeth with fillings, teeth with plaque, chipped teeth, crowns and caps. When she finally had enough, she put them in stockings, under the tree and by the fire, each with a little note for the children.

Be sure to brush twice a day and remember to see your dentist once a year.

#

Santa's switchboard lit up like a Christmas tree, with complaints.

Parents.

On her arrival back to Santa's Village, the SWAT team was waiting, with some very unfairy-like cuffs and batons.

"What's all the fuss about?" she said, before a dozen tasers latched onto her.

Cops.

The next day in the courtroom, tethered to a pair of burly guards, Tilda awaited her fate.

The judge looked up from his bench. "Seems the American Dental Association has been lobbying on your behalf to the governor. Looks like we won't get to try out old sparky after all. Next case!"

Tilda dragged her tin cup across the prison bars, *clack, clack, clack*. She called out to the sergeant at the desk, "Hey, so when do I get out of here?"

Through a gapped smile, the sergeant replied, "Releath you? How bout never? Merry Crithmuth!"

He muttered to his donut, "Faireeth."

Alternative Holidays

Midsummer with Vampire Romeo and Zombie Juliet

Keyan Bowes

Two households both alike in dignity...

The whispers have gone out: the Dead and Undead of Verona are brawling again tonight. On Midsummer Eve. Romeo, with his acute vampire senses, can smell the stink of the battle from streets away. He draws his sword and runs toward the melee, where torches held by zombie partisans light the chaotic battle. In the cobbled market square, amid the stalls set up for the Midsummer Fair, hundreds advance and clash.

BRAINNSSSS! The Dead Lord Capulet rallies the zombies with their loud battle cry. A hundred voices echo it. The vampires, led by Romeo's sire, the Undead Lord Montague, respond with a furious hiss like a disturbed nest of demon snakes.

In the grand stone-faced buildings around the square, windows go dark as humans hurriedly draw curtains and snuff candles.

Despite his age, Capulet joins the battle, whacking away at vampires and yelling threats at Montague. Romeo avoids him, darting around the edges of the fray to seek his old enemy, Tybalt.

Three zombies converge on a vampire near Romeo. The fast-moving vampire fights them off, but a fourth jumps him from behind and bites into his head. The brain-eaten vampire collapses in a pile of ashes and a taste of smoke. Romeo leaps across, wielding his sword like a battle-axe. His speed and fury easily win and the putrid stink of beheaded zombie rises into the air. Not for nothing is his sword called Zombie-killer.

The acrid scent of vampire aggression overlays the pheromones of fighting zombies. Romeo dodges through piles of debris where overturned stalls litter the ground with trodden fabric and broken pottery, mixed with the ashes of dead vampires and fast-rotting zombie corpses. Where the blazes is Tybalt?

Before he finds him, there's a sound of hooves and the smell of equine and human sweat. Into the square gallops the Prince, flanked by two mounted torch-bearers, heading a cavalcade of riders.

Rank fury rolls off the human Prince. "On pain of torture," he shouts, "from those bloody hands throw your mistempered weapons to the ground!"

The loud clang of weapons hitting stone is followed by a wary stillness with all eyes on the Prince, glaring down at them from his horse. Imperiously, he gestures for the Heads of the trouble-making Houses to come forth.

With vampire speed Romeo retrieves and sheaths his sword, and steps forward with the Undead Lord Montague. He follows his sire's lead with a showy bow to the Prince.

The Dead Lord Capulet makes his way haltingly, his cane knocking on the cobbles. There with him is Tybalt, his wife's nephew, whose ripped clothing show he's been in the thick of the battle.

Romeo glowers at Tybalt, and inwardly sniggers at how the old warrior Capulet is pretending to be feeble.

Behind Capulet's back, Tybalt growls at Romeo, threatening to draw. Romeo bares his fangs.

Capulet notices and knocks away Tybalt's sword arm.

Sullenly, the younger man steps back.

Montague scowls at Romeo, who immediately stands down.

When the Prince finally speaks, his voice is icy. "If ever you disturb our streets again," he threatens through clenched teeth, "Your Lives will pay!"

Tame Houses of the Dead and Undead, the zombies and vampires, spare the city the burden of a standing army. No foreign prince dare invade. But the Houses must behave with decorum. The human citizens of Verona are out of patience.

Romeo rolls his eyes as the Prince says something about "thrice disturbed the quiet of our streets." It's the same lecture they've heard several times already. Why should he be deferential to a short-lived human weakling who'd last about a minute in a fight and barely six decades without one?

His sire buzzes at him in warning. Romeo quickly focuses again on the still-blathering Prince. Riots ...dangerous anarchy, signaling Verona's enemies... slack and vulnerable state... He'll throw the Undead and Dead out of the city, ending their Households.

Romeo freezes. Exile? Did he threaten exile?

They need these weak short-lived humans. Cities ruled by vampires or zombies collapsed as their humans died or fled. Without strong human governments to ensure the safety of their palaces, without the orderly agreements that supply zombies with the brains of Verona's corpses, without the vampires' sanctioned blood-friends among the humans, there'd be neither Dead nor Undead. Just plain dead.

Capulet pulls at his straggly beard and glances at his rival. Montague inclines his head. The two lords kneel in submission to their Prince.

Romeo follows their lead, and so—after a minute—does Tybalt.

#

When Romeo returns home just before dawn, he's already forgotten the battle and the Prince's threat. His mind is full of love. Unrequited love, for Friar Lawrence arrives bearing a sealed letter together with Romeo's own ring. She's returned it. Again.

Rosaline, beautiful human Rosaline, is still adamant. She's refused to cross over to the Undead. She'd rather die a virgin than live a vampire.

Romeo's heart sinks. Friar Lawrence kindly advises him to leave the girl be—the same advice he gave the last time. But what does a celibate religious human know of love? All he talks about is the danger of falling into carnal sin (not that Rosaline is up for that).

What he needs, Romeo insists, is to see Rosaline and have another chance to persuade her. He'll try at the Midsummer Feast.

After Friar Lawrence departs, Romeo goes upstairs. He can't sleep, so he shutters his windows to make an artificial night. Sweet unattainable Rosaline!

#

By the time Romeo gets to the Feast, it's in full swing. This year, it's Capulet who's hosting the annual event where vampire, human and zombie mingle to celebrate the peak of summer, and everyone who's anyone makes an appearance. This is the same Capulet he was fighting only the other night, but the palazzo is neutral territory during the celebrations. Still, it's the enemy's palace, and Romeo feels a little thrill of tension as he enters.

Servers wander through the crowd offering wine and blood and little pastries made with candied fruit, partridge, and brains. A thousand candles light the halls, musicians play a vigorous tune.

From the sidelines, Romeo watches zombies in stately formal dance, vampires swirling and dipping, and humans weaving creative patterns amid the dancing throng. The aromas of spices, perfumes, perspiration, and hot candle wax waft through the room.

There's no sign of Rosaline. Romeo stands around awkwardly, wondering why he's even here.

The zombie host Lord Capulet circulates proudly among the guests, all smiles and nods instead of his usual frowns and scowls. He's introducing everyone to the Dead Count Parris, even though they all know him already.

Just when Romeo's about to give up and leave, he spots her across the room. Not Rosaline, but a stunningly lovely Dead girl in a dark red dress. Fair as the full moon, black zombie eyes, dark hair in a simple braid down her back. He catches a faint trace of her sweet pheromones.

"I never saw true beauty till this night," he whispers. He stands transfixed, barely able to look at her, barely able to look away. It drives his unrequited human love completely from his mind.

The zombie girl glances in his direction.

O, she's noticed him!

He goes up to her, offers to lead her into a dance.

She happily gives him her cold fair hand, but draws him instead into a dark corner behind the velvet curtains. The musky notes of her scent make him bold. Moving closer, he bends over her. She lifts her pale luminous face to him and he presses his lips to hers.

"You kiss by the book," she says, reaching up to touch his face. Her dark eyes are bottomless and full of wonder. Is it her first kiss, too? By her fragrance, she's as much in love as he.

He kisses her again. Her lips are firm and cold. Her arms are around his neck. Who is she? No matter. Her intoxicating zombie perfume sings with love.

"Madam!" An older human woman comes bustling through the door and they quickly move apart. "Your mother craves a word with you."

The girl gives Romeo a quick smile and follows the woman with a graceful deliberate zombie tread, her dress rustling as she walks. Romeo watches her departing back until she's hidden by the crowd.

#

A whiff of something different and dangerous hits Romeo—the smell of infuriated zombie. There in the archway with Lord Capulet stands Tybalt, sword raised.

Romeo's fangs spring out.

But instead of attacking, Lord Capulet turns on Tybalt and grabs his sword arm. It doesn't even take vampire senses to hear old Capulet rage, a human could have heard him: Is Tybalt trying to embarrass his uncle by turning the Midsummer Feast into a melee and inviting the Prince's wrath?

"I'll not endure him," Tybalt says angrily, pointing at Romeo.

The Dead Lord slaps Tybalt across the face. "Am I the master here or you?" Another hard slap. "He shall be endured!"

Jerking his arm free, Tybalt stalks from the room. Capulet keeps shouting.

Lady Capulet puts a calming hand on her husband's arm. Old Capulet starts yelling at her too, but about the Dead Count Parris and Capulet's secret sorrow. (Not secret any more, Romeo thinks, since he's telling it at the top of his voice at a gathering of most of Verona's gentlefolk.)

"The earth hath swallowed all my hopes but she," Capulet tells his lady, as though she doesn't share the same grief.

People turn to look.

Old Capulet lowers his voice, but doesn't stop. And all he's got is that disobedient princox, Tybalt. *Her* nephew, not even his own. Wealthy, well-connected and willing, the Dead Count Parris is perfect as his heir.

Romeo feels a sneaking sympathy for his old enemy. Unlike vampires who don't age, zombies eventually showed their years. Capulet has centuries on him, but since none of his get have risen from the earth except this girl, she'll probably be the only one. All his hopes for an heir will be in his son-in-law.

The girl in red enters from the other side of the hall, cutting short Capulet's harangue. She curtsies to Lady Capulet.

The Dead girl isn't just any-zombie, she's Juliet, scion of Lord Capulet.

Romeo's completely enthralled anyway.

#

Romeo leaps over the boundary wall of the Capulet Mansion, vampire nimble, lands on the ground without a rustle. Lingering in the shadows, he hears her voice—and his name.

"Romeo, Romeo... wherefore art thou Romeo?" she says. "Deny thy father and refuse thy name."

She's on a balcony above him, still in her party gown, and he realizes she's speaking to the moon or sky or herself, not to him. She doesn't know he's there. "That which we call a rose by any other name would smell as sweet," she says, plucking a rose from the climbing vine, sniffing at it, then tossing it over the railing.

Romeo catches the flower. He can't resist throwing the rose back up to her. "Call me but Love, and I'll be new baptized," he says.

Juliet gasps and peers over the balustrade into the darkness. "Art thou not Romeo, and a Montague?"

She recognizes his voice! Romeo buzzes with sheer joy.

"If they do see thee, they will murder thee!" she says urgently. The party is over, so is the truce.

He laughs. Unlike vampires, zombies can't see well in the dark. They'll never catch him. Anyway, he'd willingly die for her.

In the sweet and precipitous exchange that follows, Romeo loses track of what's said before she's called inside.

Except for the one single thing that matters.

"If that thy bent of love be honorable," Juliet says, "thy purpose marriage..."

Romeo holds his breath... "send me word tomorrow."

Overjoyed, he can hardly believe it. She loves him. Juliet, willing to be his! Ready to marry him! In his mind, she's already in his arms.

He sprints all the way to Friar Lawrence's stone cottage, and hammers on the rough wooden door. As soon as Friar Lawrence opens it, Romeo announces: "My heart's dear love is set on the fair daughter of rich Capulet!"

The friar stares. "Is Rosaline, that thou didst love so dear, so soon forsaken?"

That's the other problem with confidantes. Awkward questions.

This is altogether different, Romeo insists. "As mine on hers, so *hers* is set on *mine!*" So unlike Rosaline! He can't wait. "This I pray, that thou consent to marry us *today!*"

Romeo fidgets impatiently while the good Friar talks himself into supporting this marriage.

"This alliance may so happy prove, to turn your households' rancor to pure love," he eventually says. Romeo doubts eloping with Juliet will improve vampire-zombie relations, much less "pure love" but doesn't say it aloud. What matter if only the Friar agrees?

When Friar Lawrence finally relents, Romeo races to get Juliet.

She's peacefully asleep, fair as the autumn moon, but wakes instantly at his whisper. Taking her candle to light the way, she leads them through complicated passages to a hidden staircase and a postern gate. As a lonely pre-zombie child, she'd explored the whole mansion and knows it better than anyone, all the service corridors, all the secret passages, all the unused exits.

Outside, Romeo takes the lead, the darkness transparent to his vampire sight.

#

Juliet is exquisite in the flickering candlelight. As Romeo says his vows, she looks at him so adoringly that he stumbles over the words. The moment the Friar pronounces them wed, he scoops her into his arms.

Romeo wants to shout his wedding to the world, take his wife to bed immediately.

Friar Lawrence insists he must wait. Where can Juliet go this night but home to the Capulet mansion? And how can she brave her father's wrath alone?

Juliet slips her hand into Romeo's arm. She must go now, so no one will know anything. When they are ready, they'll tell the world.

#

As Romeo, too, makes his way homeward, the smell of zombie fury and defiance crushes his buoyant mood. Tybalt, spoiling for a fight.

"Thou art a villain!" Tybalt shouts.

Two days earlier, Romeo would have unsheathed in a moment. But now this zombie is kin by marriage—Juliet's dear cousin, practically a brother. Romeo keeps walking.

"Turn and draw!" Tybalt demands, taking out his sword. He backs Romeo into a corner.

Romeo draws his sword, Zombie-killer.

The vampire has speed, but the zombie has expertise and endurance. Zombies have as many lives as a cat.

Swords clashing, the two fight back and forth in the night. Tybalt's furious in his pursuit. Zombie-killer dances in Romeo's hand, blocking Tybalt's slashing thrusts with vampire-fast parries.

Soon a crowd gathers around the torchbearers, distracting Romeo.

Friar Lawrence yells something about the Prince's orders.

Romeo's blood-friend Mercutio waves a drawn sword, trying to stop the fight—or perhaps to join it.

Romeo leaps onto a low wall, giving him a vantage point.

Tybalt keeps coming.

Suddenly, somehow, Mercutio's there between Tybalt and the wall—and Tybalt's sword pierces him through the heart.

Romeo looks at the dying man, grief nearly choking him. Mercutio, blood-friend! Dead, dead before Romeo could make him vampire. Gone forever.

Furious, Romeo slashes down with Zombie-killer, and strikes Tybalt's head from his body. The sharp stench of dead zombie rises from the corpse. Tybalt's head rolls away and lodges against Mercutio's corpse.

The crowd gasps and whispers.

Romeo stands gaping. How has it come to this?

Friar Lawrence smacks his shoulder. "Romeo! Away! Be gone!" he urges.

Shaking, Romeo flees the dreadful death scene, the Prince's judgment ("Your lives will pay!"), and the coming daylight to his only sanctuary, Friar Lawrence's holy cottage.

#

The Friar stays on at the scene to await the Prince and plead for Romeo. After all, everyone saw Tybalt started it. Perhaps the plea works; when the Prince arrives, he condemns Romeo only to banishment, not death. Exiled, but with a full twenty-four hours to leave Verona. Relieved at this outcome, the Friar goes home to make his report.

He walks in to find Romeo curled into a whimpering ball on the floor.

"The law that threatened death becomes thy friend and turns it to exile!" he tells him. Romeo disagrees.

"Be merciful, say 'death,' for exile hath more terror," he moans. Being parted from Juliet is a fate worse than death. His sleeve is soaked with tears and snot, but he will not get off the floor.

Then—there's a messenger at the door! With word from Juliet! She'll wait for him tonight before he leaves. There'll be ropes to climb up to her balcony.

#

It's a strange secret wedding night for Romeo, stealing into his new wife's room like a thief, guilty of slaying her dear cousin. Somehow that heightens everything, their senses stretched to breaking. Intoxicated by Juliet's scent, Romeo can't get enough of her, nor she of him. Romeo strokes her wild black hair, kisses her pale lips, inhales her perfume of satisfied desire. Her skin is cold and pure as marble. He can't take his eyes off her.

"It is not yet near day," Juliet pleads. "It was the nightingale and not the lark."

"Night's candles are burnt out." He's in triple jeopardy now: in the house of his enemy; under sentence of banishment; and from his own Undead nature, which would kill him sooner than the other two.

He cups her cool face in his hands. "I must be gone and live or stay and die."

In time, in Mantua, they'll start their lives anew. But for now, morning looms and Lady Capulet is calling for Juliet. Romeo flees.

#

The Montague's distant linkage with the Mantua Clan gains Romeo only a run-down woodland cottage, and access to some inferior blood-friends who'll never be made vampire.

He's hardly unloaded and sent away the hearse that brought him to Mantua when someone bangs on the cottage door.

"Let me come in and you shall know my errand," says a soft harsh voice. It sounds like a boy trying to mimic an older man.

"I come from Lady Juliet." The hooded boy with a lantern introduces himself as Peter of the Capulet household and offers proof: "Here sir, a ring she bid me give you."

It's her wedding ring. Romeo stands aside.

Peter enters, looks around, then takes two glasses and a jug of wine from the sideboard. He gets a vial from his bag, pours the drops into a wine glass and sets it before Romeo.

"I drink to thee!" he says, explaining Lady Juliet had bid him serve a cordial of wondrous powers to Romeo.

Romeo finishes the wine. He feels—strange. The wine's blurring his senses. His hands look pink. His fangs shrink into his gums.

What cordial has the boy poured?

Now the boy pulls down his hood. It's his wife herself! But no longer the Dead Lady Juliet. She's fully human, zombie no more.

As is he. They're both mortal.

#

Just after Romeo left, Juliet explains, her mother announced they were getting her married. The. Very. Next. Day. "The Count Parris, at St Peter's Church, shall happily make thee a joyful bride!"

Aghast, Juliet protested. They wouldn't listen. If she disobeyed, she was out.

"Hang, beg, starve, die in the streets," her furious father yelled.

She'd run to Friar Lawrence. What choices had she? Bigamy? Losing Romeo? No annulling the marriage, no revealing it.

The Friar'd given her a potion to take overnight. He didn't say what it was. Poison maybe? She took it anyway.

When she awoke, she'd turned human. While her family reacted with horrified confusion, she'd grabbed some boy's clothes, a horse and her confidence, and escaped to Mantua.

#

This is the same potion. The Prince won't pursue a human Romeo. They can go home. Juliet's clever ruse will see them into safety. Peter's, he amends it. He mustn't forget, Peter.

"Hire post-horses; I will hence tonight!" Romeo says, jubilantly making plans.

First, to Friar Lawrence. Persuade the Prince to rescinded his exile. Announce their marriage to both Houses. Then have his sire quietly remake them to vampires. The zombies... well, they'll have to find a new heir. Maybe Capulet can adopt Parris or something.

Horses. First thing tomorrow. He's human, he's not restricted to the dark.

#

Traveling by daylight feels odd. The odors are more complex in the heat of the day though dimmed by his now-human senses. Colors look different, the sun feels harsh. Romeo's glad of the hooded cape Juliet's brought him.

He keeps glancing back at Juliet, this ruddy, human, boyish version of his pale zombie wife he's always seen by moonlight or candlelight. So different, still so beautiful.

They're near Verona when they see a zombie—the Dead Count Parris. Romeo tries to conceal his face. Too late.

"This is that banish'd haughty Montague!" Parris shouts, galloping at them. He leaps from his horse and advances, sword drawn. "Vile Montague!"

Romeo and Peter dismount. Trying unsuccessfully to keep the horses between himself and the rampaging zombie, Romeo draws his weapon. But he's human now, vulnerable. Parris quickly forces him down, digging his sword-point in Romeo's throat. "Condemned villain!" he snarls.

Peter launches from behind a horse, landing astride Parris's back and buries the dagger in his neck. She jumps clear as the zombie staggers.

Seizing Romeo's fallen sword, she strikes off Parris's head. He collapses, splattering them both with the putrefying stench of slain zombie.

Romeo's amazed. Where has Juliet, the sheltered zombie Lady, learned to use a dagger and sword?

A shadow crosses her face. "My dear-loved cousin..." she says, and stops.

Tybalt. Of course. Romeo imagines the two children playing in the gardens. Her cousin would have been in combat-training, and passed it on to his playmate. Romeo swallows hard.

#

Friar Lawrence gets one whiff of them and hurries them into the back room. Romeo tells their story while they wash and change, dumping their putrid garments in the outside privy.

They need to see his sire, and her parents. Someone has to get Romeo's exile revoked, and then he wants them both to be turned. Unlike Rosaline, Juliet is willing to be a vampire.

Friar Lawrence agrees to send word to the Montagues and the Capulets offering the cottage as neutral ground. Possibly the only neutral ground in Verona, as feelings about Tybalt still run high.

The Undead Lord Montague arrives just after dark. He touches Romeo's lip, wincing when he sees his fangs are fangs no longer. Romeo shivers.

Montague buzzes around the room like an angry bee. He'll turn Romeo again. But then he must return to Mantua, wait out his exile. Vampires have centuries.

Romeo flinches but accepts—but only if his sire will turn his human wife to vampire.

Montague looks at Romeo's strangely-dressed companion and shrugs. Vampires bear no children and aren't particular who they marry.

Another knock on the door and the Capulets enter. Tragedy floods their expressions when they see Juliet. Pink and human, she's lost to them.

Lady Capulet bursts into tears. "Oh me, oh me," she wails, wrapping her arms around herself. "My child, my only life!"

Juliet holds Romeo's hand. She's never before seen her mother cry. Not even when Tybalt died.

In fury, the Lady spits at him, her secret son-in-law who'd murdered her darling Tybalt.

The Undead Lord Montague looks at the tearful zombies in confusion. Friar Lawrence explains the whole story. Romeo waits anxiously, fearing his Sire's reaction.

Rightly so. There's no question of turning Juliet, Montague declares ominously. She'd be a traitor within their gates. He nods to the Friar, orders Romeo home, and leaves.

Romeo stays seated on the bench, gripping Juliet's hand.

Capulet looks at his daughter in boyish clothes, all too human, with her hand in Romeo's.

"Oh child, oh child, my soul and not my child!" He takes her other hand. If only she'll return, he'll accept Romeo as well. They can both rise as zombies.

Romeo and Juliet depart in the Capulet coach with the zombie Lord and Lady, flanked by their mounted torch-bearers.

#

Romeo stares at the richly decorated hall thronged with the zombie clan. The last occasion he was here was for the Midsummer Feast, ages ago, days ago. It's time for the Transition.

He feels traitorous, but where could they go without wealth or family support? As mortals, they'd live poor and die fast.

If only his sire hadn't refused to turn Juliet! He'd asked Friar Lawrence to plead his case, but Montague was obdurate.

Dressed in silks and heavy gold, Romeo walks up the aisle with Juliet. She grips his hand as though she can't bear to let it go. Capulet looks away, maybe wishing he was the late Count Parris. And even without vampire senses, Romeo overhears Lady Capulet say Tybalt's name.

The musicians play a dirge. With measured ceremonial steps, Lady Capulet carries to them two goblets filled with the secret potion of the zombies. The emerald-encrusted one she gives to Juliet; the diamond-jeweled goblet, to Romeo. Something in her expression makes Romeo nervous but he has no choice now.

He turns to Juliet. The room fades into insignificance as she leans into him. He bends down, kisses her. She looks into his eyes, gives him the goblet she holds, and takes the diamond goblet from him.

Lady Capulet screams. She dashes the cup from Juliet's hand before she can take a sip.

In that instant, Juliet shoulders her mother aside, grabs Romeo's hand and runs, rushing him through a labyrinth of service passages and concealed doors. As they flee, he flashes back on what Juliet had said ages—or just days?—ago. "If they do see thee, they will murder thee!" It looks like that's still the plan.

The rumble of pursuit fades as Juliet takes them deeper. The final door opens outside in a wild part of the estate. Juliet has two horses and packed bags waiting. She pulls out plain brown garments for them both, rips off her heavy gown, and tosses it in a watery ditch where it quickly sinks. Romeo follows with his silk raiment. Then they're through the postern gate and galloping away from Verona, their horses' hooves pounding on the earthen track.

They stop to rest the horses at a hidden spot on a hillside where they'll easily be able to spot their pursuers. Verona sprawls before them in the morning sunshine.

"A plague on both your Houses!" Juliet says bitterly, looking down at the city they've left behind.

#

Romeo holds Juliet's hand, keeping a watchful eye on the road. He startles at a puff of dust, but it's only a farmer's cart. Standing beside her in the unaccustomed brightness, it comes to him there will be no pursuit.

No one is chasing them. No one is coming for them.

The zombies won't bother. Rebellious and human, Juliet is no one's heir. As for himself—exiled by the Prince, rejected by his sire, nearly killed by his mother-in-law's poisoned chalice—Verona is finished with him and he is finished with Verona.

Juliet comes to his arms and raises her soft warm all-to-human lips.

"Seal with a righteous kiss a dateless bargain to engrossing death," he whispers as he kisses her. Only mortal death awaits them now as their short days run out.

Meanwhile, there's Juliet and life. He looks at her, a delicious flush of joy spreading through him. She pulls him to the ground, and they start to plan the rest of their lives. Together.

We All Have to Pitch In

David Powell

As a boy, I didn't believe in magic, but my Mom sure did.

"Listen," she'd say on Christmas Eve, standing at the window and cupping her hand behind her ear, "I hear sleigh bells!"

Mom believed in Santa Claus, the Easter Bunny, the Tooth Fairy, and Jesus, and she insisted we believe, too. The "sleigh bells" line was our cue to run to the window and celebrate the invisible. My brother Micah and I never took the bait.

When I was nine, Micah found our presents two weeks early, wrapped and stacked in an upstairs closet.

"Let's teach Mom a lesson about magic," he said.

We waited till our parents were asleep, then moved all the presents under the tree. We were careful, but confident. We knew that Mom and Dad, despite their rules and expectations, didn't know much about the nuts and bolts of wickedness; they'd sleep right through it. The next morning we let them go downstairs first, then leaped into the living room, rejoicing that Santa had come early.

"We must have been so good, he couldn't stand it!" I said.

"Look!" Micah said, pointing to the Santa footprints we'd made with Dad's boots and backyard mud.

Dad was put out, but not furious with us. He blamed himself for not hiding the presents well enough. Mom's reaction was darker.

"Well," she said, "If the Lord has blessed you with early presents, he must mean for you to share your bounty with less fortunate children."

"I thought Santa brought the presents," I said, determined not to cave in to this ominous turn. "You telling us the Lord and Santa are in cahoots?"

"Cahoots?" she snapped. "The *Lord* is certainly not *in cahoots* with anyone!"

"Then he can't tell us what to do with Santa's presents," I said, crossing my arms in defiance.

"Hey, hey," Dad said, stepping between us. "Let's just have some breakfast and sort this out later."

Mom burned the pancakes, but Micah didn't mind. He just laid on the syrup and slurped it down. He'd made his point.

Dad, on the other hand, fell into his Christmas brooding two weeks early. He was an ER nurse, and dreaded Christmas. He always got called in to work because ER cases went up by thirty-three per cent.

"Expectations of joy are too high at Christmas," he'd say, "People just crash and burn, emotionally."

With Mom furious and Dad depressed, Christmas cheer was out the window. I got desperate, thinking Mom might give away our presents. Desperate enough to plead with the invisible world.

"Please, please, whoever's out there," I said, "Grant me one Christmas wish."

I prayed till I had a headache from squeezing my eyes shut so tight, then decided I'd better check downstairs to make sure the presents were still there.

I found an elf sprawled by the fireplace, nursing a generous snort of Dad's scotch and watching the tree lights blink. He had the elf outfit—green tights, tunic, pointy hat—but he wasn't cute at all. He had claws for feet, wiry hair behind leathery ears, and a whip-like tail that idly tapped against his highball glass.

"Somebody heard me," I said, stunned.

"Uh huh," he said, yawning. He slurped scotch and sat up, hugging his knees.

"You don't look like the pictures," I said. "Had a bad night?"

"Oh," he said. His tail swished up and pulled off the hat, revealing a scalp scored with a pentagram, deep cuts glowing red like molten lava. "I'm really a demon, not an elf, but this time of year—"

"Don't tell me," I said. "Your case load goes up by thirty-three percent."

"More like sixty per cent," he said. "It's a nightmare. So we all have to pitch in. Name's Scabmire."

He creaked to his feet and downed the scotch.

"Let's get to it," he said. "Your family needs some Christmas cheer."

"Mom's mad and Dad's depressed."

Scabmire squinted, zeroing in on my forehead.

"Ha. Thought you'd knock a hole in your mom's false cheer, huh? That's dangerous. You never know what's behind false cheer. And your dad's used to working out his Christmas depression at the ER. You've brought it on early and left him defenseless. Good job kid, you've got a future."

"Okay, okay! Can you help, or not?"

"I can grant you one Christmas wish." Scabmire set the highball glass carefully on the brick fireplace and cracked his gnarled knuckles. "Be careful, now."

My first thought was to ask for a normal Christmas, but Scabmire made our normal Christmas sound pretty desperate.

"Careful how?" I asked.

He fidgeted in his too-tight outfit. "You want to be real precise with your language," he said.

"Don't know how to say it right."

He sighed and fixed his red eyes on me again, peering into my thoughts.

"Normal is too vague," he said. "Be specific about what you want."

What I wanted. I tried thinking of something to pick up the mood in the house, but kept seeing Mom's angry face and Dad's sad one. Then I had it.

"Okay. I want for Mom and Dad to have their hearts' desires granted this Christmas."

Scabmire's eyes widened.

"Wow, didn't see that coming," he said. "That sets you apart, giving away your wish. Are you really sure that's what you want?"

I thought hard, but couldn't imagine any downside.

"Let's do it," I said.

"Done," Scabmire said. He flipped his hat back on and popped out of the room like a soap bubble.

"Who're you talking to?" Micah asked from the hall doorway.

"Um, nobody."

"You seen Mom?" Micah asked. "I can't find her anywhere."

We heard a thump from upstairs, which we'd soon find out was the chair falling over as Dad hanged himself. We never found Mom. Her heart's desire, whatever it turned out to be, didn't include us.

157

Micah and I did okay, what with Social Security and insurance. We landed with Aunt Lottie, the coolest one in the family. She cooked homemade pizza, read our comics, and showed us lots of movies. We gave her not a single speck of trouble.

The Reaper of Trees

Emily Martha Sorensen

The horror had come. It was time for the reaping.

The mass of humans invaded with sharpness and harshness. Healthy trunks were beheaded and carted away. Firs were felled, leaving a quarter of her sliced open, gaping and barren.

She gusted this way and that, gathering clusters of thousands of spirits as they spilled from the trunks. Trees were not individuals: they were whole families. She was the caretaker of them all.

To each brood of spirits that spilled, she explained: "This happens in every late autumn. The quarter of me with the oldest trees is felled. I would have warned you, but I had no way to. When you're living, you speak in a language of sap, and I speak in the language of spirits."

Despite her despair, she filled her role as a comforter. It was all she could do.

The human who was here most often, the human who controlled all the others, stood off to the left of the trunk of a particularly tall fir, safe from the direction it would fall.

Or so he thought.

Rage swelled inside her.

As the bellowing sharpness gnawed towards the edge, she slammed all her force at the trunk, sending it crashing towards him.

It landed upon him, crushing an arm and slamming against his head. A liquid like sap leaked from the side, and his spirit began to leak out alongside it.

Shock and horror benumbed her. She was not meant to kill. She should not have tried to kill. Animals were different from plants. They had only one spirit. They could not regrow if a part of them leaked.

The human spirit was mostly detached. He stared around the trees with a dazed look. His eyes fell upon her, and they widened. "Who are you?"

Her frustration and rage surged again. "I am this!" She gusted a handful of brown needles into the air. "I used to be a forest. Now I'm only a reaper of trees! You only give me firs, and you never let them *live!*"

"But—" His mouth opened. "But I always harvest sustainably. I use organic pesticides and fertilizers. I keep as low a carbon footprint as possible. This farm is my livelihood. I treat it with respect. What more do you want me to do?"

His concepts made no sense. Humans were so alien. She was wise, and not clever. They were clever, and not wise.

Humans were shouting and gathering around him. The trunk was removed. The blood was stanched. The body was taken. She saw his spirit slowly seeping back in.

The slaughter of firs recommenced.

As always, she reaped until barren and went dormant weeping.

#

She awoke in the springtime to something different.

There were seedlings of an unfamiliar species growing all over her, beneath the trees.

The stumps in the barren quarter of her were still present. They had not been removed. Some were dead, but others had new sprouts growing up from the roots.

What was going on?

She wafted out of herself and drifted through the field of short-lived plants.

Where was the human? The one she had spoken to?

She found him cutting a tall patch of kale and depositing the leaves into a container on wheels. He cut high on the stems, leaving the roots to regrow.

She shoved the covering off his head.

"Whoa!" He snatched for it, but she gusted it out of his reach. He leapt up and chased after the thing. She led him to the edge of the barren portion of firs, and dropped the covering on a stump.

160

He grabbed his head-covering, shoved it back onto his head, and stopped.

"Are you real?" he whispered.

His language of sound was as nonsensical as a language of sap. But she thought he was trying to talk to her.

She blew around him and waited.

He drew in a long breath. "Look... you said you wanted the Christmas trees to live. I can't *not* harvest them, but I can let coppice shoots grow instead of putting in transplants. We'll have to cut them more carefully, leaving some branches behind to make sure the stump doesn't die, but it'll save us work in the long run, so I'm okay with that. Does that help?"

She said nothing. She didn't know what he was saying.

The human swallowed. "You also mentioned you don't like being a monocrop. I've put in some alpine strawberries. I'm pondering what else would work as an understory crop. I'm thinking about currants. I'm pretty sure I'll make enough extra profit to make the time spent worth it. I can't make you a wild forest, but I can make you a food forest. Will that do?"

She didn't know what he was saying, but he seemed to be trying to talk to her. She blew around him and toppled the thing from his head.

He laughed and picked it up. "Well, all right."

He headed back to the field, shaking his head and grinning.

She wafted around the ground, examining the tiny seedlings all over her surface. The human had seen them, and he had not pulled them out. It seemed he did not intend to.

There was more than one species. There had not been more than one species in a long time.

Perhaps someday, she would be a forest again.

Alternative Holidays

Ten Songs of Halloween

Larry Hodges

The night approaches like black smoke drifting down upon your soul. The Ten Hours of Halloween have begun. I am... but who I am is unimportant. It is enough to know that I hunger for you, like children for Halloween candy, but a thousand times greater. Trick or Treat.

The First Hour of Halloween is 3PM. The kids are getting home from school, and they are excited. They know what happens this night. *But do you?*

Now is the time for you to accept that you are going to die. Not eventually like everyone else, but tonight. On Halloween. Accept it and you'll feel less horrible. Is there a way for you to survive? Go ahead and try, but it's doubtful. Play "The Monster Mash" to help you get into the proper mood.

The Second Hour of Halloween is 4PM. The kids are trying on their costumes; once a year they temporarily change into something else, like princes and princesses into monsters and ghosts. Death is also a changing of costumes, but it's permanent. You too are about to change, from life to death, unless you find a way to escape this certain death.

Already you have an uneasy feeling that something's not right, but don't know why your heart is beating like you've been chased by a ghost. If you die, your life will blink out like a candle in the wind, and you will be no more. But you'll feel better if you think you'll go to paradise in heaven after you die. So just keep telling yourself that. Play "Candle in the Wind" and you'll never even notice when your life is snuffed.

The Third Hour of Halloween is 5PM. The kids are jumping up and down, wondering where they will trick-or-treat. Will they only visit the well-lit, decorated, in-the-spirit of Halloween houses? Or will they make the long trek down the pathways of those dark, unlit ones, where I lurk and wait?

You are uneasy, feeling your attachment to this world growing more tenuous and not sure what to do. You do not understand why your hands are cold and sweaty; if you close your eyes, it feels and smells as if they are covered in your own salty blood, which will spatter the walls as your hands begin to shake. You wonder where you will go after you die. When I slaughter you, where will you go? Upstairs? Doubtful, but you can always hope. Play "Highway to Hell" as I send you there. (Oh, I didn't mention earlier that *I'd* be the one killing you? I apologize for the omission.)

The Fourth Hour of Halloween is 6PM. The kids are now trick-or-treating, begging for candy from strangers; for all they know they are enemies, sneaking poisons and razor blades into their goodies. I would.

You are giving out candy, and so are distracted, which is a pity, for you should know thy enemy, for it is me, the one who will kill you tonight. *Hi!* Call me Ishmael, or maybe Ahab, since I am obsessed with hunting you down and killing you. I'm retired and live in the cold, spirit world, have a torture dungeon, and keep the ghost of a creepy white toy poodle—actually a Bichon Frise. My lamps are made of human skin and powered by stolen souls. I'm the Buffalo Bill of death, so play the theme music from *Silence of the Lambs* and prepare to meet me.

The Fifth Hour of Halloween is 7PM. The kids are out in force, filling their bags with sweet candy, while parents wait nearby, proudly watching to the end. Will their kids someday end up like you and I?

You are distracted, mindlessly giving out handfuls of candy to delighted children as you stare into the abyss. You look about and ponder why you feel threatened. Is it the faint smell of brimstone, like rotten eggs? The faint rustling of trees outside, like huddling wraiths plotting your doom? The dancing shadows from the window as the sun sets, like silently screaming spirits that disappear when looked at directly?

I am amorphous and unseen except in the depths of your soul and your growing awareness is not yet complete. Do not look for me, instead look to your own family and friends. Were they with you to the end, joining you this night when you die? Or just users, always there when they needed something, somewhere else when you were in need, as you are tonight? Give this a good hard deliberation, try not to think of the beetles that will gnaw at your corpse when you are dead, and play "When I'm 64."

The Sixth Hour of Halloween is 8PM. The night is coming to an end for many trick-or-treaters, especially the younger ones, and their bags are full. Who are their family and friends that they will share their candy with? Who are *your* real family and friends?

Your growing realization that you must act to save yourself is foremost in your mind, but what exactly you must do and why are only now emerging from the haze. You stare out the window, but see no escape. Your bloody demise is inevitable. You should write your will. See the fifth Hour. No rush, get it right. I'm not going anywhere. Play "I Will Be Right Here Waiting for You."

The Seventh Hour of Halloween is 9PM. Only a few teenagers are still out; the rest are home, gorging themselves as the best night of the year comes to an end. Your mind is blank, unsure of what you must do, and it's probably too late. It's time for you to prepare for your end. It's okay to be a bit sad. After all, you've lived a short life, and I plan to end it tonight, a lot sooner than you'd expected. Soon I will suck out your soul and swallow it whole. So get in the mood. Play "Speak Softly, Love," the theme music to *The Godfather*. Eat a cannoli.

The Eighth Hour of Halloween is 10PM. You sit still, eyes closed, an eerie awareness in your mind, the calm before the storm. You grit your teeth, painfully so, and cut your lip so that a drop of blood rolls down your chin. You don't notice.

The kids have eaten much of their candy and are now taking care of their candy affairs, hiding what's left from brothers and sisters. You need to put aside your resolve to act to save yourself and take a moment to take care of your own personal affairs. Only a selfish person leaves that to their next of kin. If you love them, don't make it hard for them to find all of your accounts. Besides, do you really want them poking around in your personal stuff and finding out who you *really* are? Sure, you've done some good in your life, but look at all the dreadful stuff you've done. Take a look at yourself, but it's too late to change your ways. Play Michael Jackson's "Man in the Mirror."

The Ninth Hour of Halloween is 11PM. Most of the kids are in bed earlier than they'd like—they'd rather stay up stuffing their mouths with chocolates and lollipops. And speaking of Michael Jackson, he died early, and so will you. Unless... have you found a way to survive this night?

You open your eyes and leap from your chair and pace back and forth, back and forth. You are aware of me. I am so close you can hear the beating of my frozen heart. The icy tendrils of my hands rub up and down your spine, and when you turn suddenly, you get a split-second glimmer of a smirking, leering face before I disappear into your imagination. But I am quite real. You are a fly to my spider as we stare at each other in our minds. You are caught in my icy web. You try to shake free, even as I once tried. Will you make it? I don't think so, but secretly I'm rooting for you. You continue to fight even as I throw more and more cold threads of death about your rebellious but chilling, tiring soul. Will you go meekly or make this a more thrilling night? Yes, it's close to midnight and something evil's lurking in the dark. Play "Thriller."

The Tenth Hour of Halloween is Midnight. The kids are asleep, Halloween is over. Soon you will join me. And I had such high hopes for you.

Even as I sigh, a burst of determination leaps into you, and again you battle these frosty ropes of death. *How you fight!* A Tasmanian devil you are, ironic considering who you fight. How rapid your heart now beats, sending warm blood to counter my wintry offerings. Hot, cold, hot, cold, who will win? You begin to tear free and I am full of wonderment and hope, my cold heart melting. I cannot hold you much longer. *Bravo!*

But the cold bindings hold, mental and physical. My heart again freezes over, as do you. Soon you weaken and sit still. *So close.* But now you will die.

I too am dead, of course, the restive spirit of a long-festering corpse. Your existence will end while mine does not. I'm right behind you, invisible, sucking the warm life out of you and sating my hunger even as you wave about an enfeebled, cold arm, and then it falls to your side. It'll be like going to sleep on a cool winter night, you just won't wake up. I'd say pleasant dreams, but there will be no dreams.

You were so close to breaking free and solving the mystery of life and death, but you did not succeed. Neither did I when I was in your place, which is why I too am dead, though my fate is far worse than yours. I hoped you would break free and show me the way to escape this cursed existence. But you did not, and I will not... yet. But I will keep trying, there are many more like you, many more Halloweens. So... good night. Forever. It's my treat. Play "Taps."

Alternative Holidays

Four Spirits of Christmas

Julia LaFond

Otis Drake huddled in the corner, hidden under a mink blanket: Rich and plush, like the rest of the room. Thick, velvety carpet, gray silk curtains, and linens, quilts, and coverlets piled so thick they entirely concealed the mattress. There was also the cushioned antique rocking chair, the Burmese teak desk, and the window nook bedecked with cushions and furs. He could have sat comfortably in any of them. Yet the old man eschewed all these things for the corner, shivering despite the warm blanket, and the effective heating system.

For Mr. Drake had seen not one ghost, but three.

The first had come while he was engrossed in a book. He hadn't noticed when the lights dimmed, nor when fog rolled across the floor, nor even when the ghost floated in through the door. Only when the spirit cried out, "Otis, Otis!" did Mr. Drake look up, dropping his tome with a start.

"Edwin?" He removed his reading glasses. "You can't be! The obituary—"

"Edwin Hunt, died age 84 of heart failure," his friend's ghost recited. "It is I, nonetheless."

Mr. Drake scrunched his eyebrows. "Why are you wrapped in plastic bags?"

The ghost sighed, looking down at his motley suit of interwoven white, gray, and black crinkling plastic. "In life, I cared only for my business and the money it made me. So now, in my afterlife, I am forced to wear the products I made: a reminder I left the world worse off." He looked back up, eyes blazing like embers. "You still have a chance to mend your ways! Forsake the path of greed and exploitation. Or else become like me." As the words left his lips, the spirit faded. "I am but the harbinger. Watch for the others."

Mr. Drake blinked, rubbing his eyes, and found the room exactly as it should be. He stooped down, dusting off his dropped book. "Must have been a nightmare," he grumbled, folding the pages to undo the creases. "I should go to bed."

So it was that the second spirit found him on the verge of sleep.

"Otis Drake," it boomed. "You must accompany me."

Groggy and blinking, Mr. Drake belatedly realized there was someone in the room with him. He lunged for the emergency call button. Pressing it did nothing the first time, nor did his frantic repetitions of the motion.

The intruder stepped closer.

Mr. Drake finally saw it couldn't be human, for it had an analog clock for a head. All other features were hidden beneath a suit and cape of magnetic tape.

"Another nightmare?" Mr. Drake rubbed his eyes. "Must have been bad oysters."

"I assure you, this is very real." The apparition took him by the wrist, dangling him above his bed. "Time to face your past." It produced a faded polaroid from its pocket, throwing it down onto the bed. It became a yawning portal, and they plunged down, down, down.

When Mr. Drake stopped screaming, he looked around, seeing where he was. No, when he was. The first Christmas he could remember, back in Martha's Vineyard. A joyous day shared with his nanny, private tutor, and the head chef—though he had keenly felt his parents' absence. They hadn't even bothered to call. Yet the homemade toys the staff had given him warmed his boyish heart. His younger self hadn't cared how cheap the materials were.

The spirit pulled him into another picture, another memory, one after another. Befriending classmates of similar status at boarding school. Meeting Tara, the daughter of one of his father's business partners, and falling prey to the heady infatuation of youth. Being allowed to attend executive board meetings for the first time.

The longer he watched, the fewer and further between were the happy memories. His parents remained distant. His friends drifted away. And finally Tara, sweet Tara, left him over his hostile takeover of her family's company.

"It's just business!" he repeated in tandem with his past self. Then, curiously, he watched himself break down in tears. Time had dulled the pain of that wound; he'd forgotten that it nearly tore him apart. He did remember that it was the last year he'd celebrated Christmas.

The subsequent memories blurred by unheeded. Finally, Mr. Drake found himself back in bed.

"My time has passed," the apparition declared, fading. "Watch for the others."

Mr. Drake kept himself awake by listening to music. "Don't want more nightmares," he grumbled, though he kept glancing at the door.

The third apparition came through the window, twelve minutes before midnight. "Otis!" it cried. "Come! There is much to see!"

He eyed the figure up and down, lips curled into a sneer. This spirit looked human: a pale, fat man adorned with a tacky Christmas sweater, candy-cane striped pants, a necklace of blinking red Christmas lights, and a reindeer antler headband.

"How... festive," Mr. Drake drawled.

The spirit roared with laughter, taking Mr. Drake by both hands and flying out the window. "Tonight is for celebration, after all! Let's see what *gifts* you've offered the world."

Mr. Drake silently fumed at the sarcastic tone. He couldn't complain aloud, lest the spirit decide to drop him while they were five stories up.

Their first destination was a company party: his executive assistant and the CFO casually placed bets on when he would "finally keel over." Indignant, Mr. Drake ripped free of the spirit, only to discover neither person could see, hear, or feel him.

"I'll fire them," he sputtered. "I'll fire them both!"

"Oh?" The spirit reclaimed his grip on Mr. Drake.

Mr. Drake shrieked: "Sycophants! Vultures! Disloyal—"

"Have you ever given them a reason to want you to live?"

Mr. Drake clamped his mouth shut, stewing as the spirit took him to another celebration. Tara and her family carried on a raucous, tacky, and impossibly cheap party in their suburban abode. Practically reduced to poverty.

"Good business," Mr. Drake repeated to himself.

Next was a children's hospital, where the little patients snuck peeks out the window, watching for Santa's sleigh.

"What's this have to do with anything?" Otis grumbled.

"When you pay fines rather than address your factories' outwash," replied the spirit quietly, "the pollutants enter the watershed."

Mr. Drake gritted his teeth, replying nothing.

The whirl of parties, full of people who cared nothing for him, was interrupted only by the sweatshops his foreign workers toiled in. Mr. Drake looked away from the spirit's judging gaze. He didn't complain about working over Christmas, so why should they? The overtime would help them put food on the tables.

"They don't get paid extra," deadpanned the spirit, as if hearing his thoughts.

Mr. Drake, frowning, let himself be dragged to the next destination.

Until mercifully, at the stroke of midnight, the apparition delivered him back to his room. "One spirit remains," it intoned solemnly, fading to nothing. "Watch for it."

Instead, having had his fill of the strange and unsettling, Otis Drake huddled in the corner beneath a blanket. He had previously considered ghosts to be nothing more than childish superstition. Now he employed a child's defense against the Boogeyman.

Only for the carpet beneath him to turn to rough, jagged asphalt.

He braced himself for a voice that never came. Slowly he rose, removing the blanket and wrapping himself in it.

Before him floated a swirling mass of inky shadows, vaguely resembling a hooded figure.

"What are you here to show me?" he grumbled.

An inky tendril pointed behind him.

Mr. Drake turned and gasped. His company, his life's work, stood in ruins. Crumbled walls and shattered glass. Vines clung to its concrete pillars; within, trees flourished, unimpeded by ceilings or roofs.

"It can't be." He stumbled closer to it. That's when he saw the graffiti. Curses directed at him, at his company, scrawled in scarlet spray paint.

He turned back to the shadow, flinching to find the spirit hovering over his shoulder. "But why?"

The shadow drifted into the ruins.

172

Reluctantly, Mr. Drake followed: into the deepening gloom. He dug out his phone to light his path. The flashlight was dim, but the figure shied away from it.

At last, the spirit brought him to what was once his office. Stripped of his possessions, of decorations, of everything but the desk and the mangled carcass of a laptop. Yet when the apparition floated past it, the laptop opened, good as new, to play a news report.

"Fifty years ago," narrated an unshaven newscaster with sunken eyes, "Otis Drake, more commonly known as Drake the Destroyer—"

He gawked at the screen, helplessly pointing his phone at it. He knew his rivals muttered behind his back, but surely, that was too much.

"—introduced a novel preservative through his food & beverages subsidiary." A chemical diagram appeared in a pop-up in the corner of the screen. "Everfresh, as it was dubbed, exploded across the market, due to its low price and high efficacy. The company's net worth skyrocketed. But Otis Drake didn't live long enough to see the adverse..." The newscaster looked down and took a deep breath. "The adverse effects of long-term exposure, ranging from nerve damage to organ failure."

Something loud banged off-camera, like pounding on a door. The newscaster flinched before rushing ahead: "No one foresaw the posthumous complications, occurring in about
thirty-five per—"

A distant scream trailed off into a gurgle. The newscaster paled and whimpered. "They're coming. The risen dead are ravenous." He clutched his head. "God have mercy on our souls."

The camera toppled to the floor, filling the screen with polished tile. Yet it faithfully continued recording the newscaster's wailing screams, and a slowly growing pool of blood.

"Enough!" Mr. Drake knocked away the laptop, covering his ears. "I've seen enough. I understand now. Please, take me back!"

The shadow roiled closer. Slow and hesitant. As if cocking its head, doubting his word.

Fury roiled through Mr. Drake's veins at being toyed with. "Take me back!" he shouted, turning the flashlight on the spirit.

It burst into a cloud of smoke.

Choking, Mr. Drake stumbled away, fearing he had miscalculated and stranded himself in the terrible future. Until he fell forward onto his bed, his soft, wonderful bed.

He collapsed to the floor, laughing and giggling until he gasped for breath. It was over. Now, he knew exactly what to do.

He texted the picture of the formula to the head of the research division. He called, too. "This is—Yes, I know how late it—Yes, I know what day it is! I don't care! This is our top priority. We're going to make millions! Billions! I—Fine, yes, we can discuss the details later."

Mr. Drake hung up, cracked lips curling into a smile. The spirits had shown him the truth: not one other person in this world cared about him. Why should he care if the world burned after he was dead? As long as it meant he stayed on top.

Comfort and riches for the rest of his days was the Christmas present he gave himself.

Late at Night, In the Bathtub, A Snowman Panics

Mark Teppo

"Thanks for calling the Holiday Help Line. This is Bernie. How may I be of assistance this—"

"Oh, Bernie. Thanks for answering. Thank the night stars. Thank you. Thank you."

"Ah, hi. Glad to be here for you. Um, who's this?"

"It's Seamus. I'm in trouble. Serious SERIOUS trouble. I'm in a bathtub, filled with ice. I don't know how I got here, and... and something is terribly wrong. I'm—"

"Yeah, uh huh. Right, pal. I think you've dialed the wrong number. This is the Holiday Help Line for the North Pole Consortium. We're here for—"

"I dialed the right fucking number, Bernie. It's Seamus. I'm one of the snowmen!"

"Right, right. And I'm Kris Kringle."

"I'm not kidding, Bernie! I'm—oh, God. I can't believe this is happening."

"Okay, okay. Calm down, pal. Why don't you tell me what the issue is?"

"The issue is I'm in a bathtub full of ice! There's a—I've got a shoelace in my side. It's holding me together. Bernie, I think someone stole one of my kidneys."

"Oh, hey. I recognize your voice, Seamus. That's right. You're Frosty Number—let's see, uh, Eight Four Seven Dash Six. You're in South Dakota, right? At the mall outside—"

"I'm in a shitbag motel! In a fucking bathtub! With a shoelace—a goddamned shoelace!—in my side. Oh my god, Bernie. They opened me up. They took something from me. I'm in an ice bath. That means they took a kidney, right? They took one of my kidneys!"

"Look, Seamus, you're a snowman. You don't have—Listen, are you—I'm sorry, but I have to ask—you're not riding the horse, are you?"

"The horse? What are you talking about? What horse?"

"You know... one of those substances that are on the list... one of the things you get tested for... "

"Heroin? No! I haven't... What the fuck, Bernie. I'm clean. I've been clean since last Season. Pull my case file! I gave a sample a month ago. I'm back in rotation. I've got a gig at the Mall, working the skating rink. You know, making the kids happy. That's all I want, Bernie. I just want to make the kids happy. But those little fuckers at the Mall. Yeah, it was them. They gave me a soda. I bet they put a roofie in it. Oh God, Bernie. I've been date-raped by a bunch of Mall gangbangers, and the shits took one of my kidneys, too. Little sadistic bastards."

"Listen. It's going to be—please stop crying. It's going to be okay."

"No, it's not. I can't feel my legs."

"You don't have legs, Seamus. You're a snowman."

"I'm so cold, Bernie."

"Look. Maybe that has something to do with the tub of ice you're in?"

"What? Oh... right. Yeah. That's why I'm cold."

"Take a deep breath, okay? It's going to be fine. Everything is going to be fine. Okay?"

"Y-y-yeah, okay."

"Deep breath now. Do it with me all right?"

"Deep breath."

"That's it. Let's do another one. Yeah? Okay, good. Now, let's back up and start over."

"Oh, man, Bernie. I've got this shoelace in me and—"

"Listen, Seamus. You're a snowman. You don't have—well, let's be blunt—you don't have kidneys. You don't have internal organs of any kind, really. You're made out of snow. Tip to—uh, toe. Through and through. Nothing but snow."

"But—"

"Hey, if you're missing some, that's okay. I'll just fill out a requisition for some more and one of the reindeer will parcel it down tonight, okay?"

"So... so, if, uh, oh Sweet Christmas, Bernie. They didn't take anything! They put something in. I can feel it. There's something inside of me, Bernie! They put a bomb in me. They want to blow up Santa!"

"Oh, for the love of—Seamus! You need to chi—you need to calm down. Getting hysterical isn't going to help. Just breathe. Come on, you can do it. Breathe. In. Out. Yeah, just like that. Breathe."

"Wha... what k-k-kind of bomb do you think it is, Bernie?"

"You don't have a bomb in you, Seamus. If there is anything, it's probably a rock or—"

"A rock! Those little fu—"

"Seamus!"

"Sorry. I'm... I'm calm. I'm breathing. You hear that? That's me breathing."

"Okay, that's good. One thing at a time. Now, tell me about the shoelace. The one that's been... uh, 'laced' in you. What color is it?"

"Uh, hang on. It's, um, green. Neon green. It glows in the dark."

"Really? A glow in the dark shoelace? That's kind of surprising."

"Wha—why?"

"Well, I don't see one of the Mall kids giving up a cool shoelace like that."

"Yeah, it is, and I got a yellow—oh..."

"A 'yellow' what?"

"Oh, it's... it's nothing."

"Wait. You have two shoelaces? A green one and a yellow one?"

"Uh... yeah. Yeah. I, uh, I guess I do. I didn't—I didn't notice the other one at first. I was..."

"You have one on each side, Seamus? Like maybe not so much stitching you up as adding a little 'razzle-dazzle'?"

"I don't know what that means. Razzle what? What is that?"

"Come on, Seamus. You had your first day today, didn't you? *Back in rotation.* That's what you said."

"Yeah, maybe. I don't know. I'd have to look, and it's... um... I can't move right now. 'Cause, you know..."

"Because you have no legs and you're in a bathtub filled with ice. Yes, I can certainly see where that might be a problem."

"Are you? I—I don't like your tone, Bernie. Aren't you supposed to be *helpful*? This is the Holiday Help Line, isn't it?"

"Yeah, you know? It is the Help Line, and I appreciate you calling in. How about this? You help yourself out of that tub and be on time for your shift tomorrow, which is when?"

"...ten..."

"I'm sorry? When?"

"Ten. Ten in the morning. I have the first shift at the skating rink."

"Okay, Seamus. How about this: you get yourself and your neon shoelaces down to the skating rink by 9:30. A half hour early, you hear? You get that coal smile turned upright and you keep it locked in place for two and a half hours. If I hear a peep about you poking kids with your nose or smacking baby carriages with your sticks, I'm going to have the Local 817 rip those shoelaces out of you and squirt you full of food coloring."

"You—you wouldn't dare."

"Try me, snow cone."

"..."

"You still there, Seamus?"

"Yeah, I, uh, I guess... Listen, Bernie. The kids these days? They're not like... it's not like the old days."

"Nothing is, Seamus. Everyone's a lot more scared. Everyone's worried about something."

"I don't—I don't like them, Bernie."

"Well, Seamus, you're a snowman. They like you. That's more than a lot of dads can say about their step-kids."

"It's just—it's so hard and I feel so cold and empty..."

"Look, Seamus. I know this isn't what you thought you'd be doing with your life but, yeah, there's no easy way to say it, but yeah, we don't always get what we want in life. Sorry."

"It's sucks, you know?"

"I know, Seamus. I know."

"I was going to be an artist, you know? Watercolors. But... but now, all I do is stand at the skating rink and watch those little monsters scream and howl and fall down. I can't even... I'm just supposed to stand there and do the Princess Wave with these stupid stick arms. For hours."

"Look. There's only fifteen more shopping days left in the Season. Hang in there. It'll be over soon."

"I just—I just hate this time of year, Bernie."

"I know, Seamus. Me, too. But someone has to do it, otherwise... otherwise, it's all climate change and economic collapse and reality shows on TV. That's no good for anyone. It's up to us to make a difference. We have to show them something fun, something marvelous. We have the Spirit. We have to share it. We're the only ones who can."

"Y-y-yeah, okay."

"You got this?"

"I—yeah, I got this."

"Oh, and Seamus?"

"What?"

"Ditch the shoelaces, would you? You're trying too hard. They'll read it as weakness and..."

"And what?"

"It's not important. Trust me, though. Stick with what works. And remember to smile. Get into the spirit of things. Practice saying 'Merry Christmas' without that F-word in the middle."

"There's no F-word in 'Merry Christmas."

"See? Now you're getting it. I knew you could do it."

Alternative Holidays

Crop Circles

Carter Lappin

The alien looked up at the sky, glad that the clouds had finally cleared after the morning's early snowfall. The air was still gray and cold. Few signs of the snow remained, lingering only in the occasional stubborn pile or puddle of watery slush on the ground. The more the snow melted, the more mud there was for the alien to trudge through. His boots were coated in it.

The corn stalks all around him were tall, yellow and brown with neglect and decay. Nobody would really care about what happened to them until planting season came around, which was perfect for the alien. Aside from him, the field was entirely empty of life. There wasn't even a scarecrow to keep him company.

The alien made up for the silence with a radio, which he had set on the ground near his feet. He moved it every so often, when his work took him out of range to hear it. It was set to a channel that played Christmas music. The alien hummed along as he worked. He'd developed a sort of fondness for it.

He checked his diagram, hefted his shovel, and swung. The stalks of dead corn in front of him were flattened, less than neatly. The alien used the head of the shovel to tamp the stalks down the rest of the way into the ground. Then he moved on to the next patch, right next to the one he had just been working on.

Earlier in the week, the alien had been invited to his workplace's nondenominational holiday party. It was likely in full swing about now, full of slightly drunken sandwich-shop workers having a great time exchanging gifts and having eggnog-chugging contests. The alien was a little sorry he was missing it. Rumor was, there was going to be a hot chocolate bar this year.

For a moment, he allowed himself to imagine it– the building a little too warm as the heater worked overtime to push against the cold outside, the gleaming of red and green fairy lights shining off of glass sandwich cases. Maybe someone would push a drink into the alien's hand, would clap him on the back and tell him they were glad to see him. They'd coerce him into painfully bad Christmas-themed karaoke, or dare him to eat the weird pasta salad their coworker brought, or draw him into telling a story that would have the whole room roaring with laughter. Maybe the alien would have been able to lose himself there, would be able to let himself feel human and happy, just for a little while.

But the alien had work to do, even on Christmas Eve. Perhaps especially then. The sky was free of clouds, and it was a human holiday, and the alien was homesick. Sometimes he was so homesick that it stopped feeling real anymore, like this hollowness in his heart was always going to be there. Like it always had been there.

He flattened another section of corn. He had wandered far enough away from the radio that he could only just barely make out the music that curled from its speakers. It sounded like bells, jingling against each other. Up close, stars roared, crackling with heat and fire. But down here, with the ground beneath his feet and strangers all around him, the alien looked up and imagined that the stars sounded a lot like bells did. It was a beautiful thought. It was a scary one.

It wasn't that the alien hated his life on Earth. It could be pleasant, even, much of the time. He'd bought himself a little tree for the holidays–dragged it into the wreck of his spaceship and wrapped it in fairy lights. He kept a few gifts beneath it; a small box wrapped in green paper, a bag with a cartoon snowman on it, a package so irregularly shaped that it had to have been socks. They were gifts, from coworkers, mostly, but also from friends. The alien had made friends, here. He would have marveled at the thought if it didn't also mean thinking about all that implied.

But home was a million miles away, and the alien missed it. The cracks in his spaceship's hull were hard to mend. Likely, it would never fly again. Even if it did, the chances of it safely leaving the atmosphere, let alone making it all that distance, were little to none. Sometimes the alien thought about trying anyways, on the days when the homesickness that lived in him seemed to grow extra heavy and the stars seemed extra far away.

The alien's mittens were striped, red and green. The cashier at the hardware store had wished him a happy holidays when he went to buy the shovel. His old one had broken. The alien had been here for a long time. Long enough that he had started to forget how to convert his planet's calendar system to that of Earth's. Maybe one day he'd forget that he used to use a different system at all.

The alien had started to adapt. The air was cold. The alien shivered, like a human. He couldn't remember whether it was an affection he had purposely picked up or not. The music switched to commercial. Sometimes he wished he would have had a harder time adapting.

The alien picked up the radio. He moved it to a new section of field.

He didn't know if anybody was looking for him. The alien's people lived far, far away, and when the alien crashed, he crashed hard. There were so many cracks to mend.

But the alien was going to try anyway. If ever an eye turned toward him, toward Earth, they would see what he had made. Words, huge and elegant, carved into the very planet itself. It wasn't a language any human would recognize; he doubted that they would even be able to tell that it *was* a language at all. The alien went out, when he could, and he cut crops into distress calls.

I'm here, some said. *Come and get me,* said others. *I want to tell you about Christmas. I want to go home.*

The alien made his mark in another patch of earth. In the field surrounding him, the dead corn curved out in spirals, around and around, and around. Tomorrow, the alien would see his work from above, splattered across page three of the local newspaper. He would be able to read it, be able to understand it. But nobody else would. Not unless they knew where to look. Not unless they knew *to* look. He hoped they were looking. He had to believe they were looking. He didn't know what he would do if he stopped believing.

The radio was nestled on a patch of flattened plants. The announcer was taking requests. Music filled the air again. *I'll be home for Christmas.* The alien hoped he would. The alien looked up at the color-faded sky and wished he could see stars. The world sounded like sleigh bells.

Alternative Holidays

Krampus at the Craft Fair

Sarina Dorie

The fluorescent lights from the high warehouse ceiling shone down on tables trimmed with tinsel and pine boughs. A Hanukkah song from the loudspeakers competed with the hum of the crowd.

Deedee sat in her booth, knitting green-and-red striped stockings with a steady rhythm. Her arthritic hands were stiff from the cold, one of the many disadvantages of being so close to the drafty doors. Twinkling Christmas lights illuminated the merchandise of the crystal guy, the ancient hippy selling organic soap, and the old crone at her table of cat greeting cards across from Deedee.

Two potential patrons parted from the jam of human traffic and paused to inspect her booth. Deedee smiled, her cheeks aching after doing this for days. "Welcome to Sock-It-To-Me. Let me know if you have any questions."

"Do you have any socks with six toes?" asked a woman with blonde microbraids. She wore loose layers of hemp clothes. A wave of marijuana wafted from her.

Deedee waved a knitting needle at the stockings hung from the metal display case with care. "None of my socks have toes. They'll all fit someone with six toes."

"That won't be enough room. My boyfriend has big feet. I mean, *really big*. Think bigfoot on steroids." She pointed at the white-and-blue stockings. "Can you make a pair like that with six toes?"

Deedee's familiar, Margaret, poked her head out of her shell. In the slow methodical way Deedee's pet snail always moved, Margaret nodded to the sign on the wall.

Special orders take three to five days. Payment must be in advance.

The customer's gaze followed Margaret's waving antenna. The woman must have annoyed Margaret, because the little snail didn't deign to speak.

The woman's friend asked, "What about tentacle warmers?" Her skin was an indeterminate shade of orange-copper-gold like a glittery pumpkin. From the writhing under her Rastafarian hat, she might have had a pet under there, or a headful of snakes. Neither would have surprised Deedee. This craft fair catered to eclectic tastes.

The potential customer nodded to a pair of knitted horn warmers on the wall clearly labeled with a sign large enough that even Deedee could read it. "Those look kind of small. Are those, like, child-size or something? Do you have any for adults?"

"Sorry, we're all sold out of adult tentacle warmers," Deedee lied, not wanting to explain the logic of why knitted tentacle warmers would be irrelevant underwater.

"Whatever." The woman and her friend wandered away.

"Idiots," Margaret the snail said. She had the kind of deep, scratchy voice that sounded like a woman from Brooklyn who had been a chain smoker her entire life. Or possibly her last life. Reincarnation wasn't always a step up for humans.

Deedee shook her head at her familiar. "What did we say about insulting customers?"

Margaret returned to her shell.

Two minutes later, an elderly couple perused Sock-It-To-Me's booth. Deedee went through the same spiel. The customers lingered in front of the mitten display, giving Deedee hope that she might make a sale.

Out in the packed aisle, the crowd parted, giving a towering figure in a glittering gold cape a wide berth. The man stopped before Deedee's booth. He had a dark gray beard that almost blended in with the gray-green of his skin. He wore something on his head, but Deedee's vision was too blurred to tell what it was.

"We definitely need more lights," she mumbled to herself.

Deedee reached for her glasses that she thought she had tucked onto the collar of her blouse, but they weren't there. She felt on top of her head and looked behind her mitten display, but she didn't see her glasses anywhere.

"Margaret, have you seen my glasses?" Deedee asked.

Margaret gave a phlegmy cough from her perch on the table. Apparently she wasn't going to answer.

Deedee squinted up at the tall figure, and her face lit up in a genuine smile as her old friend stepped into the booth, nodding briefly as the elderly couple carefully backed out. On top of his head was the most beautiful set of horns, gleaming like polished obsidian. He flicked back his gold cape, revealing a red-and-green one-piece jumpsuit reminiscent of something Elvis might have worn in the seventies.

Margaret slowly inched forward to greet their best customer. Krampus had come to the craft fair.

He strode directly over to Deedee, arms outstretched. "Hey, girl! How's my favorite knitter?"

His thick German accent was music to Deedee's ears.

"Krampus, it's so nice to see you!" Deedee rose to embrace her old friend. "Are you working at the market today?"

"This time of year?" He grinned slyly. "There's no rest for the wicked."

Two children about ten years old entered into the booth, halting as they stared up at Krampus with wide eyes.

"It's him," the boy whispered.

"It can't be," the girl said.

"Excuse me, sir." The little boy shifted from foot to foot in agitation. "Are you Krampus? *The* Krampus. I thought you were supposed to scare people and punish bad children."

"I do, but I'm on my break right now." Krampus winked. "And I don't just punish children. I throw adults in a sack and beat them with a stick too. If they deserve it."

This wasn't the first time Deedee had heard her friend boast about the perks of his job. Usually she disapproved of violence, but often the people he ended up beating were the villainous sort who deserved that punishment. It made her think of the woman wanting a six toed sock.

The girl crossed her arms. "You don't look very mean."

"Oh I am," he growled, leaning down and coming eye to eye with the little girl. "Especially when I'm throwing shade. But right now," he swirled in his cloak, "I need to be dressed for success—which is why I'm here." He ran a hand over his gleaming black horns.

"Speaking of dressing for success, can we interest you in a set of horn warmers?" Margaret asked.

Krampus's eyes went wide. "Please say they come in stripes!"

Deedee allowed Margaret to take the lead. She loved seeing how Krampus encouraged Margaret to come out of her shell and be more herself.

Krampus paid for a pair of gold and black striped horn warmers. As he counted out the change, he asked, "How's business this year? I'm surprised you still have merchandise left this late in the day."

Deedee squinted at the bills, trying to decipher the denominations, but she couldn't see squat without her glasses, and for the umpteenth time she wished she'd put up more lights. "Yeah, it's been really slow today. I don't know why."

He leaned in conspiratorially. "It's the competition. She's selling stockings three dollars cheaper than yours."

"What? Who?" Deedee demanded.

"She's right around the corner." Krampus waved in the general direction of a million other booths. "Knit Pickers, they call it. You know who I'm talking about, right?"

Deedee shook her head, flabbergasted. Margaret swore as only a snail could swear.

"Let me show you." Krampus gave a pointed look at Margaret. "Can you handle the booth without Deedee for two seconds?"

"Knowing you, this is going to be at least ten minutes," Margaret grumbled. "You're as slow as a snail."

Krampus was already guiding Deedee out. People edged back, giving him dirty looks. Three booths down, he nodded to a tent across the aisle.

"I can't see that far." Deedee felt for her glasses on top of her head, but they weren't there. She'd forgotten she was still missing her glasses. "Is she using magic to steal my customers?"

Krampus tsked. "The magic of a four-letter-word: sale."

As a witch, Deedee could see energies that even magical beings like Krampus might miss, but the fluorescent lights glinted off tinsel and glitter-covered displays, overwhelming Deedee's senses. Everything was so bright outside her booth.

"Whoa, cool cosplay." A teenage boy with a Christmas themed mohawk eyed Krampus.

"This isn't cosplay. This is who I am." Krampus flicked his gray hair over his shoulder indignantly.

Deedee was still squinting at her competition, trying to figure out what Knit Pickers had that she didn't. Besides customers and better lighting.

Krampus clucked his tongue. "Their merchandise is crap, machine knit acrylics. You can buy them at Walmart. Anyone with an eye for craftsmanship would know you're an artist, and she's a hack."

Deedee ventured closer. She picked up a sock from under the sign advertising Knit Pickers' prices. Krampus was right, machine woven crap. The socks weren't even shaped correctly for a comfortable fit. They were fine as decorative stockings, but they weren't wearable. The spells on them for keeping feet warm or to repel water were just layered on, not embedded in the mesh. It would be gone in one laundering.

Didn't people appreciate quality magical stockings these days?

Deedee trudged away with a heavy heart, fighting the crowd to return to her booth. "I guess I could reduce my prices," she muttered.

It was the last day after all. She usually dropped prices the last hour before the fair closed so she didn't have as much unsold merchandise to take home. But she'd already discounted her stockings at the start of the day. Each item took hours to make, plus there was the costs of materials, and the market fees. She didn't even make minimum wage when she accounted for all that.

"No, you will not reduce anything," Krampus said, placing a clawed hand consolingly on her shoulder. "Loyal customers will pay for quality. Give it another hour or two. The closer we get to lunch; the more business will pick up."

Deedee stepped back into her booth, deciding to do as her friend suggested and wait another hour to see how sales went.

"So are you going to hex that hag?" Margaret asked.

"No. What have I told you?" Deedee asked. "We are good witches. We don't hex people at the craft fair." Mostly that was because if she were caught, she would be banned next year.

Krampus turned back to the display rack. "Now, back to business. I need to buy a pair of stockings. Whichever you recommend as your most durable. I need to fill them with quarters and beat the living daylight out of a few guys down in the food court who have been extremely naughty. And then, of course, I have the usual rounds for the night."

"Goodness! What a line of work!" Deedee placed a hand on her heart, as if shocked by his admission.

Margaret squirmed forward. "We appreciate the loyal patronage."

It was true Deedee didn't know what she'd do without loyal customers. And at this point, she really couldn't be picky about who she sold products to, even if they had nefarious purposes in mind for them.

Margaret waggled her antenna flirtatiously. "When you're down at the food court, could you get us a slice of cheesecake?"

"For you, honey, anything." He winked at Margaret conspiratorially.

Krampus nodded to the knit bag that was part of Deedee's display. "Any chance you can part with that knit sack at the end of the day? My old one has a hole in it from beating it with a stick in the same place—with people inside of course."

"No problem." Deedee lowered her voice. "I'll even throw in a little spell for extra durability—just don't tell anyone."

Krampus took out his wallet again. "What do I owe you?"

Deedee grabbed her pad of paper and pen, ready to do some calculations. "Where are my glasses?"

"For crying out loud," Margaret said, her raspy voice turning shrill. "You're wearing them. On your face."

"I am?" Deedee laughed as she groped her glasses and adjusted them on her nose. "Why can't I see anything?"

Margaret sighed in exasperation. "Because you're old. And blind as a bat."

"Oh, burn!" Krampus said. "And people think I'm vicious. I need to get myself a snail sidekick."

"If you want to get *familiar* with this familiar, I'm totally fine with that," Margaret said, squirming in her shell suggestively. "Plus, I've always wanted to beat people up as a side hustle."

Deedee rolled her eyes. "Margaret, what did we talk about? No flirting with the customers."

Deedee removed her glasses and wiped them on her shirt. She felt a little zap through her belly, a tiny arch of blue light crackling between her fingers like a static charge. She could actually see better when she wasn't wearing her glasses. Her booth wasn't as dark. She squinted at the wire frames in suspicion. They looked like they were cast in shadows.

Oddly, the stench of rotten eggs wafted from her glasses.

"Do you smell that?" Deedee asked.

"You smelt it, you dealt it," Margaret muttered.

Deedee rubbed at her glasses more vigorously, the odor increasing. She understood now.

"Someone hexed my glasses." That explained why she couldn't see.

Deedee set them on the table and rummaged through one of her knitting bags for a spare pair. She found her purple tortoise shell reading glasses and put them on. They weren't meant for distance, but they were enough to help her see at least. She scanned her booth, quickly finding the lines of dark magic attached to her regular glasses.

"If I were you, I would put a pox on someone," Krampus said.

Deedee examined the signature of magic. It was the work of a witch. The market was full of magic users, but they weren't supposed to use their craft on customers. Or competition.

Deedee suspected she knew where this hex had come from.

She poked her head out of her tent, examining the energy around Knit Pickers' booth. The spell was subtle compared to the bright lights and vivid colors of the merchandise. The magic resembled shadows more than it did a spell full of smoke and sparkles that would dazzle customers into purchasing items they didn't need.

Deedee looked closer. From under her table, an almost flawless seam of magic made a crease of a line along the floor that led from her booth. The darkness in the booth she'd noted earlier hadn't been her imagination. Knit Pickers had used a cleverly disguised good luck spell.

Luck was dripping out of Deedee's booth and being funneled into Knit Pickers. Deedee observed an elderly woman studying Sock-It-To-Me's wares, a spark of interest in her eyes. The moment the potential customer stepped in Deedee's direction; the woman's gaze flickered to Knit Pickers. The woman diverted her path, her feet walking toward Deedee's rival.

Fury flared in Deedee. This was the reason her rival had hexed her glasses. She didn't want Deedee to notice the spell.

"That dirty bitch of a witch!" Deedee said.

Krampus arched an eyebrow at her. "That statement fits half the people here."

Deedee shook her head. "Knit Pickers is literally stealing my customers."

"Doesn't surprise me. Are you going to report her to the market committee?" Margaret asked.

Deedee briskly returned to her seat behind her table of wares, rummaging through her knitting back. She removed her lavender wand, a shard of obsidian crystal, and a baggie of salt.

"I have a better idea." She was tired of being Ms. Nice Witch. It was time for payback.

Krampus's eyes gleamed with delight. "You want me to beat her with a sock full of quarters?"

"Not at the moment. I need to give Knit Pickers a taste of their own medicine. And then some."

"Oooo!" Krampus said, sounding like a giddy schoolboy. "I like the sound of that."

Deedee gestured to the wall-length mirror next to the mitten display. "Krampus, dear, could you take my mirror down and hold it in front of me?"

"Anything for you, darling."

Krampus carried the mirror over, peeking around it with curiosity. Deedee cleared a space at her table where she set up her miniature alter.

"Make sure you block her from view," Margaret said. "We don't want the market committee getting word about this."

"Even if they do find out, what are they going to do?" Deedee asked. "Fine me for reflecting someone else's black magic back to them?"

But Margaret was right to be cautious.

Deedee lit incense and evoked the elements. She waved her lavender wand over the glass surface of the mirror. Her reflection rippled as she spoke, the power of her words absorbed into the glass.

She incanted:
"Mirror, mirror in my hand,
Time for me to take a stand.
Multiply ill luck by three.
Reflected to my enemy.
Let her reap what she has sown,
Give me the tidings that I'm owed.
So mote it be."

Deedee smiled in satisfaction. "You can hang the mirror back up now."

Krampus did so, admiring his own reflection afterward. He ran a hand over his horn warmers.

"You might want to stand aside," Margaret said. "We don't want a loyal customer to become injured."

He chuckled, gesturing with a flamboyant wave of his hand. "You delicious, little escargot, I am immune to witch's magic!"

Margaret cleared her throat with a phlegmy cough. "I was talking about stepping aside before the stampede rolls in."

Deedee didn't even have to wait thirty seconds before the first customer left and ambled over.

"Let me know if I can help you," Margaret offered.

Another sixty seconds went by and two more of Deedee's loyal customers from past years wandered over. Krampus backed up, the booth soon becoming crowded.

"Just remember," Krampus called over the rush of last-minute shoppers. "I have dibs on the knit sack." His gaze cut over to Knit Pickers. "I have plans."

As always, December twenty-fourth turned out to be Deedee's most lucrative day of the year.

Alternative Holidays

The Tannenbombers

James Edward O'Brien

It was my last Christmas Eve at the house. My last Christmas anywhere. At first, I thought the pipes might have frozen or the boiler was on the fritz. Old houses. Winter. Bloodless, boring, adult preoccupations.

The racket in the walls wrestled me from an Irish cream-induced slumber. I'd dozed in the midst of a newscast reporting that reindeer had quietly usurped polar bears as the apex predator of the north.

The news anchor wore a festive necktie and a look of vague consternation. "An unspecified zoonosis that renders normally docile herbivores carnivorous," he blathered. "Scientists suspect the condition is transmittable between animals and plants."

I paid little mind; it was the holiday season, after all. A sudden *crash* from the opposite side of the room drew my attention. I shot from the couch, the front of my garish snowman sweater sticky with spilled liqueur.

The sorry Douglas fir in the corner tested its limbs. It shed its hand-painted blown glass ornaments (passed down to me by my dearly departed nan) as if they were shackles. Yuletide baubles chimed and shattered against the parquet.

The tree wound back its branches and unleashed a shotgun spray of razor-sharp needles. The steel legs of its stand skittered across the floor, as my living room erupted like some fairground shooting gallery.

I shrieked as if the tree were an armed intruder, "You don't need to do this!"

Alternative Holidays

My family kept a mischievous calico when I was a child; I'd tried and failed to reason with *her* on numerous occasions. I didn't expect to fare any better against a rabid Douglas fir. So, I bolted.

As I scrambled toward the kitchen, the fir snared me in a winking lariat of lights. It is a terrible cliché to say that in moments such as this one's life flashes before one's eyes–the concept even *more* redundant on Christmas Eve, when the specters of the past are more alive than the here-and-now to begin with.

As I clawed at the string of lights that hotly constricted my jugular, all that came to mind was lying in bed as a kid on Christmas Eve, wondering if the morning might ever arrive. I remembered being driven to insomnia with the anticipation of racing to the tree and tearing open my presents. That took patience, I thought.

Now I thought of the conifers, still as statues for 370 million years, waiting for the right moment to strike—any human approximation of patience laughable by comparison. I gasped for air, forced into the frozen night at the end of my leash of festive lights.

My entire block had been occupied by a hobbled forest— sentinel evergreens helmed in tree-toppers. I wriggled dumbly as rabid pines passed me bough-to-bough in a coniferous game of hot potato. My fear boiled over to fury.

"They'll hack you to pieces!" I roared, knowing damn well there was no "they"—only *them*. Knowing damn well that even an entire *squadron* of lumberjacks with freshly sharpened, gleaming axes would fold against this yuletide armada.

The trees slammed me down. I kicked. I flailed, only managing to flense my knuckles against unforgiving bark. Tears froze on my cheeks.

I was deflated. The trees tethered me to the roof of a beat-up station wagon.

There were no sleigh bells. No snow. I prayed for sleep and solace and all those things Christmas promised. I tried to will feeling back into my limbs. The predawn sun was too far off and frigid to do much good. Its absence spared me full sight of the desiccated human husks bound in garland and cast curbside.

Cries rose block-to-block: shrill, tortured carols punctuated by the occasional *crack* from some faraway rifle, and that *smell*— chimney smoke mingling with roasted flesh.

"Help!" I croaked. "Somebody! Anybody!"

Strapped to that roof like a 10-point buck, I wished for nothing more extraordinary than I had as a kid—the intervention of some superman-saint to pass judgment upon the naughty and guerdon the good, if only for this one magical day of the year. I shifted my gaze to the pine-choked heavens in hopes of a sleigh that failed to materialize.

I'd often cringed at stories of drunks wrapping their cars around trees, but never dreamt I'd spy a tree wrap its limbs around the steering wheel of a beat-up station wagon and shuttle me off to some uncertain end. Come daybreak, the world was one big morass of tinsel: limbs and wire, splinters and burst pipes.

McMansions fell. Entire cities were reduced to shattered glass and rubble. If all those schlubs bellyaching about the Second Amendment had stockpiled chainsaws and herbicide instead of AKs and Uzis, things might have been different.

If we were a little less *evolved*, we might have taken to the branches—ridden the backs of our newfound masters like red-billed oxpeckers upon rhinos. But we'd lost the simian grace of our primate cousins eons ago.

Tree cover engulfed the last semblance of sky. The surviving world awoke to the cooing of turtledoves: a solstice resplendent with birdsong, zesty balsam—fragrant chimney smoke.

The drive took forever. My eyeballs were ice cubes. My toes burned numbly in my worn deerskin slippers. The station wagon petered out in front of a picturesque farmhouse beside a tree stump graveyard. Cruel boughs unbound me.

A knotty pine curled a crooked limb to beckon me toward the porch. My frozen limbs complied, toy-soldier rigid. The way the sky wavered like a mirage where it met the farmhouse chimney indicated that something inside had stoked the fireplace.

It had grown *fashionable* among the ecologically minded to have one's ashes interred in a biodegradable planter so that a tree might grow in one's wake. It felt remarkably *unfashionable*—downright *ignoble*—to have zero say in the matter.

It was a Christmas to remember; the first that stood out since I'd swallowed that grand ruse of adulthood: that magic was confined to fairytales, dreams and nightmares. A true pity it was to be my last.

Alternative Holidays

Chinese New Year's Resolution

Robert Jeschonek

When Dave Dixon walks through the door of the Szechuan Palace, he's bombarded with sights and sounds and smells. He smiles from ear to ear, and his mouth instantly waters, because it's Chinese New Year in his favorite restaurant in town.

For a moment, no one talks to him, they haven't seen him yet. He adjusts his glasses and takes it all in.

Every table in the dining room is full, and the customers are all talking and laughing. On his right, every stool at the bar is occupied; the bartender lights a drink on fire, and the customers in front of him ooh and ahh and clap.

Further along that side of the room, steam billows out from under the plexiglass sneeze guard on the buffet. Diners fill plates on either side, while a long line of hungry guests snake between the nearest tables, waiting their turns.

Waitresses dart through the room, bearing trays laden with tea, sodas, and bottles of beer. A tall girl with short brown hair grins and waves at Dave from across the room. Then another one, a Chinese woman, does the same, and then another.

Everybody knows him at "the Szech." He's been coming here for twelve years, two or three times a week.

Or at least he used to, until the place closed down for good.

"Shrimp-and-zucchini Dave!"

At the sound of his nickname, derived from his favorite dish at the Szech, Dave whirls. The restaurant's owner, Sam Leung, dressed in a red Tang suit, bursts out from behind the bar and charges toward him.

"Happy New Year!" Waving a cold bottle of Tsingtao beer, Sam claps him on the back. "Glad you could make it!"

"Ready for karaoke tonight?" asks Dave.

"You first!" Sam grins. "I need more of *these* before I'm ready to start singing." He sips the beer.

"You always throw the best party, Sam!"

"And you're the best customer," says Sam. "Now get over there, your friends are waiting!" He points a finger at a big round table in the back, full of people, all waving.

Dave takes a step toward them and stops. The faces are so familiar and well-loved, he chokes up.

Then it's too much for him, and he pulls off his glasses.

At which point, he sees the dining room as it really is—dark, empty, and utterly still.

He looks down at his glasses... not really glasses of course, but the newest augmented reality goggles. Images still move across the screens, and his earpieces still play the haunting sounds of a happy crowd.

#

Without the veil of A.R., the sick feeling returns to Dave's gut—the usual weight of sadness and regret that wells up whenever he thinks of the beloved Szech. The place has been closed for ten years now, ever since the early days of the pandemic.

He still misses it with all his heart and can't let go of it, not only because of nostalgia for the good times he had there, but because he feels responsible for the Szech's demise.

Why, otherwise, would he dwell in the past, returning to the shuttered restaurant once a year to relive the holiday celebration he loved? Life is good, he has a great job in software development—so why else would he indulge this morbid fantasy? Why sneak in here with his A.R. gear to imagine spending Chinese New Year with friends who've moved on long ago, if not to wallow in the guilt he feels for his role in closing down what to him was a little corner of paradise?

Almost without thinking, he finds himself putting on the goggles again and slipping effortlessly into reliving the glory days that are such a comfort to him.

#

Instantly, the world of the Szech at its height returns to full vibrancy around him.

"Dave! Hey!" His buddy Ray Henry, who moved out of town three years ago, is waving him over to the big round table. "Get your butt over here!"

Smiling, Dave weaves through the dining room. His heart beats faster as he gets closer and sees familiar faces up close, looking happy and healthy and alive.

"Hey, everybody." How to express the feeling he gets as they smile back at him?

There they are, as if in the flesh—visible and audible. Conjured from phone videos, security footage, social media, and interviews, they look and sound like loved ones.

Yet he knows all too well that they aren't.

"Happy New Year!" The image of his father grins and raises a bottle of Tsingtao. He doesn't look at all like a man who's been dead for seven years. "Here's to an even better one to come!"

Dave's cousin Mark is there, too, no longer a quadriplegic, and his estranged brother, Tom, whom he hasn't seen in 16 years.

"Hope you don't mind that we didn't wait for you!" Tom peels a salt-and-pepper shrimp and pops it in his mouth. "We wanted to hit the buffet before you tore it up!"

"Did you *leave* anything for me?" asks Dave.

"Not much!" Mark scoops the last morsel of General Jou's chicken off his plate, red sauce glistening as he shovels it in and chews it up. "About the same as *you* would've left for *us* if the roles had been reversed."

"Don't worry, D! We made sure to leave a drop of soup and half a noodle so you won't go hungry!" Uncle Pete howls with laughter, drumming a rimshot on the table with his chopsticks.

Just then, Julie, Sam's niece who works as a waitress—slim, pretty, and twentysomething—marches out of the kitchen with a pan of Dave's favorite dish. "Davey, come on! I'm refilling the shrimp and zucchini for you!"

"Check it out! They take care of me here!" At that moment, as Dave follows her to the buffet, all is as it once was. He forgets that he's immersed in an A.R. simulation and imagines that nothing has changed. He, Dave Dixon, is in the world of ten years ago, only better, and has done nothing wrong. The real Szech is right here, not the hollowed-out husk it's been reduced to.

It's the year of the tiger, not the year of the virus and the carelessness that helped sink the Szech.

#

As much as Dave tries to force back the memories, they leak in around the edges of his mind. He remembers coming down with a fever and cough, what he thought at the time was the flu...

Correction. He *hoped* it was the flu, though he suspected otherwise. He secretly worried it might be the latest round of the pandemic virus.

Though there was no vaccine or treatment for the virus yet, Dave went to the Szech for lunch with his co-workers anyway. Selfishly, he waltzed into the place, brushing aside the latest warnings in the media, dismissing them as overreactions. He wasn't worried about spreading what he had; all he cared about was having one more taste of Szechuan goodness in case he ended up sick at home for a while.

Dave sat with five coworkers at the big round table in the back of the place, lifting one plump piece of shrimp after another from the huge helping of shrimp and zucchini on his plate. He only paused in his eating when Sam Leung stopped by to give him a big handshake and pat on the back, as he sometimes did.

One week later, Sam was in the hospital...then his wife, and most of his staff. Before long, they had to close the Szech because they had no one left to run it; then, indoor dining went away everywhere for a while. Maybe they could have sustained the place with the takeout business, but they never managed to staff up enough to try. Sam, once he recovered from his illness, decided that early retirement was the option that promised the least amount of heartache and stress.

And so, the Szech was gone for good. After decades in business, the place simply went away with a whimper. The last plate of shrimp and zucchini was served, the last volcano drink lit, the last sweet-and-sour soup ladled into a chipped bowl.

And Dave, though he could never definitively prove he was to blame for the outbreak that set the process in motion, came to bear the burden on his shoulders. He decided it was his fault, and he let the guilt drag him down year after year.

The only thing that lifted his spirits was celebrating Chinese New Year's Eve via A.R. in the empty building, pretending nothing had changed.

#

Someone sets off firecrackers outside as Dave loads his plate with shrimp and zucchini and Deep Sea Delight. He tops it with General Jou's chicken and Peking Duck, then grabs a cup of champagne punch and heads for the table, resolving to go back for more ASAP.

Sam raises a flute of champagne as the audience cheers. "Almost time for karaoke, so tune up those vocal cords, people!"

"You first, Sam!" shouts Dave in a burst of enthusiasm.

"Hey, there he is, folks!" Sam lifts the champagne higher. "Let's hear it for my best customer, Dave Dixon! Get up here, Dave!"

As the crowd claps and cheers, Dave heads for the front of the room. He's almost there, about to throw an arm around his good friend Sam, when he suddenly bumps into something. He can't see what it is, but it sends him stumbling backward.

Realizing he's interacting with something outside the A.R. realm, he yanks off his goggles. That's when he sees Julie the waitress, who is also yanking off a pair of A.R. goggles.

#

"Davey?" Julie looks surprised. "Is that really you?"

"I was going to ask you the same question." Dave is dumbstruck. He hasn't seen her in ten years.

Julie tips her head to one side. "What are you doing here?"

Dave holds up his goggles and shrugs. "Chinese New Year. I, uh... I'm reliving it."

Julie frowns. "You are?" She's skinnier than he remembers, and her dark hair looks a bit scraggly. Even in the shadows of the unlit restaurant, Dave can see she looks rougher than the version in his A.R. recreation.

"I come back every year," he tells her, seeing no reason to lie about it. "I really miss the place, especially on New Year's."

"You're not the only one," says Julie. "I hear them sneaking around down here sometimes, talking about the old days."

"What do you mean? You hear them how?"

Julie looks sheepish as she points at the ceiling. "I've been living upstairs," she says. "Ever since the Szechuan closed."

"Seriously?" Dave knew there was space on the second floor. He and the gang had joked about the existence of a "party room" up there, but Sam had told them the upstairs was used only for storage. Could an apartment have been there all along? If that were true, it amazed him that Julie could have lived in it all this time.

"I didn't have anywhere else to go," she says quietly.

"Do you even have *utilities* up there? Is it safe?"

Suddenly alert, she lunges at him, grabbing hold of his shirt. "Please don't tell anyone, Davey! I'm fine, I swear!"

Dave's guilt over the end of the Szech intensifies. "I won't tell anyone," he says. "I promise."

Julie nods nervously and lets go of him. "I'll be all right, Davey. Really. People bring me food, and the churches and Salvation Army help with other things."

Dave has a knot in his stomach that tightens the longer he listens. Is he responsible for the way she's living? By infecting Sam and the others with the virus, did he inadvertently lead her to this bleak existence?

"So you're watching Chinese New Year then?" She gestures at his A.R. goggles.

He nods. "What about you?"

"Take a look." She hands over the goggles she was using. "They're borrowed from the library, by the way. A friend of mine over there programmed them for me."

Dave gives her his own goggles and puts hers on. As soon as the lenses cover his eyes, his surroundings change. The dismal, shuttered restaurant becomes the way it once was—but not the same as the vision of Chinese New Year in which he's been indulging.

Instead, he sees the Szech tidy and bright but mostly empty. He, standing in for Julie, is one of only two people in the dining room.

Though, technically speaking, he is actually *both* people at the same time.

"Julie, I'm so sorry for what happened to this place," says the other occupant of the dining room—an image of Dave himself. He looks about ten years younger than Dave does now and wears tan khaki pants and a black polo shirt with his employer's emblem on the left chest. "But I will save it. I will save *us*."

Dave frowns under the goggles, trying to wrap his head around what he sees. *This* is what Julie has been watching in her A.R. world? *This* is her idea of a fantasy?

"You and I will bring the Szechuan Palace back to life," says his image. "I *swear* it. The two of us will work together to make things right again."

It's then that Dave gets a lump in his throat. His eyes burn with tears as he stands there in Julie's virtual shoes and understands how she must feel and what she must want from him.

There's no blame in her A.R. vision, just longing and hope for the future. Just a blueprint for how to make up for what happened and set aside any guilt or sorrow weighing him down. Just a Chinese New Year's resolution for him to make and live up to.

#

"Welcome to the Szechuan Palace!"

It's a year later, and the restaurant is alive and bustling again—not in A.R., but the real world. The beloved eatery has been restored and reopened, recapturing the magic of yesterday alongside the trends and innovations of today and tomorrow.

The place is as crowded as it ever was in the Sam Leung days—maybe more so. It's been going gangbusters since the reopening six weeks ago, cleaner and brighter and better than ever.

Sam hasn't returned from retirement, though. This time, it's *Dave* welcoming guests to the big Chinese New Year party in a red silk Tang suit, playing the role of gracious and gregarious host.

But Dave isn't the only one running the place. Julie's helping keep the dream alive as his co-manager, sharing her spark and knowhow from the old days.

Together, they've got a major hit on their hands, no A.R. goggles needed... and this is their busiest day of the year. The place is really packed, especially as the busiest, craziest part of the night is about to kick off, emceed by Dave with Tsingtao bottle in hand.

"It's time for the *real* fun to start, people!" says Dave as he shows guests to their tables. "The big event you've all been waiting for! Karaoke begins in five minutes, so you'd better get your vocal cords tuned up and ready to sing!"

Alternative Holidays

The Afterthought

Jenna Hanchey

After naughty and nice, Santa had a third list. It only had one name, and no title. He couldn't figure out what to do with the belated addition. That this name was an afterthought was disturbing enough; worse, its indeterminacy. What kind of person was neither naughty nor nice?

The question plagued him.

Sometimes when he was particularly flummoxed, he would stand between the gigantic pile of presents on his right and towering stack of coal upon his left, turning his head back and forth. He built attempted solutions in the middle: a present and two pieces of coal, or a single coal and two presents. But none of the ratios felt right.

December 24 arrived too soon, finding Santa sprawled between the piles with a half-empty bottle of scotch and the troublesome list clutched in his hand.

It simply read: Mrs. Claus.

Scream Stream

Gordon Linzner

Gary knew all the best short-cuts to avoid the local bullies.

Bottlewood Cemetery had held their annual Hallowe'en bash that afternoon, so as not to compete with trick-or-treaters' schedules. To be on site on October thirty-first, however, wasn't good enough for him. The fourteen-year-old wanted to be inside the cemetery after dark, when the church clock struck midnight, watching "Archal" on his phone in total solitude.

Unless you counted the surrounding corpses.

That he'd come across multiple warnings about the sinister legendary video only deepened the temptation. For him to find a viable link had taken nearly the entire month of October. Even then, it vanished within moments.

But not before he'd downloaded "Archal" to his cellphone.

The timing could not have been better.

The boy squeezed through a gap in the rusted gate and appropriately walked along a narrow stream to the most isolated spot he knew of, behind the Paulwich family mausoleum. Their last direct descendent had been interred over a half century earlier. No one had visited the site in decades, except to pass by.

It's all about the atmosphere, he mused.

Gary had considered inviting one or two classmates to join him, but decided the moment was too good to share. He hadn't any real friends, anyway, just a few other ninth graders who tolerated his presence. One of them would certainly have blabbed to his parents; then he'd really be in trouble. No. He would show them the video tomorrow, watch their reactions even as he relived his own. Afterwards, they would realize why they should treat Gary with more respect.

He would be in a better position to pick and choose his friends.

The boy scooted up low steps to rest against the crypt. The chill of the marble penetrated his parka. All the better for the mood, he told himself, fighting his shiver.

The bell in the local church tower, half a mile away, began to toll, echoing through the still air.

Five.

Six.

Gary raised the phone in his left hand. The app had been ready to play "Archal" since the moment he entered the cemetery. He blinked, suddenly noticing the battery was down to seventy per cent. He'd charged it that afternoon; this program must use far more power than anticipated.

Still, it should be enough.

Eight.

Nine.

A cold breeze whipped around the side of the mausoleum. The boy raised his knees, pressing them against his chest to hold in the warmth.

Twelve.

And... stream!

At first, Gary saw only a dark blank screen, heard nothing beyond the wind whispering among gravesites. Disappointing.

His thumb reached to hit pause, so he could check for sound and picture.

A faint white wisp danced across the center of the screen. As the image grew, the background sound became louder: a rhythmic shattering of glass, not quite music but nonetheless intriguing enough to draw him in.

The twirling shape swayed forward, almost filling the screen. Gary made out legs, eyes, long wavy hair, an unsettling grin... but only here and there, not all at once.

His own eyes shifted back and forth. He waved the phone before him, trying to focus on the entity as a whole.

Without success.

Then he heard the voice, a whisper barely distinguishable from the background sounds.

"Welcome to Archal." The speaker's tone was neutral; male or female, he could not tell. When Gary focused on lip movement, the words seemed out of sync.

The boy started to respond, then remembered he'd be talking to a video. Might miss something important.

A hand reached forward. Gary tightened his grip on the phone.

Then realized with a shock he was gripping something else.

The phone landed with a hollow thunk! on concrete steps.

His hand felt as if plunged into ice water.

He bent to recover his phone. Nothing but darkness could be seen below him.

And above.

And all around.

Except for the white mist that continued to address him.

"What...?" Gary began.

"Welcome to Archal," the shape repeated. "A void within a void."

"This isn't what I wanted!" Gary screeched. "I want out!"

"Hush." A disembodied finger pressed against equally disembodied lips. "Your friends can hit 'escape' on your keyboard at any time. Don't you want to explore this world?"

"I have no friends. I mean, I'm watching this alone. I mean, I was watching. Now I'm wherever this is."

"Ah."

Additional disconnected wisps circled the boy in a macabre dance.

"The video's only fifteen minutes long," he continued. "When it ends, I return to my world. The real world. Right? Right?"

The figure shook its head. "Automatic replay. Still, sooner or later, someone will shut down your computer, or restart it. Meanwhile, take advantage of the situation. Think of the stories you can tell afterwards."

"I was on my phone," Gary blurted. "No computer."

"Really? That's not the best way to experience 'Archal.' Such a limited view. Again, though, you'll return when someone finds your phone and shuts it down."

Not likely in the dead of night, in the most isolated part of Bottlewood Cemetery, Gary told himself nervously.

"The battery will probably go dead first," Gary replied. "That should do it, right? I'm guessing it's half drained already. It won't be long."

Wispy lips curled in a frown. Or a gloat. Or a silent laugh.

"One must be properly signed out. It's the one essential rule for all visitors to Archal."

"But a drained battery! That should automatically sign me out!"

"Not the same."

Other wisps flauntingly echoed the phrase.

"Not the same. Not the same. Not the same."

"What, then? What will happen?"

"You will join us. There are worst fates. Ask some of the others." A disembodied hand waved toward the increasing number of wisps that began encircling Gary.

No one was near enough to the mausoleum, or even the cemetery gates, to hear the boy's final scream.

Ne'er Day

Andrew L. Roberts

It is a narrow village
of narrow houses and narrow lanes
a town of
narrow thoughts and frugal hopes
diminishing
hugging close
the weathered cliff
its crooked backbone
that separates this old place
from the rest of the world
that has long since
pressed forward and moved on
seeking out a broader sky
in which to dream much wider
dreams

And yet
this is home
stubborn and defiant
back against that wall
forever facing outward
toward its storm-blackened sea
just as
mourners must face the open grave
stoically
with grief denied and bent inward
for none to witness or betray

Lichen-mottled, stone walls
lift seaweed-thatched rooftops
chimneys yet steam
with the last fires of
Hogmanay
but all the windows
are closed and shuttered fast
hands clapped over the eyes
protecting those ancient and
irreplaceable panes of glass
that the ancestors
brought to this island
when they first came
from the mainland far away

A cock crows
and soon another
as morning breaks
announcing
the first hour of daylight
though with daylight also denied
on this stormy new year's day
the wind and rain
have rendered everything
the same shade of wearied gray
that drowns the soul
and quenches any remaining
thirst to dream

And yet those dreamers
still awake
who stumble home
from their last merriments
of the now dead year
stagger with heads hanging
loosely from their shoulders
elbows, knees, and hips
near unhinged
the joints being too well lubricated
by too much whisky and dancing

some weep for nostalgia
some laugh for the same
and some so sick with their joy
and their regrets
that it is only by a miracle
that they will find their direction
home this day

Three such men
walk shoulder to shoulder
would-be-boxers
swaying and weaving
and still singing
they nearly collide with
the young, dark-haired stranger
coming down from the
port beyond the hill
seeing him
in the last moment only
they splinter
come apart
and roll
then when once he's past
come back together
and reassemble
arms again interlacing
over each other's shoulders
becoming a gate of three pickets
with one shared cross member
a crooked gate set free
windblown
rogue
and tumbling down the road
one man swears
another quotes Burns
and the third vomits
all over his companions
they curse together
until they laugh
and carry on

Alternative Holidays

But the stranger
strides onward
head down against the wind
with his singular purpose
undeterred
until he reaches his
destination
and knocks three times
upon the oak
of Sissy McKenzie's door

He gazes up at the house
before him
struck by what has changed
and struck deeper still
by what has remained unchanged
left bewildered by the truth
eighteen years have passed for him
while eighty-seven
have passed for her
and though he has long known
this brutal equation
seeing the thing up close
is different than knowing it
as numbers upon paper
and of course
now there is no going backwards

Sissy
he says
trying to stand taller upon her step
a knapsack slung under one arm
and his Highland Pipes
wrapped in the old seal skin
tucked in close beneath the other
won't you rise
he says
and let me in
for I am the dark-haired man
for whom you've long hoped
I know you're weary

from waiting
and that your bones must
ache in this weather
but it is a new year
and I've returned
bringing gifts and a blessing
to your door
a bag of salt and a black bun
to grace your table
and sweeten your morning
whisky too
and a good dod of coal
for comfort and for warmth
and stories Sissy
—such stories and songs—
that you have never heard before
from distant stars and wider worlds
faraway
across the sky
beyond the blue and black

So
for Auld Lang Syne
listen to my voice
hear it and remember
I am your big brother
Neil
who waits upon your step
come
open the door
and let me be the first foot
to cross your threshold
on this long overdue
Ne'er Day

In reply
there is a stirring
the rumor of footsteps
and floorboards
creaking
and the slipping of the chain

and bolt
that locks the door
the knob turns
and the door opens

Peering out is an old man
of seventy years or more
once fine features now
a roadmap of wrinkles
and a head balding
yet with some silver wisps
remaining
their eyes meet
and while there is recognition
in the old man's expression
Neil knows
they have never met
before
removing his rain-soaked
bonnet
and pushing back his hair
he repeats his name
but the old man only
nods
and motions for him to enter
saying
uncle, you are late
and this dark-haired young man
replies saying
not too-late I hope
his fingers touching
the door's bolt and chain
his eyes questioning

Mother
says the old man
has me bolt the door
each Hogmanay
from midnight on
until midday
lest some other

enter by mischance
before you
stealing your
Ne'er Day

He motions again
for Neil to follow
and leads him to the room
where Sissy McKenzie
has been waiting
wrapped in a worn blanket
of storied tartan
propped up in her narrow bed
by three big pillows
and her small ragdoll
which has lost both its button eyes
and its red-stitched smile
to time

And Neil
sees now still more evidence
of time lost and misspent
for his sister has sorely been
diminished
reduced once more to the size
of the child she once was
tiny
but frail
and as ancient as the moon
and seeing this
the dark-haired young man
of thirty-six summers
falls to his knees beside
his baby sister's bed
takes her hands between his own
enfolding them
with all the tenderness
he has carried with him
across the stars
from Farhaven in Orion's Belt
and Killthunder Station

where he lost his name to war
and New Alba on Finalshore
where he found it again
in peace

Sissy
he starts to say
but she stops his words
placing her fingertips
upon his lips
before letting her hands caress
and explore his impossibly
unchanged face

And
though Neil weeps
Sissy smiles
calls him by his nickname
chiding him for being late
again
and having no better sense
than to walk in the darkness
and the rain

And Neil
wanting to smile
but unable
hangs his head
and recalls the number
of all those harried jumps
between systems
when they skipped their ships
like stones
across the event horizons
of lightless singularities
slinging themselves
through the emptiness
between the stars
courting time
distorting time
cheating time

and forever losing the time
that passed too quickly
upon this island
in the unrecoverable decades
of a lifetime missed
that can never be restored

But Sissy
pinches his chin
until he meets her eyes
again
Whit's fur ye'll no go by ye!
she says
quoting their grandmother
stop your crying
she adds
I've lived long and I have lived well
sure I have missed you
but I am not yet dead
and though much is gone
that could have been shared
some yet remains
I have only joy this morning
because
you are here
Neil
my only brother
returned from the dark
a blessing come home
flesh and bone
from across the stars
first footing my threshold
on this Ne'er Day

And Neil
nods and wipes his tears
away
reaches for his pipes that rest
beside his knee
should I play these now?
he asks

wake the neighbors as I used to?
or is it singing
that your heart desires
Auld Lang Syne perhaps
or the old Boat Song
that was your favorite?

But Sissy
shakes her head
No
she says
nothing old or familiar
play me
something shiny and new
something that will make me
feel as young as you
play me one of your own songs
brother
that you've brought home with you
from New Alba on Finalshore
let me see
those stars through your eyes
and all the places
where you've travelled
show me your life
all the way
from when you left this house
to your arrival
upon my doorstep
on this
my final Ne'er Day

Aye
says Neil
I can do that and more
and rising
he unwraps his pipes
and makes his way
back through the house
out the door again
down the narrow step

and back
into the gray dawn

Everything now
is still
the wind
has blown itself out
and the rain
that had harassed his steps
all through the night
is altogether gone
yet still the reluctant sun
plays the miser
refusing to show itself
and so Neil fills the bag
with his breath
bringing it to life
under his arm
his nephew joins him outside
unlatching the house's shutters
and throwing them wide
so that Neil sees his sister
inside
watching him from within
childlike in her expectation
her face beaming and angelic
in the firelight

With a sharp thrust
of his elbow
now
Neil strikes the drones
and begins the cèol mòr
that maps his life
starting as a slow air
sorrowfully climbing each note
one upon another
footsteps
unembellished
building the theme
of a seventeen-year-old

lad
neither eager for adventure
nor heroic in any way
just a lad
of easy laughter
with a love of his home
stifled by an uninvited duty
a lad
and no more than that
wishing to remain
with his mother and his sister
yet being marched away
from his father's funeral
leaving childhood behind
unfinished
shouldering a soldier's kit
and the family burden
assuming his father's debts
with a fifteen-year enlistment
that has him marching off to war

This slow air continues
showing little haste
yet all the while
growing darker
and more determined
gathering in tempo
and in force
becoming a stormy theme
of thunder and the gale
adopting warlike courses
that echo the anthems of
The Black Bear and
The Athol Highlanders
turning and turning
until those courses merge
and are replaced by
a song still more rampant
and the young lad, now a lad no more
finds himself in the midst of his war
on another world

circling a star in the Belt of Orion
facing the enemy in battle
on Farhaven
at the butcher's place called
Killthunder Station

The neighbors
all along the lane
begin to stir and awaken
hearing the voice of
of Neil MacCrimmon's pipes
and the song of his youth sacrificed
doors and shuttered windows
complain as they are opened
but there is only silence
from the neighbors themselves
who at first lean out only to listen
then
one by one
step out in their slippers
into the lane
drawn from their homes
to crowd about him
steaming and stern-faced
yet not entirely able
to hide all the deeper feelings
welling up inside

And seeing this
Neil eases into another theme
different from the first
altered and warmed by
grace notes and innumerable
embellishments
until the sorrow and rage are replaced
with a sense of yearning

Is that the MacCrimmon boy?
asks a voice
it must be
says another

but he's so young
says a third
then Annie MacGregor
hisses for
them to be silent and to listen

But Neil's song
is already nearing its close
having reached New Alba
on Finalshore
where his enlistment ends
and the name he lost
at Killthunder
is found again
and having both his freedom
and his name restored
he turns his heart
and he turns his eyes
towards
his home and his Sissy
once more
still watching him
from behind the glass

And so he finishes
with a tune of homecoming
of Hogmanay and Auld Lang Syne
of loving and forgiving
of pain and healing
of letting go and embracing
and most of all
remembering
and hearing this
not even the sun
could hide any longer
breaking through the cold clouds
to shimmer upon the sea of
upturned faces
who smile in the sudden warmth
and with that
all the old colors of the old town

return
yellow
green
red
and blue
all as bright as summer
and new
and this is how
a dark-haired and impossibly
young man
First Foots his entire village
and shares his baby sister's
long promised blessing
giving everything
he has and is
on this
his sister's
final
New Year's morn.

Soul For It

Mir Rainbird

Argo Lee stomped irritably through the dirty slush of last night's snow. He ought to have stayed on the main street and put up with the gaudy plastic holiday decorations and crowds of shoppers; at least it would have been clean and dry. And better lit.

Something flickered at the corner of his eye.

Just another fat man in a red velour suit. Argo's lip curled contemptuously. He could swear he'd seen a Santa on every corner today. At least they weren't those damned annoying ones with the clanging bells and metal buckets for spare change. This one had a sack: maybe collecting for a toy drive. Ugh, children.

Suddenly, something hard and cold wrapped chokingly tight around his throat and he was thrust into a snowbank beneath a heavy body reeking of sewage, coal smoke, and cinnamon streusel.

One of the amulets around Argo's neck popped and flared like a firecracker, then smoldered as it touched the wet snow.

He clawed at what felt like a chain around his neck, trying to get enough breath for a protective incantation.

A long black tongue trailed slimily across his face.

"Naughty," the Krampus rasped.

Argo's vision was beginning to go fuzzy, but he could make out the dark maw of the filthy sack as his attacker raised it toward Argo's head.

A bell chimed, quiet and clear and painfully lovely.

The Krampus gave a breathless shriek, like a boiling kettle, and was gone, taking sack and chain with it.

Argo rolled onto his back, clutching his aching throat, and lay gasping and looking up at his rescuer. She was tall and golden. Holly twined through her loose hair and around her horns.

"You're lucky I was passing by," said the Perchta. She bent and peered into Argo's eyes. Her face crinkled in distaste. "You'll put it back if you know what's good for you, fool."

She left him to pry himself out of the slushy, piss-stained snowbank where the Krampus had pinned him. It would have been embarrassing, had he still been capable of feeling embarrassment.

As it was, Argo was... vexed. Everything about the incident was irksome. Not the least because he couldn't even complain that this latest attack was unfair: he *had* been a naughty boy.

Getting rid of his soul had seemed like a great idea at the time.

It had been a solid decision, thaumaturgically speaking: he was free to practice the dark arts without the inconvenience of guilt or fear or self-doubt—all states of mind that sapped concentration and weakened the will. Now, he was focused and fierce and he never hesitated. Not even when thinking twice might have been smarter...

It was the right decision, he told himself again. No regrets.

It just hadn't occurred to him that removing his soul would leave an empty space that any number of unpleasant entities would be eager to occupy.

Many of those entities were stronger in the long, dark nights of winter, as he had discovered last Christmas. He had nearly been devoured by a daeva, dispossessed by a demon, and nobbled by a nuutipukki.

He had been more careful since then. Wards, protective sigils, and amulets had become matters of daily routine, as had avoiding the shadows. He hadn't been in serious danger since last Epiphany, but he had been inconvenienced and annoyed. And now that the anniversary of his fateful decision had come again, the longest night of the year, he was starting to think that being soul-free wasn't worth the hassle.

The winter solstice was the ideal time to undo the spell. The anniversary of its casting, and also one of the days of each year when the veil between worlds was thinnest and magic, especially dark magic, was most effective.

Not, Argo supposed, that putting one's soul back where it belonged was black magic, come to think of it. If anything, that was good magic, right? Assuming one believed in God or right and wrong or souls being divine anima or any of that. Which Argo didn't. A soul was just some amorphous medley of conscience and subconscious, various instincts and personality traits.

He hadn't thrown away the immortal part of himself, just... edited it. Trimmed the dross. Fear and shame and kindness and remorse and the pathetic desire to be liked. He cringed at the thought of feeling them again. Was it worth it, to stop being a demon-magnet?

Well, when he put it like that, yes. No point in living his best life if some monster stole his body and cast him formless into the outer dark. That would suck.

Argo made it back to his apartment, a run-down flat above a bakery. He locked the door, reinforced the wards, and took a bath with purifying salts and herbs.

Was rejoining one's soul more appropriately done at midnight, or dawn?

Eh, better just get it over with, he decided.

He toweled himself thoroughly. The black satin ritual robe wasn't machine washable, after all.

Argo rolled away the threadbare carpet that covered his containment circle, and laid out the materials he would need. His grimoire. White candles. The enchanted mirror that let him see the truth of all the planes superimposed upon one another. Ghost-offerings of bread and blood, salt and honey.

He hesitated over the silver-edged athame, then left the knife in its case; what was left to sever? Instead, he took a needle and the white thread from a tiny sewing kit he had gotten from a hotel. The thread was for symbolism—his soul should just sink right back into him where it belonged. Shouldn't it? He'd never heard of anyone getting one back before.

He sat cross-legged in the center of the circle and lit the candles with his will and the secret name of fire. He gathered his mystic strength and began to chant.

The invocation ended. The candles extinguished themselves. Argo waited. He didn't feel any different. He lit a single white candle and looked in the enchanted mirror.

"Well, shit."

#

In the morning, once the chill sun was at an optimum angle over the wet streets, he walked to the Like Magic Make-up

Mansion. The window was decorated for the holidays with mistletoe and a spray-painted gingerbread house: warnings he was sure no one got until it was too late. He wondered idly how a parasitic plant had come to be associated with Christmas kisses in the first place.

He went in. Those warnings weren't aimed at him.

"A fortunate solstice to you, Griselda," he said when he saw the witch was alone.

"You don't look like you're having a good—" She broke off to examine his face, her frown shifting to incredulity. "What the ever-loving heck, boy? Are you out of your wits?"

Yeah, this was why he hadn't been to visit his former teacher all year; he knew she'd tell him he was an idiot.

Argo flopped into a chair. "Soooo, yeah, I severed myself last solstice for very valid reasons that I won't get into and it's been fine, only apparently not having a soul opens you up to all sorts of possession so I figured I'd summon my soul back, but it didn't work and I'm not sure what to try next."

Griselda regarded him, eyebrows lost in her graying bangs. "For a smart man you sure are stupid as hell sometimes," she remarked. "At least you didn't *sell* your soul. Then you'd really be screwed."

"I'm not that dumb," Argo said, not admitting that he had considered it—why not get something in exchange, right? But the market for souls had been surprisingly weak.

She snorted, as if reading his mind. Which was possible, with Griselda. But she only asked, "You haven't noticed any other side-effects, beside demons liking the looks of you? Bad dreams? Ennui? Pleasures of the flesh losing their savor?"

"No dreams at all, anomie, and I guess pleasures do seem more transitory than they used to be, when you put it like that." Argo sighed.

"And you didn't notice? That doesn't sound like the self-indulgent hedonist I remember."

"I noticed, but I figured it was just me getting older," Argo said uncomfortably. "What about you? You look like you're pushing sixty. You changing your ways?"

She waved that off. "Nah, I got a girl lined up. I like to wait till after Christmas. Let the poor dears have a last holiday at home. She's coming in to get prettied up for a New Year's Eve party; I'll take her then."

Argo nodded. The theoretical underpinnings of the spell he had used to amputate the unwanted parts of himself were based on the spell Griselda used to steal her clients' youth and beauty. They didn't die of it, just wandered around as empty, enervated husks of their former selves.

Argo sat up with a jolt. "Gris. Do you think my soul could, well, be somewhere? I mean, physically? Like a familiar?"

"Good grief, boy, how much of yourself did you cut out?"

"Kind of a lot," he admitted reluctantly.

She narrowed her eyes. "Mirror," she ordered.

She flipped the sign in the window to *Closed* and led him upstairs, to her apartment. She had a mirror just like his—it was another piece of magic he had learned from her.

She lit a candle, handed it to Argo, and positioned him in front of the glass.

He closed his eyes, and she sucked in a breath.

"What were you thinking?" she asked, aghast. "Throwing away that much of yourself. You weren't that bad."

"That was the problem," he mumbled.

Her face softened. "Oh, Argo," she said pityingly.

He couldn't take that. "I better go look for it," he said, rising. "Should be easy enough to scry, what with it being part of me."

"Don't be a stranger," she called after him, as he headed for the door with discourteous haste.

#

His soul was not easy to scry. The damn spell kept pointing at Argo, which was, okay, reasonable.

He disassembled the locator spell and thought about what to try next.

If the soul remnant was in physical form, he ought to recognize it, right? It should remind him of himself somehow. His old self.

Argo shifted uncomfortably. He hadn't felt uncomfortable for the past year, and he had not missed it. He hadn't missed the old, obsessive introspection and self-doubt, either.

He shoved the feelings away and put on his coat.

He tried to think of places he used to go and didn't anymore. His memories were oddly vague.

He started with the campus where he had spent four years of his life. Only a few years had passed since graduation, but it felt much longer. He could only remember one professor's name—his advisor—and only a few of his friends'. Former friends... When had he last spoken to any of them?

He shook his head as he walked along the deserted quad. Of course, it was almost Christmas, classes were over and everyone was gone. He tried the student center and the Arts and Letters building, but both were locked. The library was open, although silent, and the thin, graying man at the circulation desk was the same librarian who had scolded Argo when he caught him trying to sneak into the Rare Books room.

Argo wandered the stacks for a while, meeting no one, and browsed the low 100s, where he had done most of his undergraduate reading, but nothing leaped out at him.

He sighed and headed for a bar near campus. He had been drunk there a few times and had been bounced after someone threw up on the floor. Raley, that was the name, Argo's friend who had gotten sick. Had Argo slept with Raley once, or just wanted to? Surely, he should be able to remember...

The bar was closed. He walked to another one, not the closest, but one he had liked better. It had a dance floor and drew a more mixed crowd, not just students. He had spent Christmas Eve there, senior year, refusing to go home. Not that his parents, who were Buddhist, cared about Christmas especially, but they had wanted him to visit and he hadn't wanted to, had been tired of their disappointment and nagging. Had he been home since then? He thought he hadn't. He certainly hadn't spoken to them in the last year.

Hi Spirits was fairly full for a weekday evening. Argo ordered a Campari soda and wandered past a few happy groups, mostly people reuniting with friends over the holidays. Quite a few lonely people were drinking by themselves, looking for the temporary illusion of companionship. He had come here for that himself a few times, and the memory left a bitter taste in his mouth. He turned to leave.

A raised voice by the bar caught his attention, a man saying harshly, "—saw you making eyes at him, you slut!"

Argo glanced over to see a man in his late twenties, wearing too much hair product, berating a slighter, black-haired man, whose upper arm he had in a grip that looked painfully tight. The other man's demurral or apology was inaudible, his face averted and head bowed submissively.

Argo had no interest now in strangers' drama, and what little empathy he'd possessed he had gotten rid of last year. He couldn't have said what drew him closer to the scene.

Argo had always been fairly inconspicuous, and something about the soullessness seemed to make him almost invisible, as if normal people didn't want to notice him. But as he slipped past a group of women in office clothing holding cocktails, the dark-haired man turned to him as if magnetized, even though his companion was still yelling accusations.

Him. His face.

Almost: the face Argo remembered from his student ID photo. The wide, shocked, hurt eyes he had seen in the mirror after his first break-up. He couldn't remember now what they had fought about.

The shouter, red-faced and blurry-eyed with alcohol and anger, broke off, swaying a little, to stare at Argo. "Who the fuck is this?" he demanded, shaking younger-Argo's arm. "Your brother?"

"I don't think I have a brother," the young man said.

Argo recognized the voice he'd occasionally heard when he bothered to replay voice messages before sending them, back when he had cared how he sounded. Sometimes his voice had shaken like this one.

He reached out and cupped the other Argo's cheek.

For a second the younger Argo leaned into his hand. Their eyes met.

The other Argo's eyes widened and he jerked away, stumbling backward and clutching at the man who had been berating him a moment ago.

Argo felt a flash of contempt, almost disgust.

"Hey, asshole—" the drunk said, stepping into Argo's personal space. Argo tapped the man's chest lightly, over his heart.

He collapsed, the thud of his head hitting the floor muffled by the beer-stained industrial carpet.

"Oh my God!" someone exclaimed. Someone else shouted "Call 911!"

Alter-Argo started to bend over his fallen acquaintance, but Argo caught his arm. He was annoyed to realize it was the same controlling gesture that the man he'd just given a minor myocardial infarction had used.

Alter-Argo's skin felt surreally familiar. He didn't have any tattoos.

Argo drew himself closer. Other Argo let him, although he cringed.

"You're a piece of me," Argo told him. "We need to be together."

"No! You're horrible!"

The words felt like a slap, and Argo's grip faltered.

His soul jerked free and ran.

Argo took a step in pursuit, but stopped. He could easily find his soul again now that he knew what he was looking for, and okay, maybe "We need to be together" had sounded a little stalkerish. He would give his vict—er, self, time to calm down.

God, his doppelganger was pathetic, though. He hadn't ever been such a—Oh, right. He hadn't been a wimp, because he had all those other traits, like being selfish and ambitious, to balance out the weak, soft qualities he had been so relieved to shed.

Maybe, Argo thought as he left the bar and headed home, the other Argo running away was a sign. Maybe he should forget about putting himself back together. After all, he had made it this long without—

He was knocked to his knees as something fell on him. For a moment, something cold and wet seemed to seep through his skin. Then one of his protective amulets burst into etheric flames and the dybbuk flung itself away from Argo, whining and squealing, and skittered off into the darkness. To his second sight, it looked like a gelatinous skeleton. Yuck.

Dybbuk could be dangerous, and were hard to remove once they got adhered to a physical form, but they were easily warded off. He'd have to remember to replace that seal, though; the paper inside the silver case had definitely gone up in smoke.

Argo felt slimy, and violated, and his shirt was scorched. He wanted a shower, but instead he went to Griselda's shop.

She was beautifying a sulky-looking college student with illuminating skin cream and a touch of magic. He waited in a corner, looking at eye ointments while the girl finished telling Griselda about how her boyfriend had dumped her when he was supposed to be coming to meet her parents, and how her engaged cousin was going to gloat.

"Was that your next victim?" he asked when the door had closed behind the girl.

Griselda waved dismissively. "If she was, I'd have taken her tonight and let her spend the week sick in bed rather than drinking eggnog with her petty excuse for a family. But you didn't come to admire my work."

Argo sighed and explained about his soul's being a younger version of him. And then, even more reluctantly, he described his alter-ego's aversion to him.

"Fascinating," Griselda said. "I've never heard of a spell-worker accidentally manifesting their own doppelganger like that. And I'd have expected the two of you to feel a magnetic attraction."

Argo looked away. "I did feel drawn to it, but also repelled by it."

"Him," Griselda corrected.

Argo made a face, but nodded. "Yes, he was definitely a person, if an incomplete one. What should I do? I'm not sure I can take him unawares. He seemed to sense my presence."

"Ask him to lunch."

Argo snorted. "Very funny."

"I'm not joking, Argo. I don't see any way around it," Griselda said. "To fix this mess, I think you're going to have to learn to like yourself."

#

Argo found himself the following day.

It might have been better to give his soul more time to calm down, but Argo found himself restless, unable to settle down to work or find distraction in entertainment. He slept poorly, dreaming he pursued himself through dark streets, never catching up.

He rose earlier than he had in years and went out to find himself.

He didn't even need a spell. He simply walked and let his feet lead him to the grimy, run-down apartment complex he had lived in the first year on his own after college.

At least Other Argo didn't live in his old studio; that would have been too much like fate taking an interest in him.

He was raising a hand to knock on the metal security screen when the door behind it opened.

The other Argo hadn't slept either. His eye sockets were shadowed. He was dressed but hadn't combed his hair.

"You," Other Argo breathed.

"Me," Argo said as if it were a greeting. Then, "Do you know who I am?"

"Argo," his soul whispered.

237

Argo felt a frisson of—what? Fear? Excitement? Recognition? The old magical lore about the power of true names didn't spring from nothing.

"And you?"

"Argo Lee." He sounded less confident than he had in naming Argo.

"You were never someone else?"

"I don't think so. I don't remember." Other Argo stared as if trying to read Argo's biography in the differences in their faces, and Argo realized he was doing the same.

His doppelganger didn't look exactly as Argo remembered himself in photos from college. There was some difference, some... lack. No lines. None of the small traces of years of frowning or smiling or leaning his chin on his hand while he read.

"What do you remember?"

Other Argo swallowed. "A year ago. I was walking down the street. It was night. I was naked. I didn't know how I'd gotten there, where I'd come from. I thought I lived in a dormitory. The rector remembered me. She called the police and gave them my— *your* name. They couldn't find an address or employer or anything."

"No, they wouldn't have." Like most magic-workers, Argo had put quite a lot of effort into making his name and whereabouts hard to find by both magical and mundane means.

"No Lees in town were missing a son, and, well, you can guess how many Lees there are in the country."

"No one's looking for you," Argo said absently, and Other Argo flinched.

"No one is looking for me, either," Argo added.

Other Argo clutched the metal grating of the security door. "What are we?"

"I'm a wizard, and you're... a piece of me."

Other Argo shivered. "Is that why I can't leave town? I tried twice and I got so sick, so panicked. The first time I thought I was having a heart attack."

"I don't know. Probably. I didn't expect this. I thought the things I was getting rid of would just..." Argo waved at the air. "I didn't expect anything to materialize."

Argo had always hated having to admit ignorance or acknowledge mistakes. But he was only telling himself, wasn't he?

"Why did you? Get rid of me?"

"I thought it would make me stronger. Happier, too, maybe."

"But it didn't?"

"It did, but it turns out there are drawbacks."

"And now you want to undo whatever you did. Undo *me*." Other Argo shook his head. "I may be weak and lonely but I wouldn't rather be *dead*."

"You wouldn't be dead, you'd be me."

"I don't want to be you!" Other Argo snapped, for once sounding like Argo.

Argo sighed. Did he want to be himself? He wasn't sure. "Maybe we'd both be someone else. I told you, I didn't know you would appear. So, I don't know what will happen next, either. But don't you feel like you're missing something?"

Argo touched Alter-Argo's chilled fingers and they both trembled.

"Yes, but—I don't know. I don't know. I'm scared."

"I'm scared, too," came out before Argo could stop it. And he was. Afraid and uncertain. He could feel those things again, touching the other part of himself.

"Look, this isn't something that has to be decided today." Argo wasn't eager to take that step either. In fact, reluctance to join together seemed to be the one thing the two Argos had in common. "Maybe we can spend some time together and see what we think."

"Well." Other-Argo looked at their joined hands. "I guess that would be... interesting. What are you doing for Christmas?"

"Christmas?" That was right, it was the twenty-fifth. "I don't celebrate Christmas."

"It's my first time. Last Christmas, I was in the hospital getting brain scans. But it looks nice on TV. Colored lights, cookies, family..." Other Argo trailed off wistfully.

"That does sound nice," Argo admitted.

"Then come in."

And his soul stepped back and opened the door and let him in.

Alternative Holidays

Twelve Silver Candles

Emily Munro

Ellie paced the length of our kitchen, splitting her attention between the gravy on the stove and the turkey resting under foil on the counter.

"Relax," I said, pouring her a glass of wine, "You've already met my family. Don't tell me your mom is worse than my Aunt Carol." I offered the wine, but she just gave the glass a death glare.

"No," she said, fiddling with the bundle of herbs hung over the window, "No wine yet. I need to be on my toes."

The doorbell rang.

Ellie turned white like she'd heard a ghost.

I set the wineglass on the counter near her hand, stood very close, and kissed her on the cheek.

"Hey, I love you," I said.

Her expression went gushy.

I whirled and ran to the door before she could change her mind.

Ellie almost never talked about her family. All I knew were bits and fragments. She'd told me once that her mother was a real witch while she was growing up and another time that her father worked in contract negotiation and was rarely around. So when Ellie told me her mother wanted us to visit for Thanksgiving dinner, I immediately suggested that we host instead with the idea that she might be more comfortable in her own space. To my surprise both Ellie and her mom accepted, with the caveat that it be just the three of us.

As I opened the door, I thought that maybe I'd missed a holiday.

The woman at the door was exceedingly tall, wearing a long black gown with subtle sparkles, and had long black hair down to her waist. Her pale skin was accentuated by smoky gray eyeshadow and shocking red lips. It took me a second to see the faint lines on her face that said she was older than me by more than a few years, and a second more to notice the large cardboard box she was holding.

Her face lit up to see me. "You must be Casey," she said in a honeyed voice.

"Uh, hello," I said, still working my way through the logic train to conclude that yes, this was Ellie's mother, and not an extremely late trick-or-treater. "Can I help you with that?" I asked on reflex.

"Oh, no. I'll just set it on a chair over there."

I held the door as she swept past me into our apartment.

I turned in time to see Ellie's eyes go wide with horror. "Mom, you didn't. Please tell me that's not what I think it is."

Her mom, having left the box on a chair with a loud thud, glided over to wrap her in an embrace. "And why not? Your father deserves to have Thanksgiving with us, too. I know he's dying to meet your lover."

"MOM!" My girlfriend's face blushed furiously red, and I felt my own heat a little, too. It's not like we hadn't been open about it but—

"Please, darling. You were always so prudish." She turned an arch gaze in my direction. "I'm so glad you're helping her out of that dear, I'm sure she took a lot of work."

"Mom!"

"You know it's true darling," her mother said.

"Can I get you a glass of wine?" I asked before things could swing further in that direction.

"Yes, that would be lovely dear."

I took refuge in the kitchen.

Ellie followed, eyes wide.

"Oh gods, it's worse than I thought," she muttered under her breath. She looked at me with fear in her eyes. "Just promise me one thing?"

"Anything," I said.

She winced.

"Just," she glanced away, "Just don't leave, Ok? Whatever happens?"

"I'm not going anywhere," I kissed her again and she melted against me, relaxing just a little.

"If you two are done necking in there," her mother called from the living room, "I think I smell the gravy burning."

My girlfriend's eyes went wide and she squeaked. "The gravy!" She ran towards the stove.

I laughed and brought another wineglass and the bottle out to the table. Where I stopped in surprise.

Ellie's mother had somehow gotten the rug out from underneath our card table, leaving the tablecloth and setting completely undisturbed, and had poured salt in a huge ring directly on our hardwood floor. She was now busily tracing an apparently random mix of Latin and Greek characters around the circle with quick, precise strokes from the pour spout of the saltbox.

"Thank you, darling," she said, looking up from her work. "Just put it on the table would you? And be a dear and grab another glass? You're a doll."

I turned around and went back into the kitchen.

Ellie looked at me anxiously from where she was pouring gravy into our large glass measuring cup, waiting for my reaction.

"Your mother wanted another glass," I said, like she couldn't have heard the entire conversation.

She just nodded, resigned. "Would you take the cranberry sauce, too?"

I grabbed the last of our four wineglasses from the cupboard, and the cut-glass dish I'd found at the flea market, now full of cranberry gel still in the shape of the can, from the counter.

"Anything else?" I asked.

Ellie sighed. "Remind her to put the collars on the candles? I don't want to spend a week scraping up wax."

I nodded, walking back out to the living room.

The circle of salt with symbols was finished, and now her mother was pulling twelve shining silver candles from the box, complete with silver candlesticks.

"Help me put these up?" she said.

"Ellie said to remember to use the collars?"

"Damn, yes, I almost forgot." She rummaged in the box and came out with a stack of tiny glass plates, each with a hole in the center the size of a taper candle. "Be a dear and slip these over each one?"

I slipped little glass rings over candles while Ellie's mother set three of the candles in a triangle on the table. Then she began pacing back and forth, placing the rest of the candles in a ring.

Ellie came out with the cornbread and stuffing, saw the ring around the table, and rolled her eyes. "Is all this really necessary Mom?" she asked.

"It wouldn't be if you'd bothered to put more than a general ward up on your threshold," her mother groused.

"It's an apartment, Mom," Ellie shot back on her return to the kitchen, "It's not like anything stronger would stick anyway."

Her mother paused in her work and tilted her head from side to side in a 'maybe you've got a point' motion, before taking a sip from her wineglass and going back to sweeping stray grains of salt into the circle with the edge of a knife.

I went back to the kitchen and grabbed a second, and then a third bottle of wine for the table. Ellie hoisted the platter of turkey she'd carved like it was a shield, squared her shoulders, and marched out into the living room ahead of me.

"All set dearies?" her mother asked.

I checked my pocket for the small box I'd put there this morning, then looked at all the candles, still unlit. "Matches?" I asked.

"Not a problem," her mother said, "Mind the salt when you sit down. I had to make the circle a little small. Ellie's sister's been in my stash again."

Ellie gave an aggrieved sigh, and set the turkey down. "Better your stash than mine," she said. She sat herself down, then jumped back up again. "The pie!" She rushed back into the kitchen.

I sat down at the table, careful to keep the legs of my chair off the edge of the salt circle, now uncomfortably close.

"I thought we were doing pie after dinner?" I called into the kitchen.

Ellie rushed back in with the pumpkin pie in both hands and a can of whipped cream tucked in the crook of her elbow. "Dad loves pie," she said.

I shrugged and took a sip of wine. Ellie's dad loves pie. Noted.

"Got everything now, dear?" Her mother asked. She looked less spooky with a glass of wine in her hand.

We both checked the table.

Turkey still under tinfoil in a losing battle to keep it warm. Mismatched crockery full of stuffing, mashed potatoes, yams and green beans alternately scorching or too cold, your guess as to which. A basket of cornbread muffins I'd made this morning with their little dish of honey butter. A basket of biscuits with their dish of maple butter, because Ellie and I argued about which had to be there and we'd settled on both. Cranberry sauce sparkling alone and majestic in Euclidean near perfection on its crystal dish. Gravy in our good measuring cup with a towel wrapped around it. Pumpkin pie from a bakery in town, because neither of us wanted to go through the trouble of making pie crust on top of everything else.

It was definitely a Thanksgiving dinner.

"Yep," Ellie said, reaching the same conclusion.

"Excellent," Ellie's mother said. She clapped her hands a single time, and everything went dark at once.

I froze. That was... more than I'd been expecting.

All of a sudden, an eerie blue glow rose all around us. The salt was on fire.

Ellie put her hand firmly on my knee and squeezed. "Don't leave the circle," she hissed through clenched teeth, with a heavy implication of *don't leave me.*

A crawling sensation skittered over my skin as Ellie's mother began to chant. It wasn't quite Latin, but they don't hand out medieval history PhD's to just anyone. I could make out the meaning.

"Come to me my darling,
We've good food and wine,
Your daughter, her lover, and I
Invite you now to dine."

The chanting took less time than I expected, but the light show was something else. After a pause somewhere between a nervous freshman's midterm presentation and one of Aunt Carol's marathon graces, the candles flickered back to life with a silvery glow. And all of a sudden, there was an older man sitting to my right.

I startled like a cat spotting a cucumber, and only Ellie's hand shooting out to catch the top of my chair kept me from toppling out of the ring of salt. My heart pounded in my chest. *What? How?* Ellie patted me on the shoulder with a worried glance. *Anything,*

I'd said. I took a deep breath and settled back in my chair, patting her leg. "Still here," I mouthed to her.

Tall and upright, the man wore a tweed coat with worn leather patches, *pince nez* glasses, long red hair in a ponytail, and a goatee straight out of a cliché. He looked at Ellie's mom with an expression of such devotion and delight. I could only hope I looked at Ellie like that.

"Hello my love," Ellie's mom said.

"Hello my love," he replied. His voice was thick like he'd been breathing too much smoke.

"Daddy!" Ellie said, taking his hand into hers from across the table. I half expected her hand to pass through his, but she was able to grip it tight. "Daddy, how are you?"

"Hello pumpkin," he said with a grin, "Better now that I'm here with you. Is that pie?"

Ellie and her mother both laughed.

"You must be Casey," Ellie's father said to me, "It's a pleasure to meet you, I've heard so much about you."

"Nice to meet you too," I said, my heart still racing.

After that, it was a fairly normal Thanksgiving dinner, for a bit, if you ignored the shimmering circular wall rising from the salt ring. My heart rate gradually slowed back to normal as everyone passed serving dishes and piled them high with food before working steadily through a week's worth of calories in one sitting. Ellie talked about her dissertation topic like her parents had never heard of it before, and if I babbled a little—well, I had more than one reason to be nervous tonight.

We ate all of the biscuits and all of the cornbread, and got into a too-elaborate debate on the merits of each.

Her father asked relevant questions and cast gooey eyes across the table at Ellie's mother when he thought no one was looking. Ellie's mother gave as good as she got.

I was pretty sure they were playing footsie under the table too.

I answered a few mostly friendly probing questions like "And what do you do for work, Casey?" to which I replied, "I write, mostly, but I'm lecturing now, too. Medieval History at the University."

"Shaping minds, a fine profession. I did a bit of that myself once."

But mostly, I basked in how happy Ellie looked with both of her parents there. And I realized she'd been fearing introducing me to them. She glanced my way when her father was telling me a story (someone messed up big time upstairs at his work) and there was such a happy look in her eyes; I just had to lean over and kiss her on the cheek. Her mother made happy sounds.

It wasn't until the pie was making its second round that her father's gaze turned suddenly serious.

"Now Casey," he said, his smoker's voice gone quiet as an assassin's velvet, "I think I've been pretty patient here, but we don't have all night. Are you going to show my daughter what you've got in your pocket or not?"

I swallowed, my mouth suddenly very dry.

Ellie raised an eyebrow at me.

"I wasn't sure it was going to be the right time."

"Oh, there's never a perfect time," he said with a devil's wink. "Best just to get it out and over with."

"If you say so," I said. How much more of a prompt do you need? I stood, being oh so careful of that damned salt, still glowing all around us.

I went down on one knee.

Ellie went even whiter than when she'd seen her mother with the box.

I pulled the little velvet case from my pocket.

"Ellanore—my Ellie," I said, "I love you more than I've ever loved anything. More than my heart can bear. Would you make me the happiest person in this world or any other, and marry me?"

I opened the box, exposing the modest engagement ring within.

She tackled me with a kiss and we both tilted towards the shimmering wall along the salt circle. I made a grab for the table but missed and we fell past the line with a flash of light and thunder. I waited for oblivion or disintegration or I don't know what, happy at least to be in Ellie's arms. Instead we fell heavily on a hard floor, Ellie on top of me, still kissing me.

I let out a gasp of surprise and pain, that made Ellie stop and look around.

"Oh damn," she muttered.

We were no longer in the apartment. The room around us was at least three times the size of our tiny living room, with walls of deep crimson and a floor of dark marble with white streaks throughout. A window across from us cast shifting shadows that moved across the walls and pooled along the baseboards in a disturbing manner.

Something oozed towards us from one of the corners, moving with a disjointed fluidity that made it hard to track in the shifting light.

"Ahh!" I screamed, until I noticed Ellie's eyes go wide with panic. I snapped my mouth shut, cutting off the scream.

Ellie gave a sharp look at the roiling mass moving towards us and it shifted, abruptly, into the form of a young man in a black and red suit. He winced as he straightened up. "Miss Ellie, we weren't expecting you."

Ellie sighed, "We fell through the barrier Reggie, it's my fault."

"Sorry I screamed," I said, "I was just surprised."

Reggie nodded at us, "It's alright. Miss, can you get yourself back?" Ellie nodded and he took himself back towards the wall, disappearing through a doorway I'm sure was more for my comfort than his convenience.

Ellie looked at me, "You still want me? You're sure? Really sure? You're okay with this?" She made a vague gesture, to the room, herself, the whole situation.

I swallowed, my mouth still dry, "I was surprised. You made such a big deal about the salt. I thought it was going to hurt us."

Ellie laughed, somewhat manic, "What? No. Touching the barrier makes the candles sputter. It gets wax everywhere." Her expression turned annoyed, "It's going to take an age to clean up."

I laughed a little too hard. I couldn't help it. I kissed her on the cheek. "I will clean up a thousand candles worth of wax if it means staying with you, darling."

"You say that now," she muttered.

"Seriously," I said, "You told my Aunt Carol to take a long walk off a short pier during Sunday dinner. I'll never forget the expression on her face."

"Well somebody had to, the things she was saying."

We both chuckled. She squeezed my arm and picked up the small velvet box from the floor.

"Let's head back." She took me by the hand and led me back towards the wall, which still rippled. I closed my eyes and we stepped through.

When I opened my eyes again, her father quipped at us from the table, "I guess that's a yes then?"

"Yes!" Ellie said. I slipped the ring on her finger and we both sat back down at the table. A bottle of scotch and tumblers had appeared, and I was well past caring how they'd got there.

We chatted happily until well past dark, the silver candles slowly dwindling to pools of wax around their candlesticks.

"Well my dears," her father said rising, "I am so happy for you."

I rose too.

He gave me a huge, back slapping man-hug. "Treat my daughter right now." No *or-else* was even needed. Shades of Hieronymus Bosch paintings floated through my mind, but I dismissed them since it was Ellie and giving her up was an impossibility. He gave me a knowing smile.

He kissed his daughter on both cheeks. "Be happy my dear," he said.

"Love you, Daddy," she said, "See you soon."

He embraced Ellie's mother, then gave her a kiss that left Ellie and I red-faced again and the both of them panting.

"See you soon."

"See you soon, darling."

The candles guttered out, as one, and the light returned to reality, leaving the three of us standing in a circle of steaming salt with a pile of dirty dishes to do.

Standing, Ellie sighed, soft and wistful. "That was nice. Thanks, Mom."

"Yes, thank you," I said.

Ellie's mom just laughed. "Thank me after the wedding, you two. He'll insist on coming, and all our relatives as well." She shook her head and raised her glass. "To love," she said.

"To love," we echoed, and drank the last in our glasses.

Ellie glanced at the table and went for the Tupperware, debating with her mother which of her cousins it would be safe to preemptively uninvite from the wedding, and which were likely to try to curse them for it.

Now all we had to do was survive telling my side of the family. Maybe Ellie had an uncle we could sit next to Aunt Carol at the wedding.

Grinning, I grabbed a butter knife and started scraping candle wax off the floor.

Alternative Holidays

Something Wicked

Evan Davies

The house on Randall Street groaned like a sinking ship.

Allen took three steps up the leaf-strewn walkway, before realizing his father hadn't followed.

"You're a big kid now," he said, when Allen looked back hesitantly. "Remember your manners."

Brown leaves squished beneath bright red boots as Brian scampered on ahead. Allen's ghost costume dragged in the muck as he followed.

Brian was not afraid of the house on Randall Street. The Murphys had just moved to Lynchfield, Massachusetts and didn't know the rules. There were only five costumes allowed in Lynchfield: Vampire, Ghost, Frankenstein, Mummy, Wolfman.

Not Witch, though.

Never Witch.

The old bedsheet billowed up around Allen as wind snickered through the trees. When he pulled the holes back over his eyes, Brian was waiting for him to catch up.

Brian looked around at the shuttered windows and empty yard. "There's no decorations," he said, as they reached the end of the walkway. "Are you sure this house gives out the best candy?"

Allen's hands twisted around the handle of his pail. He hadn't said that. His father had. The bedsheet rustled as he nodded.

The porch smelled of tide pools and week-old fruit, and the dark wood groaned when they knocked. The door crackled like logs on a fire as it opened just a hair. Allen saw an orange eye peering through the gap. "Trick or treat," he said, holding his pail out with hands that trembled.

The eye flicked up and down. "Such a *nice* costume." The voice was old and dry as crinkled paper. A long, thin arm slithered out to drop a candy in his pail.

The hand reached up, and Allen felt a set of shriveled fingernails brush against the fabric of his costume. They lingered just beside his neck until he swallowed and said, "Th-thank you."

The arm slid back behind the door, and the glowing eye snapped towards Brian.

"And... *what*... pray tell... are you?"

"I'm a Power Ranger," Brian said.

"*Power... Ranger...*"

Allen saw a smile cut through the darkness like a knife.

"I don't have a Power Ranger yet."

Silent Night

Liam Hogan

It was the night that everything was silent.

In homes across the country people cowered beneath their Christmas trees. Only real ones would do, the pine scent masking the fear. The trees groaned with brightly coloured baubles, the more the merrier to try and confuse Santa's sensors. It used to be said that he knew if you were naughty or nice and that he'd come for you if you'd been bad, but the truth was much simpler. Any noise, any movement, *anything* that gave away your hiding place and that would be that.

In one living room, made double height by the collapse of the floor above, there were two such trees. Under the larger, a family huddled. The youngest was a mere four years old and small for her age and so, perhaps, the only one among them who would be truly safe. But the sooner she learnt the dangers of this night, the better. Her sister, eighteen months her senior, held her hand and snuggled close, stilling her whimpers. The night was cold and the small fire eating away at the dampened Yule log offered little in the way of either heat or light.

Under the smaller tree the eldest child, Tommy, lay listening to the wind howl, his grandpa beside him. He'd begged and cajoled to be allowed this privilege. Earlier, Gramps had ruined the traditional telling of the holiday tale and had been in disgrace ever since, but, as the long night had dragged on and the danger lurked ever closer, Mother and Father had finally relented. Besides, Tommy was getting bigger every year and there really wasn't that much space under either tree.

After a long while listening to the noises of the night, Tommy finally said, "Gramps...?"

Gramps started and fearfully checked his watch. It was still early; Santa wasn't due for another hour. He let out his breath in a plume of vapour.

"Yes Tommy?" he said quietly. As they were lying close together under the prickly cover of branches and needles, he could speak just above a whisper and still have Tommy hear him.

"That story you told. Is it true?"

Gramps sighed. He'd already gotten into a heap of trouble on that account. And yet he was the oldest person in the village. At 43 he was perhaps the oldest for miles around. It was hard to tell because travelling wasn't as easy as it had once been. When his time came—which could very well be tonight—who then would know the truth?

"About the presents? Yes, Tommy, it's true."

Tommy took a moment to digest the full horror of this. His parents had passed it off as a sick joke, but he'd known it wasn't the sort of thing that Gramps did. Which was why he'd been so eager to leave the family tree for the first time and join Gramps under his.

"What sort of presents?" he asked.

Gramps blinked. Truth be told, he could hardly remember. He'd been younger than Tommy was now, that first year.

"Oh," he muttered, "Wonderful things. Magical things. Games that made moving pictures and sounds. Make believe worlds of bright colours, toy cars..."

Tommy knew all about cars, but couldn't understand why you'd want to make a toy out of them. They were dull, uninteresting things and only good for hiding in or sheltering from the rain.

"Why," Tommy gulped, "Why did he... it ... change?"

Gramps thought for a moment. This was the crux of it and he wished he understood it better, but he'd been so young. On that first night, very few kids his age or older had survived; those who had been lucky enough to take shelter beneath the Christmas tree, amongst the presents that would never be opened.

"There was a war," he began tentatively. Of this, he was quite certain. He remembered one of the toys he'd gotten the year before, a tank. Remembered how his mother had not approved of the way he'd lined it up against his other toys, the foam shells knocking them over one by one to the sound of electronic explosions, while his dad looked on beaming.

"There was a war," he repeated, "A war in distant lands, a war won by drones. There were no prisoners, no wounded, and no civilian casualties. Nobody who wasn't a terrorist, wasn't a baddie. The drones went from house to house looking for hidden weapons, seeking out and killing the enemy. And that was that. The war that had lasted forever came to an end in a single fortnight."

It was amazing how it all came back. For almost 40 years, he'd hardly thought of it, he'd been too busy surviving. They all had. After the adults had gone...

But he was getting ahead of himself.

"It was the first Christmas after. The celebrations were barely over and everyone was happy, everyone was joyous. You know that word? I haven't used it in a long while. Joyous. We all went to bed that Christmas Eve, certain that there were only good things in our future."

"Under the Christmas tree?" asked Tommy.

"What?" Gramps said, a moment of confusion. "No... This was before all of that. We slept in our normal beds, but with stockings hung on the bedposts and a plate of mince pies and carrots put out for Santa."

Tommy looked at him disbelieving. "Carrots? For Santa?"

Gramps laughed, a muffled exhalation that shook the broken red bauble nearest his head and showered them in pine needles. "No, not for Santa. For the reindeer. Donner, and Blitzen. And, of course, good ol' Rudolph!"

Tommy bit his lip. So many things that he didn't understand. It was like a nonsense poem, like the battered copy of *Alice in Wonderland* Gramps used to read to them, until one of the wild dogs ripped it apart. Was this all made up as well, he wondered?

Gramps shook his head, slowly. "But the reindeer didn't come that year, or ever again. Nor did Santa. Not the Santa I remember. The *real* one. Not these killing ones." He patted Tommy's head lightly and fell silent.

Tommy waited for a moment, then another. "What happened?"

Gramps took a deep breath, shaking his head to hide his trembling. "I awoke to the sound of screams, of guns. I didn't know where I was for a moment and then the bedroom door was flung open and a dark figure stood in the doorway. "Hide!" my father said. "Quick! They're coming! Hide! For God's sake, hide!"

"It was the last I ever saw of him... alive. I hid under the bed with my brother. I heard more shouts, my mom screaming at my dad for the combination to the gun safe, my dad telling her not to be stupid, that guns wouldn't help, not against *them*. My dad was in the army, before the drones, so I guess he knew. The front door slammed open, or perhaps shut, and there were a couple of loud bangs and then... and then there was silence."

"We could still hear the shots, but they were distant and growing more so. I was shaking and desperately needed to use the bathroom, so I edged out from under the bed while my brother hissed at me to stay put. I crept downstairs. The front room flickered with coloured lights from the tree and, as I looked about wondering where my parents had gone, something red flitted past the window, a strange humming noise that suddenly stopped."

Gramps ran his worn hands over his face. "I dived under the Christmas tree just as the door was blown off its hinges, just as my brother was creeping down the stairs to see where I'd got to. I... I like to think it was quick for him and that from what everyone who survived said, he wouldn't have been safe under the bed anyway. But I sometimes think I should have stayed and shared my brother's fate, whatever it was to be." There was a tremor in Gramps's voice and something hot and wet splashed onto Tommy's hand.

"You see, in those days there were so very many targets, they didn't check as closely as they do now. I even pushed aside a branch and *saw* the damned thing hovering over a lifeless body. You don't do that anymore. You see it, it sees you, end of. But somehow I survived. It was a drone, of course, dressed in a red cloak. Someone's sick idea of a Santa."

Tommy gasped. "But... I thought you said we'd *won* the war?"

"We did," Gramps said grimly. "All the drones were ours. They were brought home and put into storage. We don't know for sure what happened next, but smarter boys than I have guessed, and it makes a strange kind of sense."

Gramps levered himself up slightly so he could look Tommy straight in the face. "Some idiot down the depot gets bored of standing guard over a warehouse of tin soldiers. Maybe he's had a Christmas drink or two, so he decides to reprogram them. Decides to turn them into the Military's very own Santas, delivering presents to the whole country.

"Only, he didn't do a very good job of it. We guess he managed to remove most of the safeguards and retarget the drones on the civilians: the children, the adults. Everyone except the very young. Thank God he left that protocol in! The least capable of hiding, of staying quiet; they're the only ones who turned out to be safe."

"He probably tried to disable the weapon systems as well, but... Did they re-arm themselves? Or did he simply mess up?"

"I hope he was their first victim, when they awoke as programmed that first Christmas Eve," Gramps said bitterly, shaking his head. "When I think of my parents, my brother and all the many others... I hope he was the first."

He was silent a moment and then, wearily, he finished his tale.

"We survivors didn't know then that Santa would be back. That he would be an annual event. We lost a lot of people that second year: all those who laughed at the childish fears of the more timid kids, or were simply too busy looking after all the little babies to count the days."

"We lost more the year we thought we were grown up enough to attack the depot. I was there, on the fringes. We thought, since it wasn't Christmas, they'd be defenseless. We were wrong. We did manage to kill a few of them and more have fallen by the wayside since. There's no one to repair them, after all. Perhaps, one day, they'll all be dead. Perhaps even in your lifetime. Until then... thank God they weren't programmed to cope with Christmas trees."

"Gramps?" whispered Tommy. "What was Santa like, before?"

"Before? Oh, he was a big, jolly man. Dressed in red, just like the drones, but with a flowing white beard and a hearty laugh. He had a sack of presents slung over his shoulder and everywhere he went, he used to call out, 'Peace and goodwill to all men,' he used to say, 'Peace—'"

Gramps fell abruptly silent and held his roughened finger against Tommy's lips. In the distance, the first shots rang out in the cold night air.

Santa had arrived.

Alternative Holidays

The Apocalypse Was Glorious, My Darlings

Paula Hammond

I gave up being a dragon in the mid '90s. My heart simply wasn't in it anymore. Oh, I still switched skins on moonlit nights to skim mountain tops and scare sheep, but it wasn't the same. I missed the fair ladies. The bold knights. The shiny armor. All that jazz.

If I'm honest, I never really understood what the villagers expected me to do with all those damsels in the first place. So I did what came naturally: I seduced them. Medieval women were surprisingly open-minded, but it never lasted. How could it? I was in the first flush of youth when the pyramids were built. Talk about an age-gap.

Still, for the first three thousand years or so, life was sweet. Women were adored; worshipped. The miracle of childbirth and the turning of the seasons were all reflected in a matriarchal world.

Then around the year zero, there was a definite sea-change. Goddesses were replaced by gods, queens were displaced by kings. Dynasties rose and suddenly it was all about power, succession, and legitimacy. Women—their minds and their bodies—needed to be controlled.

In the blink of an eye, everything shifted. Women went from being the embodiment of Mother Nature, to objects passed from father to husband like so much bartered chattel.

Now, My Darlings, it's true that I was never in any real danger. Having skin like crushed diamonds and the ability to breathe fire, gives you certain freedoms. But, in human form, I'm a six-foot-three woman, with a mess of fire-red hair, jade eyes, and skin the color of tanned leather. Even hidden under robes and veils, I stand out from the crowd. So, for a thousand years or so, I kept my head down and waited to see what the world would do next.

When I finally dipped my claws back into society, I was pleased to see that things had moved on apace.

The Renaissance was a blast. It felt like the world was young again: a riot of Technicolor after centuries of monochrome utility.

Then came the Age of Reason which, for all its dour empiricism, was a time of bold people, doing bold things. I decided that I'd had enough of sitting on the sidelines: I wanted in. I set up a salon and became the toast of London. It was liberating to find that, for once, I wasn't the most outrageous person in the room.

Things took a definite downturn when that awful German woman came to the throne. Really quite spoiled my century. So I set off on a Grand Tour. Boy did money buy a lot of fun in those days!

Well, My Darlings, I moved to the States in the 1930s and drifted around a while, getting the measure of a continent I'd last seen covered in buffalo. In the '60s, I settled in Frisco and spent my days barefoot, with flowers in my hair, just like the song says.

In the '70s, I made my way to New York. With a 12-inch beehive and a faux leather cat-suit I caused quite a stir, I can tell you. Oh! How the punks adored me—bless their little rebel souls.

In the '90s, I swapped the communal squats and riot grrrl gigs for a small apartment on the Lower East Side and carefully coordinated Dior. True, I was barely middle-aged for a dragon, but there was something about city living that seemed to sap the strength. The days drifted past and I found myself doing the one thing I swore I never would: puttering. Watching daytime TV, dusting, filling in online petitions.

Somehow, some when, I'd lost the ability to care. I'd always kicked against the pricks. Fought my corner. Not just with flame and brimstone, either, 'tho that was fun. I'd wielded axe and spear against the Romans. Loosed arrows against mailed knights. Raised sabred-hell with privateers in the Caribbean. Yet, as the centuries moved on, I'd started to see patterns repeating themselves. The world didn't make me angry anymore. It made me tired. I was feeling like I'd reached the sticky end, and that's the truth My

Darlings. Something had to give, but I never imagined things would work out the way they did.

#

It started small, in the superheated hallway of an Art Deco condo. It started with a UPS lady, in dour Pullman brown, in a tug-o-war with the building superintendent.

"You can't leave that there Miss," he sputtered, lifting a package off the wax-sheened floor. "I can't be held responsible for any losses."

"And you, Sir," said the UPS lady, with surprising force, "have no right to touch government property."

While it was clear she was no brawler, she had a sort of quiet determination that caught my attention. Set me tingling.

Now, I hadn't seen a good fight in decades, and I was half inclined to see just how far things went. In the end, I took pity on the red-faced super and shooed him away.

"Ignore him. Leave it anywhere you like," I said with a toothy smile. "I'll take responsibility for any losses. It's my hallway. Hell, it's my damn building. I'm Amanfirys by the way."

The UPS lady was small, impossibly pale, with white hair pulled into a pair of fearsome pigtails, and eyes the color of magic. "Snædís", she replied.

Well, I know an ice witch when I see one, so I invited her in.

"You're a long way from the North Pole," I began, conversationally.

Snædís shrugged. "Global warming. I figured I could stay put and watch the world shrink around me or strike out and try something new."

"Huh... UPS tho?"

"Oh, it's not as dull as you think. I keep myself amused."

There was something in the way she said that last word that caught my attention. "Oh?" I hazarded. "How so?"

"I tamper with the mail."

"Isn't that illegal?"

"Oh, totally," Snædís agreed, then flashed an arch smile that set the two of us blushing.

For a while, neither of us spoke. Tea was stirred. Biscuits—cookies—were nibbled then, quietly, Snædís continued.

"From the day they're born, boys are given toys that let them play at being astronauts, explorers, soldiers. They're promised that their world will be one of endless possibilities, instant gratification, action. Girls? They're told that fulfillment comes from being pretty, popular, patient, passive. And what's the result? Boys grow into men who believe they're in competition with everyone, destined to rule the world. And when the pressure of living up to all those expectations gets too much for them, they're told to suck it up. Be a man. They end up depressed, suicidal, eating and drinking themselves to death. Meantime, girls grow into women who are afraid to be themselves. Desperately trying to find contentment in the mundane. They end up bulimic, OCD, trapped in dead-end jobs and abusive relationships. The world is broken. So, every package I deliver includes a little extra Something."

Snædís lingered over that last word in a way that promised delicious surprises. I raised a quizzical eyebrow. "Something?"

"Let's just say, Something Magical."

Let me tell you, My Darlings, at that point I snorted so hard, I almost set the tablecloth on fire. Ice magic is like taking a dip in a plunge pool. It leaves you gasping, reeling, seeing the world afresh. Whatever Snædís was up to, it was sure to be interesting.

"I don't suppose... you need a hand?" I hazarded.

Snædís leaned forward, her teacup balanced on one knee, a biscuit in each hand. "What do you have in mind?"

"Oh. Something a little dragon-y."

"Actually," Snædís replied, with a twinkle of those impossible eyes. "I have a project brewing for the holiday season and a little transformative magic could be just the thing."

I sat back and regarded my unexpected guest with an appreciative smile. For the first time in decades, I felt indomitable.

#

Real magic, it should be said, isn't like the movies. There are no wands, no power words, potions, or cauldrons.

Us folk who are not-quite human, owe our existence to a certain flexibility in the way the universe works. The scientific term is quantum entanglement, but Einstein was closer to the mark when he talked about spooky action at a distance.

Magical beings are connected, not to each other, but to forces generated elsewhere. They're able to draw on, and interact with, dimensions and realities where physics works in a very different way to our own. No one has yet discovered why, but every creature resonates on its own quantum frequency and this gives us certain special abilities, which for want of a better word, can be called magic.

Once you accept that ice witches and dragons exist, it's not hard to imagine that extraordinary creatures might have extraordinary abilities, or that each might have a different specialism, magically speaking. Combining forces though—that's the tricky bit, requiring strategic thinking, and lots and lots of tea.

We talked late into the afternoon. The conversation, nostalgic at first, morphed into the sort of warm, intimate chat that only very old friends have. There was, perhaps, a little flirting, too. Maybe more than a little, but if anyone asks where you heard it, it wasn't from me. I wouldn't want you to think I was the sort of dragon to kiss and tell.

The wild tales and laughter warmed the balmy afternoon even more until, when the last digestive biscuit had been dunked into the last cup of Darjeeling, Snædís finally headed off to deliver the rest of the mail.

Naturally, My Darlings, I've never been afraid of a good fight. Quite the contrary. I love getting my scales mussed once in a while. But Snædís had reminded me that not all battles are fought with talons and teeth. Words and ideas are just as important as weapons and warriors. And, if everything went to plan, the opening salvos would have been fired before anyone even noticed.

#

Christmas might be a relatively new festival—at least on a dragon's timescale—but people have always marked the passing of the seasons. The result is dozens of holidays, celebrated on or near the Winter solstice. We had four months to prepare. We weren't sure it would be long enough.

Luckily, Snædís had a friend who ran a small print-shop. In another life, in another time, she'd been Seshat, the leopard-skinned Goddess of Writing. She'd packed her bags and left Egypt when she'd been downgraded to divine concubine. Truth be told, she was still a bit pissed about it. But, if you needed some specialist printing, then Seshat was the best in the business. Once Snædís had explained what we had in mind, she even threw in a bit of Heka witchcraft, free of charge.

Finally, the cards were done and all that was left was to slip one in every package that passed through the UPS sorting office. They looked harmless enough. Just some gold embossed text and lots of glitter. What might have seemed curious, if you were paying attention, was that while the words read "Happy Holidays!" everyone read it in their native tongue. The cards also felt enticingly warm to the touch—like bread fresh from the oven. Seshat's contribution ensured that recipients were compelled to pass the card onto a friend or family member, helping to spread the word, so to speak.

Well, My Darlings, it took a couple of days after the first deliveries for social media to start filling up with those little things. Everywhere a card was delivered, weary calorie-counters canceled spin classes, ordered cake, and thought 'the hell with it.' It started in America—countless little rebellions. Then slowly, inexorably, the cards reached further afield.

In Pretoria, Susan Jaimeson, had spent two days preparing a meal for people she loathed. After opening the card, she switched off the oven, dimmed the lights and took to bed with a good book. In Madrid, twins Maria and Carlo opened their very traditional gifts—a Barbie for her, and a lightsaber for him. Without a word, the children swapped toys, and deaf to their mother's insistence that they'd opened the wrong parcels, spent the day blissfully playing. In Sydney, an exhausted pizza delivery girl told her boss where he could stick his minimum-wage slavery, and sat down to paint for the first time in a decade. In Paris, Joshua Marlow, 18-years-old, a Mormon Missionary with the fever of belief etched on his face, tore off his name tag and headed out to enjoy the city he'd been living in for six months, but had never seen. In London, Susan Etherington finally realized that, despite what her family had been telling her for years, she was not—and never had been—the problem.

The Internet went dark. People switched off their phones, got drunk, made love, came out, lay in the park, took duvet days, called old friends.

By then, the shards of Snædís' ice magic had begun to work their way in deep. I don't think either of us anticipated what we were setting into motion, if we're totally truthful.

#

We all live with lies. The little ones that are supposed to smooth life's rough edges but somehow erode something essential in the process. And the big ones. The things we ignore or tell ourselves we can't change. Poverty. Injustice. Hate. Suddenly, it was like someone had held up a mirror to the world and showed us, not how things were, but how they could be. Factories fell quiet. Borders opened. Armies laid down their guns. People embraced strangers and wondered why they'd ever been persuaded to hate them. Governments panicked.

The President came on TV and declared war on the unnamed enemies who, she said, had poisoned our water, drugged our food, and were intent on destroying our way of life. The way she told it, this was the end of days—the apocalypse was coming. Well, my Darlings, if this was the apocalypse, it was bloody glorious. Three-days later, she went walkabout in a dalmatian-patterned onesie, leaving a scrawled note saying that anyone who fancied running the country was free to take a shot.

Hand on heart, I probably overdid my part in the whole business. Dragon magic is like that. Air into fire, wood into cinders. It transforms. It can strip you to the bone if you're not careful. Snædís' cool touch ensured that things didn't get bloody. Passionate, angry—yes—but never violent. We had no desire to add to the world's problems.

Now, My Darlings, I know what you're thinking: how dare we. How dare we try and change people. Make them do what we wanted. As though The Powers-That-Be haven't been doing that forever. The truth is, we don't have the ability, the power, to subsume beings of anima and free-will. We just gave you a glimpse of your better selves. Your true selves. And just to be fair, to ensure that we shared the same risks and rewards, Snædís and I sent each other cards, too.

We opened them together, on Christmas Eve, in front of the picture window in my apartment. We watched as the wintery sidewalk, below, filled with children playing and couples dancing. We listened to the laughter. Saw old Nate Mackie drag a piano out of his music shop and set fire to it. How he'd always hated teaching scales to rich brats. In the apartment above us, a woman tossed her bra and heels out the window. They landed in a tree. Pretty soon, you could barely see the foliage for all the shoes and bras. It was like some otherworld Christmas tree.

For a moment, watching it all unfold, I had flashes of the '20s, the '60s. Of Christmases centuries of old, when the holiday really meant something.

I won't lie, it wasn't all fun and frolics. There were raised voices, doors breaking, long suppressed bitterness, secrets and desires boiling and spilling-over. The world shrugged off its torpor and decided that life was about more than getting and keeping, after all. People were reassessing their priorities and maybe that left some feeling untethered, a little lost.

Then it was our turn. We set down our wards and looked at the cards. When it was done, Snædís peeled off that god-awful UPS uniform. I looked at her, naked and glistening, and despite the chill evening air, I felt the glow of her irrépressible spirit. I shrugged off my skin, and she climbed on my back. I took a breath, blew out the window with a gust of sulphur and smoke, and jumped. I don't even think anyone saw us fly away. They were too busy doing all the things they had been told they shouldn't, couldn't do. And you know what, My Darlings? Even though I'm old enough to remember the world when it was impossibly young and unimaginably lush, it had never looked as beautiful as it did then.

Last Mission

Alex J. Smith

The first sign of trouble was the book. The Naughty or Nice book.

The book had always had a nice heft to it. It seemed... less substantial today.

Santa shrugged. After all, he'd been spending some time in the gym. You had to do something about the cookies. For heaven's sake, when had three home cooked gingersnaps of years past turned into triple stacked cream filled monstrosities?

But, so be it. He opened the tome to the slender red ribbon that told him where he'd left off.

Ah yes, the "G" section. He started at the top. Gaarwain Williams, such a nice boy. Helped in the garden, took out the rubbish, nice to animals. There was that one incident when he lied about who ate the last piece of kidney pie, but.. It was kidney pie. Forgivable. Six years old, lived in Lancashire.

Santa picked up his pen, and as he went to make his mark, the name faded. He hung his head. He knew what that meant. A soul had left the mortal plane. It happened too often. Too many died young. Not so bad as during the plague, but bad. He flipped the pages. Gaarwain had a sister, she would get a little something extra. Her name too was gone. The parents as well.

Santa felt a cold chill crawl down his spine.

Name after name was gone, some vanishing before his eyes. Even as he sat the book shrank visibly. He knew time passed differently on the other planes, but this spoke of disaster.

He closed the book and carried it back to its shelf. He sighed heavily and opened another door. Seldom used, the hinges squeaked. The opening revealed the mirror, a simple thing in a pewter frame. He picked it up and carried it to the table.

He rubbed a hand over the glass until it glowed. "Mother," he said and waited.

She looked terrible.

"You've heard?" she said.

"No, I just know that humanity is dying."

She turned her head and spat.

"No," she said. "They are un-dying."

"I don't understand," Santa said.

He looked over at the book. No longer a tome, but a slender volume.

"Zombies," she said.

"Everywhere?"

She nodded.

After a moment of silence he asked hesitantly, "And England? Has it fallen?" Memories of the sweet smell of hay being gathered on the last days of summer. A mental glimpse of his mother's red cheeks. Of times long ago, before...

"One village survives," she said, interrupting his memories. "Plockton, it is called. But the hoards do approach."

Santa sighed. Names and faces. He knew them all. It came with the job. "Thank you," was all he said as he turned away from the mirror.

He shouted for the sleigh to be made ready. Minutes later, he looked again in the mirror. His armor gleamed in the lamplight. His great axe almost glowed.

He stepped out and went to where the sleigh waited.

The world needed a Santa Claus.

Cupid's Confession

Alicia Hilton

A nude sphinx knelt in front of my throne. Yellow sapphires set in gold dangled from her pierced nipples, jingling. "May I offer you refreshment? A massage?" She leaned closer.

Her *purr* promised sensual delights, but I said, "Not today, darling."

Being the God of Passionate Desire sounded like a scintillating, sexy occupation, but after engaging in hedonistic exploits for millennia, I sought a higher purpose. Of course, Cupid couldn't abdicate his erotic duties, but if my plan worked, more young mortals would grow up to become lovable adults.

I strode across the gilded chamber and cleared my throat when I reached Jupiter's throne.

My father was mediating a dispute between a dragon and a cyclops with a broken arm.

"She attacked me!" the one-eyed giant said.

Steam shot from the dragon's nostrils. "Trespasser," she hissed.

Jupiter pointed at the giant. "Cyclops, you violated Olympian Edict #33. No monster shall enter another's abode without an invitation."

My father flicked his wrist, and lightning shot from his fingertips.

The electrostatic charge enveloped the cyclops.

The giant battered her fists against the force field.

Pulsating light lifted her off the floor. Her body spun as it levitated higher and higher, rising more than fifty feet to the domed ceiling.

Jupiter turned towards me. "I can't persuade you to stay?" He grasped my shoulder. His hand was as heavy as an anvil.

I tried not to flinch, but my knees wobbled. "I'll return for Vinalia," I said. My father was particularly fond of the festival that celebrated the grape harvest.

He squeezed my shoulder tighter. "Do not make me regret trusting you."

#

Shopping mall photo booth attendants were paid $15 per hour, crappy compensation for the one and only Cupid, but working at *Cupid's Photo Booth* was an ideal vantage point for conducting surveillance as a winged crusader.

February 8th, my first customer was a voluptuous brunette wearing scarlet thigh-high stockings and a mini dress. When she climbed on the fake swan for her photos, her skirt rode up, flashing thong panties.

Her smile was salacious. "Want to ride with me?" she said.

No other customers had arrived, but from the scent of her pheromones, she was ovulating.

I fluttered my wings. "Not today, sweetheart," I said.

Olympian Edict #23: Cupid Shall Not Sire Demigods

#

February 9th, I'll never forget the twin boys who wore matching tracksuits and glittery silver sneakers. The brats whacked my swan with their skateboards, busting the beak. Since there were no witnesses, I shot them with my magic arrows and turned them into squeaking mice. Not permanently—they'll become boys again in seven hours.

Olympian Edict #17: Cupid Shall Not Harm Children

#

February 10th, I'd never seen a child more terrified of a plastic swan, and my bow and arrows made him scream. When I gave the little darling a chocolate heart, he stopped wailing. Mummy was so grateful; she bought the deluxe photo package and asked me if I wanted to babysit.

Our rendezvous was unexpectedly pleasant. Mummy and little Jimmy lived in a posh apartment on Nob Hill. The fridge was loaded with tasty snacks, but I only devoured one pint of cherry sorbet while Jimmy played video games.

Mummy was despondent when she returned from her blind date because the bloke was a rude dolt. After I comforted her, she gave me a kiss, and invited me to her bedroom. I figured she'd be a freak in the sack because she was into cosplay, but when she realized that my wings didn't come off, wow, what a ride!

After we rutted, I wiped her memory, so she'd believe that she'd banged an ordinary guy she'd met in a bar.

I said, "Goodbye," to her adorable tyke, patted his head, and erased his recollection of me.

Olympian Edict #2: Cupid Shall Not Reveal That He Is A God

#

February 11th, strolling the mall on my lunch break, I spied two nymphets arguing outside the lingerie shop.

"Skank!" the filly who wore a crop top and daisy dukes said. She punched the lass who wore a sundress and combat boots.

Blood gushed from her nose. She nailed her attacker with a swift kick to the knee.

Another punch from the instigator, and they were rolling on the floor. Hair pulling. Scratching.

Their screams drew a crowd.

I rubbed my hands together and said, "Let there be love."

Suddenly, the catfight stopped.

The girl with the bloody nose kissed her enemy.

Instead of giving her another slug, the filly who'd started the fight deepened the kiss and caressed her tit.

A gawker with a buzz cut was filming with his cellphone. I put my hand over the camera lens and said, "Don't be a perv."

He shoved me. Hard.

My back smacked against the shop front, making the glass shake.

The galoot was stocky and three inches taller than me. If I'd been an ordinary mortal, the blow would've left a bruise.

"Fight!" a teenage boy said.

Heads swiveled as the crowd's attention was diverted from the girls who were still making out.

I rubbed my hands together.

The big galoot yelped and pissed his pants.

Sweet revenge.

Olympian Edict #27: Cupid Is Permitted To Use Appropriate Force In Self-Defense

#

February 12th was a special day, the sixty-sixth time I had a car date with a man. His breath tasted like cinnamon. He said he would be gentle, but we both got carried away. His boxers matched his socks—red with white stripes.

Spicy.

While I was zipping my pants, he offered to buy me dinner. A real gentleman.

"I'd love to, but I have an audition," I lied.

He glanced at the clock on the dashboard. "At 9:30 at night?"

I smiled. "It's a beer commercial."

Olympian Edict #49: Cupid Shall Not Dine With Mortals

#

February 13th, my favorite customer was a nurse who wore fishnet pantyhose. She slipped me a $20 tip and confessed that she liked to be tied up. She took me home to show me. The stockings looked lovely wrapped around her wrists.

After we screwed, she recited sonnets. Her poetic repartee was as delightful as the sex.

Parting was sweet sorrow. I wanted to ask for a second date, but feared Jupiter's wrath.

Olympian Edict #7: Cupid Shall Not Fall In Love With Humans

#

February 14th, my last customer was a middle-aged woman who wore a hideous flowered hat and a pink polyester skirt suit. A little girl stood beside her. The child stared at the floor, like she wanted it to open up and swallow her whole.

"$19.99 for four photos?" the granny grumbled.

"The package includes a deluxe key chain." I pointed at the price chart.

I smiled when she swiped her credit card.

She didn't smile back. She snapped her fingers at the child and said, "Get on the swan."

The girl raised her head. "Do I have to?"

"Get on the damn swan!" She slapped her granddaughter.

The poor child's lip bled.

Of course, I couldn't let such a despicable act go unpunished.

I tailed them when they left the photo booth.

Since it was late, there weren't many shoppers lingering. I kept enough distance between us so they wouldn't notice me skulking.

A silver minivan was parked near the exit door. The passenger side window rolled down.

The driver had curly brown hair like the little girl. "Did you have fun?" she said.

"Uh, huh. Thanks, Grandma," the child said. She climbed into the van, and it drove away.

Indignation coiled inside me. My gut clenched.

The granny walked towards a station wagon with fake wood paneling.

I glanced behind me. The exit area was deserted.

I rubbed my hands together.

In an instant, my face morphed. Horns sprouted from my skull. My flesh reddened, deepening to the color of a ripe tomato.

"Hey," I said.

Granny turned around. Her eyes widened.

"Welcome to hell, bitch." I grinned, flashing my demon fangs.

She clutched her chest and keeled over.

I sort of tried CPR, but it didn't revive her.

The shapeshifting gave me a horrid headache, and I strained my back when I lifted the corpse and set it in my sedan's trunk. I'd make sure it didn't go to waste.

As I drove home, I heard a thunking noise coming from the trunk.

I pulled over to the side of the road, and checked on Granny.

She still wasn't breathing.

My heart hammered as I thought about Jupiter's wrath.

Olympian Edict #1: Cupid Shall Not Use Deadly Force

#

Valentine's Eve at 8:51 PM, I arrived at my apartment, and took a shower.

Venus had promised to visit. My mother wasn't judgmental, but she'd be worried if she discovered that I'd become a vigilante.

Mother charged up the transporter and beamed herself from Olympus to California at least once a month. She sent text messages before she arrived. Venus didn't want to see me engaged in trysts.

I opened a bottle of Beaujolais and fixed supper. No meat, Mother and I were vegan. I'd have to wait until Venus left to finish my project in the basement.

It was too soon for the body to stink of decay, but paranoia made me light incense.

The frankincense aroma was soothing, but I couldn't stop fidgeting.

I stirred the minestrone soup and added more garlic powder.

My stomach churned as I thought about carving Granny's flesh and mopping up blood. At least the meat would be savored by my furry friends. Stray kitties and doggies loved me.

I'm a god, not a monster.

About the Authors

Daniel Ausema
Daniel Ausema's short fiction and poetry have appeared in *Strange Horizons, Daily Science Fiction, Fantasy Magazine,* and *Diabolical Plots.* His published novels include the *Arcist Chronicles*, published by Guardbridge Books, and the steampunk-fantasy *Spire City* series. He lives in Colorado at the foot of the Rockies. His website is https://danielausema.com. Follow him on Twitter: @ausema.

Keyan Bowes
A peripatetic writer of short fiction, Keyan Bowes currently calls the West Coast of the US home. She's occasionally ambushed by stories, and writes when inspiration bites. Her work can be found online and on paper in a dozen print anthologies. She's a Clarion graduate and a SFWA member. Website: www.keyanbowes.org

Gregg Chamberlain
Gregg Chamberlain lives in rural Ontario, Canada, with his missus, Anne, and their two cats, who enjoy Christmas every day with treats and bellyrubs. He writes speculative fiction for fun and has appeared in other B Cubed Press anthologies.

Evan Davies
Evan Davies is an avid reader and writer of fantasy, science fiction, and horror. He attributes his success to the better authors whose works inspired him and to the many beleaguered friends who were too nice to tell him how terrible his first stories really were. His writing has appeared in several anthologies, including *We Who Are About to Die* by Rogue Blades Entertainment. Follow him on Facebook: https://www.facebook.com/evan.davies.73594.

Sarina Dorie
Sarina Dorie is a science fiction, fantasy, and mystery author who has sold over 200 short stories to magazines like *Analog, F & SF, and Daily Science Fiction.* Her award-winning series, *Womby's School for Wayward Witches* is available on Amazon, along with 80 other titles she has available. In her free time, Sarina Dorie enjoys chocolate, gluten-free brownies, Jack Sparrow, steampunk aesthetics, fairies, Mr. Darcy, and Captain Picard. For more information about her newest releases, free short stories, or to sign up for her newsletter, go to her website: www.sarinadorie.com.

Alternative Holidays

Louis Evans

He's coming to sing you the old song of ice/He hopes that you think that his poem's quite nice. Louis Evans's work has previously appeared in *Nature: Futures*, *Analog SF&F*, *Interzone*, and more. He's a graduate of Clarion West. He's online at evanslouis.com and on twitter (rarely) @louisevanswrite.

Katharina Gerlach

Katharina Gerlach was raised in the middle of a German forest where she and her three brothers roamed and dreamed. But even tomboys grow up. She got an education and returned to the love of her life, her husband, with a PhD in science and a head filled with weird facts. By now Katharina has dabbled in several genres, mainly Fantasy, SciFi, and Historical for readers of all ages. Find heronline: www.katharinagerlach.com and www.facebook.com/KatharinaGerlach.Autorin

J.C.G. Goelz

J.C.G. Goelz is your common garden-variety polymath. He writes because he hopes someone will read it.

Paula Hammond

Paula Hammond is a professional writer and digital artist. Her fiction has been nominated for the Pushcart Prize and a British Science Fiction Association award. If you should spot her in the pub, she'll be the one in the corner mumbling Ghostbusters quotes and waiting for the transporter to lock on to her signal. She'd be delighted if you shared pictures of puppies with her on Twitter: @writer_paula.

Jenna Hanchey

Jenna Hanchey is a critical/cultural communication professor by day and a speculative fiction writer by...uhhh...earlier in the day. Her stories appear in *Nature: Futures*, *Daily Science Fiction*, *Medusa Tales*, *Wyngraf,* and *Martian Magazine*, among other venues. She lives in Phoenix, AZ with her mysterious mutt, Mystic. Follow her adventures on Twitter (@jennahanchey) or at www.jennahanchey.com.

Alicia Hilton

Alicia Hilton is an author, editor, arbitrator, law professor, and former FBI Special Agent. Her work has appeared in *Akashic Books, Best Asian Speculative Fiction, Daily Science Fiction, Vastarien, Year's Best Hardcore Horror Volumes 4, 5 & 6*, and elsewhere. She is a member of the Horror Writers Association, the Science Fiction and Fantasy Poetry Association, and the Science Fiction and Fantasy Writers Association. Her website is https://aliciahilton.com. Follow her on Twitter: @aliciahilton01.

Larry Hodges

Larry Hodges has sold over 130 short stories and 4 SF novels. He writes professionally, with 17 books and over 2000 published articles in 170+ different publications. He's a member of Codexwriters, and a graduate of the Odyssey and Taos Toolbox Writers Workshops. He's also a professional table tennis coach, and claims to be the best science fiction writer in USA Table Tennis, and the best table tennis player in SFWA! Visit him at www.larryhodges.com.

Nina Kiriki Hoffman writing as Robin Aurelian

Over the past four decades, Nina Kiriki Hoffman has sold adult and young adult novels and more than 350 short stories. Her works have been finalists for the World Fantasy, Mythopoeic, Sturgeon, Philip K. Dick, and Endeavor awards. Her novel *The Thread that Binds the Bones* won a HWA Stoker Award, and her short story "Trophy Wives" won a SFWA Nebula Award. For a list of Nina's publications, check out: https://ofearna.us/books/hoffman.html.

Liam Hogan

Liam Hogan is an award-winning short story writer, with stories in *Best of British Science Fiction* and in *Best of British Fantasy* (NewCon Press). He's been published by *Analog, Daily Science Fiction*, and Flame Tree Press, among others. He helps host Liars' League London, volunteers at the creative writing charity Ministry of Stories, lives in London and waits impatiently for Halloween. More details at http://happyendingnotguaranteed.blogspot.co.uk.

Robert Jeschonek

Robert Jeschonek is an envelope-pushing, *USA Today* bestselling author whose fiction, comics, and non-fiction have been published around the world. His stories have appeared in *Clarkesworld, Pulphouse, Fiction River*, *Black Cat Mystery Magazine,* and many other publications. He has written official *Star Trek* and *Doctor Who* fiction and has scripted comics for DC, AHOY, and other publishers. Visit him online at www.bobscribe.com.

Simon Kewin

Simon Kewin is the author of the *Cloven Land* fantasy trilogy, cyberpunk thriller *The Genehunter*, "steampunk Gormenghast" saga *Engn*, the *Triple Stars* sci/fi trilogy and the *Office of the Witchfinder General* books, published by Elsewhen Press. He's the author of several short story collections, with shorter fiction appearing in Analog, Nature and many other magazines. His novel *Dead Star* was an SPSFC award semi-finalist and his short story *#buttonsinweirdplaces* was nominated for a Utopia award.

Julia LaFond

Julia LaFond is a geoscience/astrobiology PhD candidate at Penn State University. She's had short stories published via *Utopia Science Fiction Magazine, Caustic Frolic*, and *The Night's End Podcast*. In her spare time, Julia enjoys reading and gaming. Her website is https://jklafondwriter.wordpress.com/.

Carter Lappin

Carter Lappin is an author from California. She mostly writes speculative fiction. Her short stories have appeared in publications such as *Apparition Lit, Timber Ghost Press, Improbable Press, Sunlight Press, Manawaker Studio,* and *Air* and *Nothingness Press.* You can find her on Twitter at @CarterLappin.

Richard Lau

Richard Lau is an award-winning writer who has been published in newspapers, magazines, anthologies, online, and the high-tech industry. He thanks Barbara, who makes every day a holiday.

Gerri Leen

Gerri Leen lives in Northern Virginia and originally hails from Seattle. In addition to being an avid reader, she's passionate about horse racing, tea, and collecting encaustic art and raku pottery. She has work appearing or accepted by *The Magazine of Fantasy & Science Fiction, Strange Horizons, Galaxy's Edge,* and others. She's edited several anthologies for independent presses, is finishing some longer projects, and is a member of SFWA and HWA. See more at gerrileen.com.

Gordon Linzner

Gordon Linzner is founder and former editor of *Space and Time Magazine,* author of three published novels and scores of short stories in *F&SF, Twilight Zone, Sherlock Holmes Mystery Magazine,* and numerous other magazines and anthologies. He is a full member of the Horror Writers Association and a lifetime member of the Science Fiction & Fantasy Writers Association.

Judy Lunsford

Born and raised in California, Judy now lives in Arizona with her husband and Giant Schnoodle, Amos. She writes with dyslexia and a chronic illness (Meniere's Disease), is hard of hearing, & is a breast cancer survivor. She writes mostly fantasy, but occasionally delves into other genres, and has written books and short stories for all ages. Her website is: https://judylunsford.com/author/judylunsfordwrites/.

Jeremy Mallory

Jeremy Mallory is an attorney and writer living in Reston, Virginia. He has studied religions, philosophy, and the occult, as well as magic of all sorts—both spells and sleight-of-hand. Jeremy writes contemporary dark/urban fantasy, and speculative fiction. His work has appeared in the journals *13 Myna*

Birds and *Drunk Monkeys*, and the Writers of the Future Contest has recognized two of his stories as a semi-finalist and an honorable mention. His website is jeremymallory.com. Follow him on Twitter: @inkstainedwords.

Samuel Marzioli

Samuel Marzioli is a Filipino-American writer of mostly dark fiction. His work has appeared in numerous publications and podcasts, including the *Best of Apex Magazine, Flame Tree's Asian Ghost Short Stories*, and *LeVar Burton Reads*. His chapbook, Symphony of the Night, was released by Aurelia Leo and his collection, *Hollow Skulls and Other Stories*, was released by JournalStone Publishing. You can check out his infrequently updated blog at marzioli.blogspot.com.

Kevin McCarty

Kevin McCarty took up writing as a hobby because it's safer than alligator wrestling and cheaper than owning a Monster Truck. He is an Associate Professor of Computer Science at a small liberal arts college because otherwise, he would starve. Follow Kevin on Twitter: @KevCSProf.

Lawrence Miller

Lawrence Miller (he/him) grew up in Tampa, spending most of his formative years attending Trek, Comic, and Anime conventions, and playing D&D in the living room as there are no basements in Tampa. He currently lives in Pennsylvania with his spouse, two children, and a dog, and spends his weekdays writing software to help physicians become better physicians. He can be found on Twitter at @ldpm.

Emily Munro

Emily Munro is pretty sure she'll get the hang of this whole author thing any-day-now. In the meantime, she reads anything that sits still long enough, knits her own socks, and drinks far too much tea. She can be found scribbling away in a variety of Brooklyn and Manhattan coffee shops and on Twitter @thatEmilyMunro. She has two previous short stories published in the *Of Gods and Globes* anthologies.

Marie Noorani

Marie Noorani is a visual artist, musician, and author. She enjoys writing fables, personal narratives, and essays. With a particular interest in surviving grief, she has shared her thoughts as a TedX speaker and contributor to art and mental health magazines. She currently lives in southeastern Washington State.

James Edward O'Brien

James Edward O'Brien grew up in North Jersey in the US where he graduated from *Dungeons & Dragons* and *Doctor Who* to punk rock and weird fiction. His speculative work has appeared in *The Deadlands, On Spec,* and on the *Tales to Terrify* podcast, among others. He currently resides in Queens, NY with his wife, three dogs, and two cats. Follow Jim on Twitter: @UnagiYojimbo.

Kelly Piner
Kelly Piner is a Clinical Psychologist who in her free time, tends to feral cats and searches for Bigfoot in nearby forests. Her writing is inspired by *The Twilight Zone.* Ms. Piner's short stories have been featured in *Weirdbook's* annual zombie issue, *Scarlet Leaf Review's* anniversary issue, *Storgy, The Literary Hatchet, Drunken Pen Writing* and others as well as multiple anthologies. Follow her on Facebook: https://www.facebook.com/profile.php?id=100083043362509.

David Powell
David Powell has taught school, directed plays, and portrayed zombies, but now he writes full-time, seeking out the pockets of chaos brewing in the corners of the grid. You can find his writings in magazines such as Calliope and First Line Literary Journal, and anthologies such as *Shattered Veil* and *Georgia Gothic.* You'll find a complete list, as well as free reads, on his website, davidlpowell.net.

Mir Rainbird
Mir Rainbird is composed primarily of words. Mir's other hobbies include arguing with cats and being bad at art. Visit Cosmic Horror Monthly for more words (and cat pictures) or follow mir_rainy on Instagram.

Andrew L. Roberts
Andrew L. Roberts is a northern California author and poet. His poems and stories have appeared in *Bourbon Penn, Polu Texni*, and *New Myths Magazine.* His book *Duramen Rose* is a WWI novel written entirely in verse. His current book project is a story of spirit possession, murder and revenge set in seventeenth century Japan. When not writing, he enjoys soulful conversations with his dog and cat. Find him at Twitter as @AndrewLRoberts1.

Alex Shvartsman
Alex Shvartsman is a writer, translator, and anthologist from Brooklyn, NY. He's the author of *The Middling Affliction* (2022) and *Eridani's Crown* (2019) fantasy novels. Over 120 of his short stories have appeared in *Analog, Nature, Strange Horizons*, and many other venues. His website is www.alexshvartsman.com.

Emily Martha Sorensen
Emily Martha Sorensen is a bit of an oddball. She's allergic to clichés, and she has a boredom intolerance. She particularly likes clever characters who

charge straight through her plot and send it spinning wildly off the rails. (Those brats.) You can find her books at http://www.emilymarthasorensen.com.

Mark Teppo

Mark Teppo lives in the Pacific Northwest, where he watches a lot of movies when he's not selling books. In addition to writing more than a dozen novels across multiple genres, he's also the publisher at Underland Press. His favorite Tarot card is The Moon. You can find him on Instagram (@mark.teppo) and Twitter (@markteppo).

Richard Thomas

Richard Thomas is the award-winning author of eight books: *Incarnate, Disintegration, Breaker, Transubstantiate, Spontaneous Human Combustion, Tribulations, Staring Into the Abyss,* and *Herniated Roots.* He has been nominated for the Bram Stoker, Shirley Jackson, and Thriller awards. His over 165 stories in print include *The Best Horror of the Year (Volume Eleven), Behold!: Oddities, Curiosities* and *Undefinable Wonders* (Bram Stoker winner), *Cemetery Dance* (twice), *Weird Fiction Review, Chiral Mad (#2-4),* and *Shivers VI.* Visit http://www.whatdoesnotkillme.com for more information.

Jenniffer Wardell

Jenniffer Wardell is always on the lookout for the weird and wonderful hidden stories in the world. She's the author of three novels, including the award-winning *Fighting Sleep,* and several shorter works. You can find more about her online at jennifferwardell.blogspot.com.

Sheri White

Sheri White's stories have been published in many anthologies, including *Tales from the Crust* (edited by Max Booth III and David James Keaton), *Halldark Holidays* (edited by Gabino Iglesias), and the HWA publication *Don't Turn Out the Lights* (edited by Jonathan Maberry). Her first and only collection (so far), *Sacrificial Lambs and Others,* was published in 2018. Follow Sheri on Facebook: https://www.facebook.com/sheriw1965 and Twitter: https://twitter.com/sheriw1965.

Alex J. Smith

Alex J. Smith makes his home in Fort Worth Texas where he spends his time escorting women and their families to Kansas, a state where reproductive health is still allowed.

Publishing *Alternative Holidays* has been a great ride with some wonderful people. I can only hope you all enjoyed this anthology as much as I enjoyed collaborating with Alicia and all of these excellent writers.

Bob B.

About B-Cubed Press

B Cubed Press is a small press that publishes big books about things that matter.

A percentage of EVERY book we publish is donated to Charity. Usually the ACLU.

We can be reached at Kionadad@aol.com.

Our writers gather routinely on the "B Cubed Project Page" on Facebook and we can also be found at BCubedPress.com.

Made in the USA
Middletown, DE
08 February 2024

49318267R00177